Praise for K.L. Brady

AWARDS & PRAISES FOR K.L. BRADY

Winner — Next Generation Indie Book Award for Multicultural Fiction (2010)
  Winner — Next Generation Indie Book Award for Multicultural Fiction (2013)
  Winner — Next Generation Indie Book Award for Multicultural Fiction (2014)

Publisher's Weekly calls K.L. Brady's work "comic and charming..."

***

RT Book Reviews calls Brady's work "Hilarious!"... and says she "draws readers in immediately...and propels them straight through the drama, humor and the various twists and turns that will leave you exhausted but satisfied."

***

"12 Honeymoons had me laughing from the first page. Miki is a hoot, with a smart, sarcastic sense of humor and mouth that won't quit (and gets her in trouble quite regularly)." – San Francisco Review of Books

"I don't know how KL Brady manages to write romance that is equal parts emotional tug and belly laugh. The plot twists keep coming...always with humor...until girl gets her guy and readers get the happily ever after. Fast-paced, this is such a fun holiday read." – Amazon Reviewer

"Cue the Mistletoe! Five Golden Rings is the perfect holiday read."

"K.L. Brady delivered again with Her Perfect Catch. This is a quick but fulfilling romance novel and combines two of my favorite things, football, and love." ~ Good-reads Reviewer

"Her perfect catch is the perfect read for the romantic at heart. Add sports and you have a recipe for the perfect love story." – Goodreads reviewer

"As always, K.L. Brady does not disappoint with her hilarity, her sensual moments, and tension. Her Perfect Catch is a perfect read." ~Amazon Reviewer

Her Perfect Catch and The Player's Option

"Great series can't wait for book 3. Very heartwarming shared a few tears. Loved the drama. Looking forward to reading book 3...." ~Amazon Reviewer

LOVE IS IN THE CARDS

A Second Chance Romance

K.L. BRADY

LADYLITPRESS

Keep It Real Cards

CONGRATULATIONS!
You took a Risk. You're Following Your Dream!
Good Things Come to Those Who Wait…

Let's Keep It Real—Your new gig may give you freedom from
the man, but *the man* pays biweekly and you've got bills.
DON'T QUIT your day job!

Prologue

"Welcome, everybody. This is day one of Keep It Real Cards. We're standing on the leading edge of the greeting card industry, and here is where success lives."

Bright smiles accompanied vigorous applause in the wide-open room. She'd hired a small team, ten of the best poets, graphic artists, and illustrators she could afford.

"We're all here because we're committed to a single mission: delivering the hard truths, even when it hurts—especially when it hurts."

Today, she'd leased a Capitol Hill loft for rent too cheap to pass up and gathered her newly recruited creative staff there. For future operations, Tessa longed for a location on the Georgetown waterfront—her dream location—but this would do for now.

"This team, our sales mission, isn't for the faint of heart. The truth's often harder to tell than fiction," she said. "Did you join our team because you've bottled up sweet memories of drawing feel-good, warm and fuzzy cards in your onesie pajamas? And now you want to sell them to vulnerable consumers?" She paused and waited for responses. No one made an outward movement. "I've got news for you— you're in the wrong place."

A burst of laughs and chuckles helped set her jittery nerves at ease.

"Grab an Uber, go home, and submit your application to Signed & Sealed, GetEcards, or American Salutations. We don't do ooey-gooey sweetness here."

She'd pinched her pennies until the eagles cried and sacrificed much of her liquid assets to give her life purpose after Cody Hart abandoned her. To afford her staff, she kept the budgets as tight as her best friend Mia's Spanx. Having joined the journey from day one, Mia had witnessed every second of pain and glory that brought her here.

Now—three-hundred sixty-five days.

She could finance operations for twelve months without earning a penny. If the company took off, she'd operate longer, but her deadline had been set.

"The Keep It Real mission is simple: we use humor to communicate difficult messages that are hard to speak, but that we need to hear. Life is a series of lessons learned. And you can only become the best version of yourself if you listen and apply them. That's what our art will help people accomplish."

Fail or flourish—her path could trail in either direction. In a year, she'd crawl back into her feelings or take this venture to new levels. Where would this path lead?

"As I warn you about the difficulties that lie ahead, I'd like to see a show of hands. Anyone in here seen The Wiz?"

All hands went up, a few reluctantly.

"Do you remember Evilene, the wicked witch? She sang 'Don't Nobody Bring Me No Bad News?'"

All heads nodded.

"Keep It Real exists for people like her. By all accounts, she was clinging to power by a thin thread but living a content existence. When the flying monkeys arrived with the truth, she wanted no part of it. They tried to warn her, told her danger was afoot. She heard the warning...but did she listen?"

Tessa privately concluded one vital fact: Cody's cowardliness had led her to her destiny.

"Evilene didn't encourage her minions to keep it real. No. The question is why a lie is easier to handle?"

Tessa well understood, better than anyone, how much easier it was to embrace denial than reality. Her bitterness toward Cody had phased from an over-boil to a low simmer, at least in her estimation. She'd kept her distance from him to keep the heat down. Now, she was on her own.

Everyone craned their necks around and then back at her.

"The illusion of power and control. If anything went wrong, she could blame fate or the universe, everyone and everything except herself. I'll bet she hit the pile of crap and thought, 'I'd rather have a V8 and the truth than this.'"

A round of chuckles filled the silence.

"At Keep It Real, we don't allow friends, or our customers, to plummet to the pile of crap. We gift the truth. Someone did me this favor once. I can't lie. It hurt like nothing before, but it made me wiser, a little more cautious, discerning, independent, and a lot shrewder. We're all here today because of it."

Tessa smiled and clasped her hands as in a prayer.

"Truth is not a curse; it's a gift, one we will deliver to our consumers, one card at a time."

Without Cody's brutal delivery, would she have found the motivation, drive, and grit to make her dream come true?

Tessa would never know.

Chapter One

T essa

THE SWIRLING RUST- AND GOLD-COLORED LEAVES MIRRORED TESSA'S uneasiness as she entered the newly renovated Keep It Real offices. Her suites sat on the campus of Sweet Media, her father's publishing company that owned Ebony Books, the nationwide chain where she sold her greeting cards.

What a difference the passing of time made.

Five years ago, almost to the day, she wore uncombed hair that was kinked to Rastaman proportions and a bougie yoga outfit as she hoisted her butt into an upside-down headstand. Tears and snot had rolled over her forehead as she mourned her ex-boyfriend, Cody Hart. He didn't die—unfortunately. No, he dished her a serving of heartbreak with a cold callousness she'd not experience since Signed & Sealed rejected her greeting card ideas.

Today, she celebrated her manifested dream, but still hoped for one last blessing to take her business over the top.

The wall clock read a quarter of nine, signaling she had only fifteen minutes before her first meeting of the day. She passed through the lobby of her swanky creative studios and stopped at the receptionist's desk; the cheery space buzzed with innovative energy and incessant phone rings.

"Keep It Real Cards, where we always keep it one-hundred," Mabel said, at last ending the irritating ringing. The executive assistant, with her schoolmarm hair porn boobs, was a defector from Hart Enterprises, her ex's company. If Confucius had been a motherly black woman who didn't answer phones (well), Tessa's version would present herself in the form of this gem who'd become the knower-of-all-things-that-must-be-known.

"Ms. Sweet is scheduled to attend a meeting as we speak." After a few seconds, she ended the exchange with her trademarked quip. "No, I'm sorry, I don't take messages. You should call back in two hours. You're welcome." To hear Mabel tell it, she was born to welcome guests to Keep It Real. In Tessa's estimation, it was the only skill she hadn't quite honed.

Tessa waved a hello and flittered into her contemporary-styled executive suite. She stopped, inhaled, and held a cleansing breath, a ritual she repeated to slow down, stay in the moment, and burn off nervous energy before reaching her desk. The brief reprieve gave her time to recognize her success and the challenges she faced, as the latter were many.

Through her office's glass walls, only partially frosted, she surveyed her kingdom before lifting the quarterly sales report. One glance at the trend lines caused her stomach to lurch. She'd clung to a sliver of hope that she'd see enough evidence to relay some positive, reassuring news at the huddle up with Mia before the creative meeting. One glance at the crappy update killed that thought.

Moments later, Mia entered lugging the weekly mailbags, mostly feedback from consumers. One bag overflowed with letters; the second mini-sack, much smaller, left Tessa believing for improvement. They letters had grown from short-stacks to wide loads over the past five years; they'd also changed in tenor.

She supposed she preferred hate mail over the alternative. Five years ago, instead of mailbags, Mia carried a double wine-tote containing Pinot over her shoulder; the spoils of her Trader Joe's excursion were designed to help Tessa nurse her broken heart.

"Please tell me those aren't filled with hate mail...this time. I liked it better when you brought me wine."

Mia dropped them where she stood and didn't crack even a half-smile; Tessa's glimmer dissipated. "I brought you wine because your doormat says to bring you Pinot Grigio or leave," she said with a laugh. "You've come a long way from the hippo butts under your eyes, and smelling like Pepper dragged your dead carcass through the house."

Pepper was her sweet black cat. He'd never eat her...she didn't think.

"So, what's the verdict?"

"Let me put it this way, if negative feedback represented one of these sacks, it'd be the really really big one," Mia said. She slumped back into a guest seat, crossed her legs, and caught her breath. "Check this out. While in the mailroom, I read a letter from a woman who received one of Keep It Real's 'better-not-bitter' divorce cards. She wishes death on you, your unborn chil-dren...and your children's kids, uncles, aunts, and first, second, and third cousins. Basically, your whole family."

Tessa groaned and lifted the report from her desk. "That would explain these sales numbers. Flatter than French pancakes. What happened? Last year, we did so well."

Mia tightened her lips. "Hmm. Yes, we did. Well, perhaps not so much last year as the one before the one before. We've done exceptionally well with a certain demographic, a niche group of consumers. If we put a label on those types of people, we'd call them witches and sons of, except we'd use the letter 'b.' That's the upside. The downside is that some of our messaging, a significant portion, in fact, fails to resonate with kind, considerate, decent, tactful people."

It's clear Mia claimed truth-when-it-hurts as her superpower.

Tessa let out a long sigh, and her shoulders slumped. "We always understood our brand wouldn't align with everyone's values, right? Some people will never understand what we're doing here."

"Do you know what we're doing here?" Mia asked. "Any more?"

Tessa steamrolled over Mia's question. "What I need to do is inject some fat into these numbers—or we'll all be looking for jobs sooner than later."

There were two truths Tessa had to face: she used to have a winning formula, and her can't-miss approach was no longer netting new customers. Instead of facing her problems head-on, she may have drifted into Evilene territory—no bad news. Speak, hear, and see no truth. This strategy, two years strong, had faltered and correlated with the sales slump...along with one other occurrence.

"It'll take a smidge more than a fat injection to make a turnaround in this market," Mia said. "We're on the verge of needing a defibrillator, intensive care, and some life support. Did you ever review the research I prepared for you? The sad, sad focus group results?"

"Not really," Tessa's lips pursed. "My schedule's been insane. You know."

Mia's brutal honesty remained core to the engine that kept Keep It Real running. At this moment, however, Tessa wished Mia would keep the hard facts to herself.

"I'm just keeping it real. That's what we do around here, isn't it?"

"Unfortunately, I may revise the mission statement. I need you to infuse me with false optimism."

Mia laughed. "Don't you remember what you told us on day

one? Friends don't let friends plummet into a pile of crap. We gift the truth. No optimism that isn't backed by numbers."

"The more I think about solutions, the more I think a refresh with a new line is the answer to our trouble. Something sticky. Something viral," Tessa said. "We've got to get it off the ground— and soon."

"Respectfully, I'd recommend we develop the *right* concept. We've got one idea on the table, but—Straight Talk? That thought is all wrong. You'd know that if you looked at the numbers and focus group results."

"Fine, where are they?" Tessa said before glancing at her watch. Truth be told, she didn't want to review them. She'd had enough facts and reality for a lifetime. "Shoot! I can't right this second. Saved by the bell. We're meeting with the writing team."

"Don't fret. In three minutes, our team will flood us with fresh and original ideas," Mia said with every ounce of sarcasm she could muster.

Tessa expelled a woeful sigh. "Keep It Real can't fail, Mia." She clenched her eyes shut, and her head fell back against her chair. "Too many people count on me, on this thing of ours. And we're so close. One more year in the black, only one more, and I'll have enough cash to buy Keep It Real outright from my dad. But I dunno. I'm always chasing. No matter how close I come to the things I want, I'll never catch them. Everything stays in view, but just out of reach."

"We'll come up with something. We'll pull through. I've got faith that a turnaround is coming, but I strongly recommend we leave the Straight Talk idea where it is—unseen."

After fumbling for words, Mia offered an understanding nod and mimed a violin serenade. "No one is more sympathetic to your plight than I am, but c'mon, Sis. You've successfully run an award-winning business for five years. I have no doubt you'll win over new customers...as soon as you learn to stay in your own lane and abandon your hyper-focus on one-upping Hart Cards."

She'd acknowledge to herself, if not to Mia, that her sales slump directly correlated to the point at which Hart Cards had risen to the number three greeting card company in the country. Hart rose on the brilliance of her plan for Sweet-Hart Cards, a fact that wasn't lost on her although it seemed to be lost on Cody.

"Humph. Why would I need to outdo myself? He-who-shall-not-be-named could never conceive the idea on his own."

Mia remained unmoved by Tessa's protest. "You sound a whole lot like a bird with ruffled feathers to me. Seeing he-who-shall-not-be-named at the Charity Gala last week isn't the source of this latest wave of angst, is it?"

"The gala? Pshh." Tessa batted her hand in the air, playing off her agitation. "Child, please. I have no idea what you're jabbering about."

Lying to herself had come easy for Tessa—deceiving Mia was harder.

Her mind drifted back to the moment at the ball she and Cody locked eyes on one another. The event, all glitter and glam, hosted throngs of D.C.'s best and brightest. They assembled to donate to the Historically Black College and University scholarship fund. Cody, Mia, and Tessa were A&T Aggies.

At various events over the years, she'd passed him with nary a stolen glance, but for some reason, on gala night, her eyes lingered on him. To her surprise, she did not stay there alone, even as he stood across the room with the Pop-Tart on his arm. Tessa didn't think much of it; he'd displayed many fill-ins over the years, no doubt attempting to burrow in her skin. But this time was different—Tessa not only gazed at him, she saw him, the man she remembered and the man he'd become. He materialized all wrapped up in an Armani tux and clinging to Miss Frosted Blueberry.

"Oh, you're not picking up what I'm putting down, huh? You haven't dated anyone, at least not seriously or long-term, since the infamous card delivery. Methinks someone doth protest too much."

"I beg to differ. I doth not protest at all. In fact, I doth not wish to continue this conversation. Cody Hart is a non-factor."

The mere sound of his name caused the shattered pieces of her heart to crumble to dust.

"Good thing. This morning, I read he's engaged and getting married soon. The announcement's in *The Post*, Style section, page seven." Mia retrieved the article from one of the bags and slid it across Tessa's desk until it was so far under her nose, Tessa couldn't deny it.

Of course, she refused to acknowledge the article, even as her eyes glued to the photos and the couple's toothy grins.

Married? Tessa heard the sound of flushing in her mind. It was the toilet that was her life...right before it stopped up and flooded. *Married.*

"You're not bothered, are you?" Mia asked.

"Bothered." She shrugged. "By Mr. and Mrs. Poptart? Whoop-de-ding-dang-do for them." Tessa both loved and hated how well Mia knew her. Right now, she wanted to pluck her in the forehead. An alarm beeped at her wrist. "It's meeting time! Let's go see what fresh and original ideas Creative will deliver."

"Mmm-hmm. I see what you did there. We're not finished. This conversation will rise like Lazarus. We'll pick it up later...whether you like it or not."

Cody and the Poptart. Married. Five years ago, she tried to kill herself with Hershey's kisses and struggle yoga because of her breakup with him. What would she do now? She hated healthy meditation crap.

"You're doing it wrong," Mia had told her back then. "There's no crying in yoga. What do you think happened? Is he seeing someone else?"

"If he had another woman, I could just maim him, do some jail time and be over it. No, sadly, what happened between us is worse—an obstacle emerged between us, one neither of us could overcome."

As they gathered their things to head for the writers' meeting, Mabel knocked on the door and poked her head inside. The whine session drew to an abrupt halt when she entered.

"Uh, Tessa, can I speak to you for a second? We've got a situation needing your immediate attention. *Right now.*"

"Message received," she replied. She had no idea what nightmare had befallen the company, but Mabel's scrunched eyes and pursed lips spelled direness and doom.

The urgency in her voice pushed Tessa up from her chair as she announced her swift exit. "I'll be back shortly."

"No, she won't," Mabel countered. "She'll return this evening...or tomorrow if we're lucky."

In the hall, Mabel took quick paces, led Tessa toward the reception area, and stopped abruptly, increasing Tessa's panic.

What the heck is going on?

"All right," Tessa said. "Spit it out."

"You've been summoned...by Mr. Hart."

"Mr. Hart?" She jerked her head back and sunk into a hard denial. She couldn't possibly be hearing Mabel correctly. There were only two Mr. Hart options, and one was deceased. "Last time I checked, Devon Hart was dead, wasn't he? God rest his soul."

Mabel shook her head. "Really, Tessa? I think we firmly established that...at the funeral. You sat on the second row, remember?"

"Then, you meant Cody?"

"Who else?"

After five years of stone silence? Tessa had read everything he needed to say about their relationship in the message Cody had couriered to her. "Why in the world does he want to speak with me?"

They were kids of publishing magnates, heirs to their respective thrones. Greeting cards were their perfect niche. Tessa

Sweet. Cody Hart. Sweet-Hart. That was the plan before the split.

"So, you're giving up on Sweet-Hart Cards?" Mia had asked Tessa. "You dreamed of starting that company with Cody for so long. If you go forward with Keep It Real, you're quitting."

Tessa didn't give up; Cody did. She'd planned to crush him like a roach, but Mia said Tessa was more Dr. Spock than Khan. When all was said and done, she put everyone ahead of herself...and she was right. Mia believed Tessa'd always come out on top in the end; Tessa wasn't so sure.

In fact, a pit in Tessa's stomach told her this meeting with Cody would reveal otherwise.

"All I can say is this—it's about the business, and it's urgent," Mabel said. "He needs to see you. Honestly, I'm as shocked by this day as you are. I thought he must be pranking me, at least until your father called."

"Dad?" she asked.

"Yes, he rang, insisting I put you in a car. Right now! The service is waiting out front."

"I'd rather drive myself." Tessa huffed. She disappeared into her office, now vacant, and reappeared with her purse. At the elevator, she glanced over her shoulder. "You know what's going on, don't you?"

Mabel inhaled a frustrated breath, tightened her lips, and shrugged. "Take the service. Also, this might be an ideal time for some of that yoga breathing...and a headstand."

As Tessa made her way to Hart, the pain from the old heartache resurrected. She recalled when she finally gathered up the strength to tell Mia what happened.

"This is about Cody. Tell me he didn't," Mia had said on that infamous day.

No longer able to maintain her fragile composure, she descended from her pose and made an ungraceful landing into an Indian-style position.

"Mmm-hmm." Through snot and tears, Tessa strained to say,

"Got me all gussied up and took me to dinner with his dad, who I've known most of my life. I can't lie. I felt like I was auditioning for a role I'd already won. Guess I failed. Afterward, he broke it off. Dumped me like last week's trash—with that."

He'd couriered a greeting card—one of the Dear Jane variety. He'd used a proxy, a stranger, to deliver the message that would erase what they'd been building since they were kids.

"A square peg in a round hole? We don't 'fit' anymore?" Mia's brow furrowed. "He must have brain damage because it's clear he bumped his whole entire head. He's writing this as if he's tossing out an old sweater, not ending a years' long relationship with his childhood sweetheart. He's a coward."

Tessa hadn't seen or heard from him from that day to this.

This meeting should prove eventful, if not enlightening.

Chapter Two

C ody

FROM AN UPSCALE, WATERFRONT PENTHOUSE BEFITTING THE HART Enterprises CEO, Cody enjoyed the city's panoramic view in his spacious home office. Waves of red, yellow, and orange leaves dotted the Georgetown harbor as cool winds dusted them into loose swirls. The end of the autumn season approached just as new troubles had begun. As his eyes roamed the tree-line, he held his cell to his ear with one hand and maneuvered his iMac mouse with the other.

"Yes, Uncle Brian. I've couriered the paperwork. It's en route," Cody said, turning his attention to Tessa's Keep It Real website. "I transferred the payment an hour ago." Guilt flooded his conscience, along with some apprehension. He inhaled deeply and exhaled to release the tension. "No problem. It's my pleasure."

After hanging up, a brief burst of contentment transformed into more unease. His latest business move had come with a hefty bill, one much costlier than his financial outlay—and this debt was long overdue. Avoiding the inevitable wasn't an option.

He could no longer deny the fact that he and Tessa, and their futures, sat on a collision course.

Wouldn't be the first time they were destined to clash.

They were on summer vacation, and she strolled into the Hart Enterprises grand entrance hall on her father's arm. Pops and Uncle Brian Sweet, Tessa's dad, together had built the media giant in an eclectic nook of the city. Every summer vacation, their fathers invited the heirs to the throne to learn the publishing business.

Each time he saw Tessa felt like the first time; on this day, she wore a blue dress covered in pink flowers and butterflies. A brief reintroduction reminded him that her name suited her perfectly. *Tessa*. It sounded like a whisper, a sweet one. Gazing at her reminded him of opening his favorite present, the giant one with his train set inside.

The youthfulness that left him secretly crushing on her also rendered him clueless about the difference between being the boss and being bossy. He leaned into his father's advice to be aggressive, pushy, never take no for an answer—but, for him, bad things happened. Even then, he remembered thinking that making Tessa fall in line wasn't supposed to be so hard.

Perhaps he should've considered those things when he made critical decisions about their companies' futures, especially now that he had risen to serve as the Hart Enterprise CEO.

After scanning Keep It Real's newest web collection, he stared at the "About Us" link. He resisted looking at it for months, but after a brief hesitation, he gave in to his desire and clicked. There she was, the girl he crushed on, the girl who once wore the butterfly dress. It seemed like minutes, not weeks, had passed since they last saw one another.

When they crossed paths at the charity auction, he wanted to take his eyes off of her, he'd even tried to avoid her, but he failed.

She glowed with confidence and seemed to possess a strength beyond mortals like him. She wore a grown-woman blue dress split to her hip, and her eyes sparkled as if she were lit from within. Her whole vibe unearthed sweet memories of endless days Cody had spent worshipping in the church of *her*.

His eyes drifted closed as he remembered the way he used to trace the line of her cheek with his index finger until he reached into the depths of her dimples. Back then, his sole purpose in life had been to expose them to the world.

She'd become so much more than Pops ever gave her credit for. He once called Tessa a chicken and Cody an eagle before their breakup. He said eagles and chickens could not coexist; he all but threatened Cody to let her go—but looking at Tessa in that blue dress at the ball, she was no chicken, and he wondered if he should have caved to his father's request.

Perhaps he wouldn't have if he had the courage and fight of a young Tessa wearing Chuck Taylors. He'd never forget those shoes.

Her Chucks had spent more than a few days in the sandbox. They were capped with frilly white ruffled socks. From her head sprung twin kinky puffs; they finished off her sweet face, like a bow on a gift. Her cuteness stole his heart; and he started on a mission to win hers way back then.

He'd made up the game they played, Big Business, to impress her. In his mind, he'd take the role of CEO and sit in the coveted big chair; she'd play receptionist and admire and adore him.

She had an entirely different idea.

"First of all, you don't tell me what I'm gonna be!" She had placed a sassy hand on her hip and fixed her mouth to tell him all the way off. After notifying him that her daddy told her she could be anything she wanted to be, she added, "That's why I'm going to be the CEO, too. The chair's big enough. Why can't we both sit in it?"

When he refused, well, Cody met Chuck in a way that branded on his brain.

He couldn't blame her. Tessa's dad declared she would succeed and someday lead; he was a girl-dad.

Now, looking at her webpage, it's clear she'd taken him at his word.

She'd been more than a lover. She was the best friend he'd ever known. They laughed about everything and nothing. The connection they shared—a once-in-a-lifetime bond—could not be replicated with anyone, including his fiancée. The latter now stood in his office doorway, wielding a spatula and wearing a "Kiss the Cook" apron. She was as opposite of Tessa as he could find—light, not dark brown, thin, not curvy, compliant, not unpredictable. He tried to offer a genuine smile in the face of his impending deception. The struggle was real.

"Ahhh," Cody said. "Nothing like the fresh smell of burnt toast and crunchy grits to start the day."

"Hey, you better be glad we're still in the honeymoon phase, or you'd pay for that." In good humor, she snickered and flipped her thick mane over her shoulder.

Her laugh bounced like an old, familiar song. It had a decent beat even if he too often struggled to dance to its groove. The pleasant moment sobered in a hurry as she breached the long-established boundaries and crept into his work zone—headed straight for his computer.

Tessa's photo consumed fourteen inches of his twenty-seven-inch monitor.

Surprised by her incursion, he rushed to grab the mouse—but she beat him. He proved too slow to minimize the Keep It Real window in time.

She leaned over to kiss him and flashed a nosy eye toward the screen. Her baby browns narrowed into fire-spitting slits. Her entire body stiffened.

"Really?" She pressed her palms together as if praying for strength not to wallop him. "See, what you're not gonna do is gawk at your ex-girlfriend's picture and expect to sit here and eat your breakfast without fearing for your life."

Before he could stop the words, he quipped, "What are you talking about? Every time I eat your cooking, I fear for my life."

An awkward laugh slipped out, one that nearly cost him his ability to inhale oxygen, based on the evil eye she flashed.

"Too soon," she snapped.

"I just hung up the phone with my Uncle Brian...Brian Sweet, the head of Sweet Media and Tessa's father. I'm working with him to solve a problem, a business challenge."

Her perfectly sculpted eyebrows scrunched. "*Humph.* I call B-S."

She stood there, unamused. Her face blanked to the point at which he couldn't figure out which way to duck. Before she fixed her mouth to curse him out in the manner to which he probably deserved, he attempted to quell the storm by speaking the words men never should say in the heat of battle. "Baby, it's not what you think."

To his surprise and relief, she only crossed her arms over her chest and huffed, waiting for him to reach into one of his orifices and pull out a satisfactory excuse.

So, how and why did Tessa consume his mind? And why didn't he confess the business deal to Chandra? After all, he'd been planning it for weeks.

He suspected he had lingering questions neither he nor Chandra could answer.

"Why are you behaving this way? Nothing's going on. This is business," he lied. If the mere sight of Tessa's likeness on his screen angered her to this degree, she'd go a mile past off when she learned the full truth. He couldn't tell her yet, not until he'd broken the news to the person who most needed to hear it first.

Chandra's Tina Turner legs got a full two steps into stride when Cody jumped up and tugged her elbow. Hurt flooded her eyes. The entire scene that morning—Tessa's picture, the half-truths—all conspired to worsen already bad optics. The situation might appear shady, but his intentions weren't, not in the least.

"What could you possibly have to say to Brian Sweet? Didn't your father all but ban the Harts from engaging with that family?" she said, her voice brimming with unnecessary contempt. "Your sisters go into anaphylactic shock at the sound of the name Sweet."

"Well, my father's not here anymore. This is a new day. I respected his choices, even though I disagreed with them. But, understand this—they've never been enemies to this family, our business, or me, despite chatter to the contrary. I'd advise you to ignore Renee and Regina."

He frequently referred to his sisters as The Devilment Twins —the most accurate way to describe them with so few clean words.

"So." She huffed and jerked out of his grip. "What kind of deal requires you to sit around gawking at...her picture on your screen?"

"Gawking?" An angry heat rose into his chest and up through his collar. "Listen, I can't discuss the details yet. This is a private matter, and I'm going to keep the information exactly that— private. The only place you'll find anything nefarious about this situation is in your mind. My hands are clean."

"Is that right?" she snipped.

He nodded. "I'm not only right, but I'm also correct. Your suspicion is not only unnecessary, but it's also unattractive. Inse-cure's not a good look on you."

Shot fired.

Her nostrils flared. Instead of consoling her, pulling her into his arms, and loving reassurance into her, he'd crossed the line, deepening the divide between them. On a positive note, the distraction of this terse discussion about Mr. Sweet would help him conceal the truth...a little while longer.

"Excuse me?" she said. "First of all, you've got me all twisted up."

There she blows.

"I don't—" he began before Chandra cut him off.

Chandra Barrington, of the Washington D.C. Barrington's, daughter of "doctor and wife of," was well positioned in the upper echelon among DC's socialites. At a Barrington family dinner party at their Potomac estate, he'd eavesdropped on the conversation between Chandra and her mother, at the precise moment her mother called him "the catch of the century" and "Mr.-Oh-So-Right." She cautioned Chandra not to release Cody from her clutches.

Well, she said the words 'get away,' but he heard the clutch part.

Regardless, the goal was to keep their relationship in tact at all costs. Thus, Chandra became a chief tactician who never met an argument she couldn't avoid, especially if it didn't suit her agenda. This wasn't one of those times.

"One thing is clear in this situation: you've got one heck of an imagination. Did you believe this place existed?"

He shrugged. "What place?"

"The place where I don't get justifiably ticked off about your little business secrets. Apparently you've conjured up some fantasy location where obedient girls suck up their anger and don't speak."

Maybe she meant the place where the event-of-the-season wedding becomes more important than the marriage. In every moment they shared since the dinner, he questioned Chandra's motives. Even worse, he'd begun to feel smothered, as if she'd pushed the pedal to the floor and accelerated their lives straight into a whirlwind to manipulate him. They'd scheduled the wedding inside of a month. He proposed, frankly, because loving Chandra was easier, simpler, and required much less energy from him than doing the same for Tessa, precisely what he thought he wanted. Cody accepted his fate because he'd rejected all other relationships, especially long-term ones, since Tessa.

With the wedding weeks away, their life integration was underway. She had started the move to his place a full month ahead of schedule—a trinket here, an appliance there—taking Cody's suffocation to critical levels. She'd scheduled every detail, made every decision, planned every aspect of their future —all at a much faster pace than he expected. He hardly had time to fuse two cogent thoughts together, a state of mind that seemed core to their survival and her ability to maintain the status quo.

So, she must have really felt threatened to snap like this.

"Chandra, you lost me."

"Well, pull up Google maps so I can explain where we are."

He gulped hard and swallowed. At once, she'd reminded him of someone—a woman who was neither easy nor easily fooled.

"We took a U-turn at you-must-be-kidding-me and finally have arrived at you-must've-bumped-your-head." She charged toward his office door and glanced back over her shoulder.

"Stop, please. I've heard you, Chandra. I've listened to you," he said, calling after her. "And one thing is obvious to me right now."

"What?!" By now, she'd done an about-face and stared at him. The emphasis she put on the "T" confirmed his suspicions.

"You're hangry. We should eat," he said, revealing a sliver of a smile. "Look, Baby, have I ever given you the slightest cause to mistrust me? I've never been missing-in-action, never unreachable. You've got access to my cell phone, though you've chosen not to check it. Every free moment I have, I spend with you."

She breathed an audible sigh of relief. As the hard edges of her expression softened, he moved in.

"I love you. We're getting married in a month," he continued. "You hold not only the key to my home but also my heart."

"You're so cheesy."

"And you love it. Now, let's go eat your crunchy grits." He chuckled when he took steps toward his office door to meet her, and she jabbed him in the arm. "But, I'll reserve the first bite for you...just in case."

"Ha. Ha!" She started past the threshold. "You're right, baby. I've got nothing to worry about. After all, you've got me. What more could you want?"

He followed her out the door, but not before glancing back over his shoulder to catch a glimpse of Tessa, anticipating the drama that lay ahead. The girl in the butterfly dress was a woman of many moods—a full range—but he dreaded the calm. He'd experienced the lethality of it when they were kids.

Back in the day, after he declared himself the CEO and Tessa the receptionist, he offered her the opportunity to take dictation, including their McDonald's order.

"You sit in there," he said, pointing to the receptionist's area. "When I'm ready, I'll call you in, so you can answer my phone. Your first assignment is to place our Happy Meal orders with Ms. Mabel. My treat. I've been saving my milk money."

"Why can't we both be CEOs and sit in the big chair, again?" she had asked.

"Because I make the rules. It's my job, my seat." He positioned his body to block her path. Then he took a deep breath to inflate the scrawniness in his chest. "The only one who's gonna sit there is me."

"Okay," she said, flattening her voice into an eerie calm. "If you say so."

He'd impressed himself. She'd folded more quickly than a Hart Card.

He now, as a grown man, understood the realities of a calmly spoken "okay" from an angry woman's mouth.

As he envisioned the days to come, it was Tessa's "okay, if you say so" that scared him most.

Keep It Real Cards

When fortune favors the bold, wonderful things happen to courageous people who deserve the best.

Let's Keep It Real—You're neither courageous nor deserving. But, luckily, fortune favors people like you, too. Congratulations!

Chapter Three

C ody

CODY TOOK REFUGE BEHIND THE SAFETY OF HIS EXPANSIVE EXECUTIVE desk, bracing himself as he waited for Tessa's broom to swoop in. Through Mabel, he called her in to talk. Whatever their differences and her grudges, she deserved the respect and consideration of hearing the news from him.

He anticipated an awkward civility dance; he was more practiced in that art than Tessa. He'd offer a reasonable explanation if she'd give him a chance. She'd come to understand he never intended his dealing with Uncle Brian to be perceived as an act of war.

Even if Tessa rolled in like thunder and lightning and unleashed her fury, she'd calm when she understood what happened...and why. He'd be prepared to accept her gratitude, but he may be waiting a long time for it.

No sooner than the thought crossed his mind, thunder clapped. The storm had arrived.

Quick hard steps clacked against the marble floor, and then he heard the voice of Ms. Dee, his long-time Hart Enterprise executive assistant, and ally. She'd been with the company since Uncle Brian and Pops ran it with attached hips.

"Oh, my goodness, Tessa. You're...all grown up and stunning!" Ms. Dee sang. She loved Tessa as an auntie would her favorite niece.

"It's been too long," Tessa replied. "I've been ridiculously busy, but that's no excuse. We must do dinner...soon!"

Chill bumps raised in Cody's arms at the sound of the sweet lilt in her voice.

"Only if you serve that fondue again. Thank you for that recipe," Ms. Dee said excitedly. "Anyway, we can catch up later. Right now, Mr. Hart's expecting you. Please, go right inside."

Within seconds, the door whipped opened. Before he could catch his breath, she materialized in front of him, and they stood there—eye to eye, face to face. She strolled inside like a Chuck Taylored boss. She'd blossomed and straightened the kinky curls she wore during their union into bone-straight grown woman locks; they bobbed over her shoulder with each stride. She seemed to move in slow motion as in the tense moments of a John Wu flick.

He'd anticipated the worst but reality proved to be less frightening. Her presence blanketed him like a refreshing breeze. Everything about her mesmerized him still. He allowed his eyes to roam the contours of her cheekbones, her button nose...until he reached the steely gaze.

"Tessa." He masked his attempt to inhale her signature lavender and jasmine scent. She caused a seismic shift in his mind without speaking a word.

A timely recollection brought him back to a cold reality—he'd put a ring on it, and Chandra was the one he chose the second time around. Still, he couldn't deny his feelings for the one standing front and center, even if he refused to act on them.

"Cody," she barked. "You beckoned?"

"It's been a long time," he said. "How many years now?"

"Oh, I dunno. Five?" she replied.

His eyes lowered to take in her sleek, black tailored suit molded to every hill and valley on her glorious body. After his thorough once-over, she returned the favor. Then a heavy silence hung between them before she nipped it.

"Color me surprised. You called me in for a face-to-face instead of sending me a card." An empty, angry chill had replaced the adoration and devotion that once filled expressions reserved for him. "By the way, I understand congratulations are in order. A month away from the big day, right? I think I spotted that somewhere."

"*The Post.*" What could he do except nod? "You're too kind. Thank you."

"How perfect." He sensed sarcasm and so much of it. She paused as if she'd expected him to say something else. Then the sound of her voice cut into the heavy silence. "May fortune favor you both."

"Fortune favors the bold, right?" He smirked, having read that copy years ago when she wrote it the first time. "Tessa." His voice broke the tension. "Please, have a seat."

He gestured his palm toward the guest chair and watched her stroll over, her gait smooth and sure as if she traveled on a people mover. His head wanted to turn away, but his neck refused.

Until now, he'd forgotten Tornado Tessa's vampire powers. She'd only been in his office for two minutes, and she'd already begun to suck the joy out of him.

"We should get to it, the reason you beckoned me." Her entire demeanor screamed "unbothered," a state that wouldn't last long.

Cody worked up the nerve to tell her, but it choked in his throat. A long awkward pause settled between them.

"Okay, I'll go first," she said. "So! I see you finally wrested control of Hart Enterprises from the Cruella twins. Good to see you remained committed to...something."

The shot fired brought him to a fork in the road. He could follow her lead and veer off the high one or keep the discussion civil. He opted to do the latter...sort of.

"Yes, that's the way companies work. When you get ready to take them to the next level, they come along for the ride. You understand that better than anyone." He steepled his fingers together. "I've followed Keep It Real since day one. What you've achieved is nothing short of amazing."

"Amazing? Wow. Coming from you, that's...well, that's almost like a compliment." She cocked her head to the side and gazed at him in disbelief, allowing space for another uncomfortable silence. "Can we get on with this? Some business at my office needs my attention."

Cody cleared his throat. "When you say, 'my office,' we should define the word 'my.'" He'd finally collected the nerve to break the news, so, of course, her cell phone rang, and she glanced down.

"It's my father. Excuse me for one minute. I need to take this." She held up her index finger. "He never calls me during the day. It must be important."

Tessa didn't know the reason for the call, but he did. Cody shuddered, imagining what Uncle Brian was saying. A quick clock-check reminded Cody that his warm-up small talk with Tessa had taken longer than expected. Cody's plan ran late while Uncle Brian had called right on time. He was supposed to be consoling her after she received the news. Instead, inadvertently, he was breaking it to her. Cody had stalled for too long.

"Dad, I'm in a meeting." She shifted in her seat and turned her back to Cody. "What can I—"

In an instant faster than a flicker, Tessa quieted and then went silent. First, she nodded and froze like a mannequin, sat perfectly still. She didn't grunt or move. Nothing. Then the bomb dropped. "You. Did. What!" She yelped. Through her intense shock, the words "To whom?" rolled off of her tongue.

In an exorcist-like whirl, her head wheeled toward Cody, and her eye, the left one alone, narrowed into a slit and locked on him. "Dad, I'll see you in an hour. Goodbye." The deadly glare could've broken his bones. She fell back against her chair, her expression now one of complete and utter disbelief.

"What the hell, Cody?" Her voice boomed, and he felt his body fracture. He did the only thing a man could do in this situation—offered her a bottle of Fiji water.

"You thirsty?" he asked.

She reluctantly accepted it, seemingly more out of shock than need. Then she untwisted the cap. She sniffed it as if he'd poison her instead of killing her with his bare hands or piercing her heart with a wooden stake.

"Congratulations?" Cody shrugged and revealed a sheepish grin.

"You bought Keep It Real. My company. You bought—you acquired my company!" Her arms flailed; water splashed everywhere. "What in the entire, Cody? You could've purchased a gazillion other things if you had a little spare cash sitting around. Shares in Apple. A yacht in the Mediterranean. Waterfront property on some distant island. Heck, you could've named your own island. Why in heaven's name would you buy my thing, my only thing, Keep It Real?"

"I can't disclose the terms of the deal—per the non-disclosure agreement, which was your father's idea, by the way. But you should know this gesture is a kindness. Really. And I don't want you to—"

"Excuse me? A kindness? You wouldn't know compassion if it chewed off half your face." She jutted her hands in the air as her voice erupted. "I can't believe this—my own father, the man who gave me life, sold me out for thirty pieces of silver."

"I wouldn't exactly call the price I paid thirty pieces."

"Oh, yeah. What would you call it? Twenty? Ten? I'm sure you snapped it up for a tidy little bargain."

Tessa had apparently planned to break off another piece of her mind and hurl it at Cody, but it stuck in her throat, causing her to swallow down the wrong pipe and choke. She took a sip of water to calm the coughing.

"A little more than twenty, I'd say," Cody started. "Ten-point-two million is a lot of waterfront property. Or Apple shares, as you recommended."

Tessa sprayed Cody's face with the water that filled her mouth and cheeks. Cody winced and rode the wave. He retrieved a handkerchief from his pant pocket and dabbed his face. He was old-school that way. Learned it from Pops.

"Wait. What?" She dangled on the edge of her seat.

"You heard, right. I'm disclosing the price, despite the NDA, so you'll understand I didn't pay a 'little' money for Keep It Real. No way will I dismantle it. You have my word."

"Ha! Your word. How rich! That and a quarter wouldn't buy me a free cup of coffee."

"Listen, please. I'm not laying off or firing any of your staff, and your leadership will remain unchanged. But after reviewing your accounting books— "

"My...my—you reviewed my books?"

"Of course, as part of the acquisition." He nodded and jerked his head back. "Your sales are sluggish. You must be aware of the financial hit you're taking."

"Wow. Your powers of deduction? Still astounding. I'm in awe."

There it was. The sarcasm. He'd hit the dead-end on the high road. The snark forced him low. There was no turning back. "Keep It Real found its initial success because it filled a niche demand in an underserved market," he began, "but your bang has fizzled, and now you're struggling for survival. Sales projections don't appear promising. The current numbers suggest the novelty's worn off."

"Novelty." She sounded breathless as if he'd sucked the oxygen from her lungs.

"Yes, you've got more competition—"

"Copycats. Hart knows that better than anyone."

He ignored the dig. "And expanding your market share is critical. Hart Cards outsell yours two-to-one."

"You're kidding me, right? Apples and oranges. With all of its business interests combined, Hart is more than fifty times the size of Keep It Real. Yet you're only outselling us two-to-one and, in certain markets, we outperform you."

"Someone's been doing her homework on Hart's sales."

"What can I say? I like reading things that make me laugh...hard...out loud."

"Regardless, I can take you where you need to go, and, frankly, I know you're capable of more than...this."

She fell back into her seat, and hope left her eyes. He remembered that look.

"This? Exactly what do you mean by...this?"

He'd wounded her; it was her fault. She veered onto the low road, and he followed. Now, he'd deliver the final blow. "Do you know what they call Keep It Real in industry circles?"

"An award-winning company?"

"I mean, behind your back."

She shrugged.

"Bitter Witch Greetings." He went straight for the jugular. "No one else will tell you, but I will because I've never been anything but honest with you. Your ideas are stale and mean, and no one likes your products anymore."

She turned away.

"Keep It Real needs a change in direction. You, more than anyone, must realize I'm telling you the truth," Cody continued. "And I've developed a strategy, a roadmap, to help you find a higher level of success than, frankly, you could reach on your own."

"Roadmap."

"I won't completely alter your vision, but, together, we'll....
let's say we'll pivot a little."

Her jaw tensed, and he could almost see steam rising out of
her ears. Tornado Tessa launched into a deadly spin and would
touch down any second. Cody braced himself, knowing she'd
acknowledge the truth...eventually.

"Pivot? You've got some audacity. Who do you think you
are?"

"I'm the CEO of Hart Enterprises and now the head of Keep It
Real Cards. You should get used to that. Sometimes it helps to
say it out loud. CEO."

"Please. I wish I would." She sucked her tongue. "And don't
let your little performance here detract from what I'm trying to
say. Yes, our profits may be a little on the flat side, but to suggest
we're struggling for survival is a tad dramatic, even for you, Mr.
Square-Peg Round-hole. Furthermore, we've already developed
a plan to increase our market share."

"Perfect. I look forward to reviewing and approving it."

She bolted to her feet. "First of all, I have several suggestions
about what you can do with your little approval."

"Tessa—"

"Secondly, I'll get my company out of Hart Enterprises and
your clutches if it's the last thing I do. If you've got a roadmap
for that, I'm all ears."

"Come on..."

"Lastly, you can't be my CEO if I quit. And be warned, I
always keep a pair of Chuck Taylors handy."

"Are you finished?" He shrugged and waited for a response
that didn't come. "If that's how you feel, it would seem that you
and I have come to an impasse."

"No, we're at the end...again."

Tessa hovered over his desk with a menacing glare and
snorted like a bull before making her exit.

He allowed his head to fall on the mahogany wood and
banged it repeatedly. Then he picked up the phone to warn the

next victim. "Brace yourself. Tornado Tessa just left here. I'd bet two-to-one she's on the way to you."

Tornado Tessa. He introduced her to the Big Business game all those years ago, and refused her the chance to sit in the "big chair." Adding insult to injury, he told her she could grab a notebook and take their Happy Meal orders.

His chest had puffed with pride as he put her in her place. He'd run the show like Pops, let her know who was boss early and often. In twenty-twenty hindsight, he was a child unacquainted with women or the ways of the world. Under her seemingly placid façade was Tornado Tessa.

In lockstep with him, Tessa made a play for the chair and reached out to grab it. He strong-armed her to prevent her incursion, planted his hand against her shoulder to hold her back. He was determined to keep her from getting what she wanted. She'd need to settle for what he gave her.

That's when it happened—she planted her Chuck Taylor's so far into his chicken nuggets they jiggled in the back of his throat. The kick sent Cody crumbling into a heap on the floor, howling in pain. Through unfallen tears and blinding agony, he glimpsed her form as she nonchalantly stepped over his soon-to-be corpse with the boldness of a cold-blooded boss she later proved herself to be.

Even in her youth, Tessa was unflappable. Little did he realize at the time, the kick that could've marked their ending sparked a new beginning.

He hoped for a similar outcome this time…except he'd rather avoid the kick, proverbial or otherwise.

Chapter Four

T essa

CODY'S ANNOUNCEMENT, THE ACQUISITION (TAKEOVER) OF KEEP IT
Real Cards, cut into Tessa like brutal, jagged blades. Her mind
flooded with a litany of unspoken clap back responses that she
wished she'd delivered with the fury of dragon fire, but nothing
could come close to the sting in his retort.

Bitter Witch Greetings.

Well played.

She'd think of the perfect, snappy response about an hour
after their meeting ended. Too late to matter.

His quip, his well-chosen strike weapon, pierced through her
veneer of self-assured success. His words compounded her
persistent doubts that she'd strayed from her purpose, her goal,
to gift the truth rather than curse people with it. She'd never
intended her brand to sound bitter or witchy. She'd only wanted
to help people, to "keep it real" while using humor to soften the
blow of hard, cold realities.

But her failing did not diminish the weight of her message to him—the nerve! Cody had the gall to criticize her when he built Hart Cards on the idea she conceived; he was the one who sent the "Dear Jane" cow dung that crushed any possibility of building Sweet-Hart Cards. Shame on him for judging her. She could recommend a location or two where he could shove his wisecracks.

However, Codys beef with Keep It Real put the spotlight on underlying issues that were more significant than acquisitions and roadmaps and could be boiled down to two salient points: Tessa had succeeded without him...and he hated her for it.

With her life and sanity in shambles after the clash with Cody, Tessa left Hart Enterprises and lurked outside as she pulled herself together. She wandered across the parking lot to her car, and the wind rudely greeted her like the frost between her and Cody. Between the break-up card and the acquisition, Cody was two-for-two in hitting his intended target—back-to-back bull's eyes.

The farther she moved from the building, the steadier and harder the stream of frustrated tears flowed down her nippy cheeks. Her eyes rained more from the disappointment than the pain; she'd been deceived...again.

Tessa had only trusted two men in her lifetime—Cody and her father. With the sale of Keep it Real completed behind her back and with zero notification, it was clear they'd conspired to ambush her. Once upon a time, she didn't believe either capable of this DEFCON 1 betrayal. Together, they'd not only taken her life's work but robbed her of time to wallow in the mire. She'd now set on a new mission—to find the shortest distance from defense to offense and make her move.

She mopped her eyes dry with the back of her hand and stiffened her spine. She put her well-deserved pity party on pause while she wheeled her car out of the parking lot and pulled onto the road to get answers.

The drive gave her time to regroup. The journey to redemption would begin in the place where her new trouble with the Harts really began—her father's office.

Dad's got some explaining to do.

In one fell ambush, Sweet Media, her former refuge from the world of Hart, became enemy camp. Now she'd storm the building like a ticked off Marine on a beachhead, kicking butt and taking names all the way up to the seventh floor.

Determined and fierce, she ripped into the lobby and bolted toward the elevator banks.

Security usually recognized her as the boss's daughter, so they never stopped her...until today. A giant neophyte officer, unschooled in the company way, defended the Sweet Media territory like Davie Crockett at the Alamo. Before she reached out to the call button, the towering man-mountain materialized and blocked her.

"Sorry, ma'am," he said as if he was talking to her grandma. "I can't permit you to go upstairs. Strict orders." He pointed upward.

She tilted her head back to take in his altitude. He stood man-wall tall.

"Listen...Mr. Shorty."

"Mr. Little."

"Stop, really?"

He pointed to his name badge.

"My father owns the building. I'm Tessa Sweet." She batted the air with her hand and dismissed his refusal as she leaned forward to call her ride to the seventh floor. He obstructed her with a Kung Fu arm block.

"I know who you are. Your father not only posted a picture of you, but he also called down and ordered us to prevent you from entering if you arrived in, quote, Tornado Tessa mode, unquote. I failed mind-reading 101, but my keen talents for observation suggest the cyclone has touched down. Your journey ends here. Sorry! I can't allow you upstairs."

Allow? Hello! I own this building.

By her calculation, he weighed three or four of her. She'd be a next-level fool to get ready for that rumble. Instead, she ducked and dodged, danced on her toes like a prizefighter—but instead of sticking and moving, she moved without sticking. She flounced from side to side until she bobbed and weaved herself breathless. Then she huffed and puffed, searching for a place to perch herself so she could catch her breath; she noticed lobby benches that sat too far out of reach, so she planted her hands on her hips. By now, beads of sweat had collected along her hairline.

The man-wall, unlike Tessa, was unflappable. He hadn't wheezed, gasped, or missed a single inhale while she stood there sucking air like a Hoover. She vowed to resume her workout routine...next week...after a few days of carb loading.

For now, she raised her white flag. The fight was over. Tessa bent over to grasp her knees, praying they steadied her while she collected herself; she held up her index finger before foolishly failing in her second and last physical attempt to breach the barrier.

"You don't understand," Tessa said. "I own part of this company. I demand to see my father."

Mr. Little had the nerve to start laughing. "Mr. Sweet told me you'd say that. He directed me to remind you that your company has been sold and, technically, neither you nor Keep It Real are part of Sweet Media."

Tessa's shoulder sagged. She wanted to argue, but her fancy feet routine had turned her from a storming Marine into a napping-Norma.

Defeated, at last, she pivoted but left him with words to remember before walking away. "One day, maybe sooner than you think, my father's gonna die. As his sole heir, I'll own everything the light touches in here." She jabbed her index finger in his face; she'd save the middle finger salute for a safer distance. "If you're still working here when that day comes, pack it up, my friend—you're so fired!"

She cranked up her inner toddler and mumbled her verbal tantrum all the way to the exit.

"If I'm still here," he called out to her, "I'll let you go upstairs."

What am I gonna do now?

Back on the street again (in a non-hooker way), she hung her hands on her hips and allowed her thoughts to churn for a moment. There had to be a way inside besides scaling the man-wall. She'd practically designed Sweet's new building, well, two snack rooms, and the daycare center. No one knew the interior better than she and her father, especially not the man-wall.

That's when an epiphany cracked through her exhaustion. She'd use the insider information to her advantage. All those summer vacations spent at Sweet exploring the halls were about to pay off.

Wearing a floppy straw hat and dark glasses purchased from a nearby street vendor, she dropped her chin to her chest and piggybacked on a UPS delivery driver rolling a stack of Amazon's smiling boxes on a hand truck.

Once beyond the threshold and unnoticed, she slipped into the emergency stairwell and slogged up seven flights of steps. She opened the door at the destination, and her eyes volleyed between the elevator banks and her dad's office as she scanned for Sweet bounty hunters.

With a clear coast, Tessa trotted into her father's posh, newly decorated suite where she found him tucked away behind his desk reading, no doubt the sales reports. The unschooled eye would see an executive suit with silver hair. To her, he was a dimpled, kind-eyed angel and doting father who stayed up half the night assembling and reassembling her Huffy bike for her eighth birthday. Usually.

Today, he was the Judas who traded her company for, well, ten-point-two million cannoli.

"Buttons! I wondered how long it would take you to make it by security."

"Don't Buttons me, Dad. Really? It's Miss Sweet to you."

Flashbacks to childhood threats to knock her eyes in the back of her head squelched her desire to curse him like a man off the streets. She much preferred her peepers to stay where they were.

"Oh, don't be angry with your dad. You needed time to cool off. So, my plan worked. How did you escape Tiny?"

"You mean, Mr. Little? Yeah, if he's Tiny, I'm Michelle Obama." She snickered from her gut. "There's not an inch of this space I haven't explored. You're lucky I used the door. I could've dropped through the ceiling like Tom Cruise in *Mission Impossible* and given you a heart attack," she said, spreading her arms as if in a hover pose.

Angry or not, Tessa kept her father in stitches, and today he laughed with his belly and shoulders, emitting almost a honking noise from his left nostril. She closed the door behind her and scowled at his plush new couch before collapsing on it. During the recent redecoration, he'd rid the office of the worn leather sofa that served as Tessa's sole remaining source of nostalgia, the monument to Tessa's and Cody's first kiss. She didn't want to keep the cast-off furniture, but she also didn't want to let it go...much like her relationship with Cody.

"Do you remember bring-your-daughter-to-work day? My absolute favorite. Not Christmas. Not my birthday, but spending the day with you at Hart and then Sweet. This place. I thought you intended to pass Sweet Media to me, as part of our family's legacy from you to me, me to my future kids, and so on."

Pride tilted his head upward. His smile was the evidence of it. "How could I forget? You've always burned so bright, with this fire, this hunger for success. I admired that quality in you, even though you were a little artsy for my tastes. It takes some people years to learn in business what you know by nature. That's flare. I can't teach that."

He spun around and shifted his eyes from her face to his hands. She could feel the hurt in her expression, and he avoided it but continued. "You asked me a hundred questions. What is this? What is that? What does the line on this report mean? How do you use this? What does this key do? Who is that? What does he do? I've worked with some of the most powerful and talented people in this industry, and, to date, I've only been stumped by the litany of questions from my excessively inquisitive daughter."

"And to think Mom wanted me to earn an MBA."

"Or get a Juris Doctor so you could join corporate counsel," he added.

"She even suggested medicine. Me of all people. I can't even stand the sight of blood...on a Band-Aid."

"Yeah, you're a touch too bougie for bodily fluids...but, I must admit, Dr. Tessa Sweet had a nice ring to it," he replied.

Tessa smiled. "She hated the idea of me writing. Too unpredictable, she warned. But not you. You said go for it—you told me that I might find a hundred things I'm capable of succeeding at, but I'd only find one passion, one pursuit that I'd love so much that, if I was lucky enough to earn a living doing it, I'd never work a day in my lifetime. You all but ordered me to find that thing and commit myself to it. You remember?"

"Sure do."

"You allowed me to discover and choose my own destiny. You said you'd always have my back."

"True to this second."

"Is it? The knife lodged in my back begs to differ," she said. "You sold Keep It Real like a used Toyota...and to none other than Cody Hart, for the love of all that's good and holy."

"Here we go. I didn't sell you out."

His words hung in the air like smog. "Since you left Hart Enterprises, the Harts have been plotting to destroy Sweet Media at every turn," she said. "On top of that, you watched me circle the drain for months after Cody abandoned me. I cried like the chief slicer in an onion factory for weeks. Then I crawled my way out of that darkness and found my dream; I struggled to build my company. Some days I didn't think I'd make it, but you helped me put the pieces back together. For what? To auction them off to the highest bidder?"

"I didn't agree to this arrangement to hurt you. Whether or not you understand the rationale, I did what I needed to do to help you, ensure your future, but I can't disclose—"

"The terms of the deal. Blah. Blah. Blah. Spare me the spiel. It didn't go down well the first time when I heard it from Cody," she said with a shrug. "I'll quit Keep It Real, abandon it as Cody did me. Let him try to run my company without me; he wouldn't last a day."

"Buttons. You built Keep It Real from little more than a dream....and so much pain. You and Mia used almost all of your savings, your imagination, and card stock. You turned paper and ideas into a multi-million-dollar corporation. And, now, I mean, what? You're really going to abandon everything and everyone, your family as you call them because your pride's a little bruised?"

"Bruised? No, Cody opted out of Sweet-Hart cards, not me. Now, he's emerged from the muck to steal my life's work, and you've welcomed him to use you as a proxy."

Her dad paused, and his lips turned down at the corners. "Six thousand, three hundred and seventy-nine."

Tessa's shoulder-shrug reflected a question about the source of that number, a question she didn't ask but wanted him to answer.

"That's the number of employees in my charge," he continued. "You are one of them." He lifted a single index finger in the air to put an exclamation mark on his point.

"I used to be the most important one."

"You still are...but you equal one person. When I make decisions involving this company, Buttons, I have a fiduciary responsibility and a professional commitment to think about what's best for all. This deal was best for everyone—you included."

"How did we even get here, Dad? You didn't even hint that selling Keep It Real was under consideration."

He took careful steps toward the slick new sofa before filling the seat next to her. He wrapped his arm around her shoulder, hugged her close, and she became his sweet girl again.

She resisted and pulled away at first but conceded before leaning into him; her eyes gave way to a flourish of tears.

"Buttons, you are a part of me. I would never make a decision of this magnitude without ensuring your survival. There were *stipulations*...several."

She wiped her eyes and jerked her head backward. "Such as?"

"Hart Enterprises voting shares, for starters. As you know, Devon loved surprises, positive and negative. Firing his final shot to his kids, given the rivalry between him and me, he bequeathed some of his shares to me—as it turns out, just enough. As part of the acquisition agreement, you will receive mine."

"But that means—"

"Exactly. Except there's a but..." He paused, leaving her hanging in the silence. "In his final letter to me, Devon asked me to do the impossible—keep the peace between Cody and his sisters, serve as a check and balance. I think his request demonstrates how well he understood his kids, especially in light of the recent court battles. Handing over my shares to you is a gesture to show you how much I trust you."

The wheels in her mind began to turn. Ten minutes ago, her predicament appeared hopeless, bleak. Now, not so much.

"It's not a sizeable percentage, but it's critical—vital to Hart's operations." He left her side and returned to his desk. "Cody holds forty-nine percent, a combination of his and his brother Jackson's shares. The twins hold forty-seven. Four percent tips the balance either way."

"If both sides were on fire, I wouldn't spit on one, so they could save the other, especially not Things One and Two," she said of the sisters, Renee and Regina.

"The girls were good kids...once."

"Good. The way an eagle is good to a rabbit. They went

straight witch—north to west—ever since Devon divorced their mother and married Cody's," she said.

"The thing is," he said, "these sibling personality clashes mean zero-zilch-nada. What matters, truly, is the people—the staff and the consumers. If you keep their interests first, you will always succeed."

"You've always said we don't build companies; we create families."

"Devon and I differed on many issues, but this principle was never one of them. We were brothers in every way except blood." He appeared wistful, exposing the ache in his heart. "I didn't stop loving my brother. We quit speaking. My greatest regret is that I stopped trying. I gave up on us, and maybe I shouldn't have."

"What more could you do?"

"Who knows? The point is, I shouldn't have stopped. It's our job to do all we can do until our loved ones are gone," he said. "I realize the rocky past you two shared clouds your view of Cody, but I've watched him over the years."

She tightened her lips and narrowed her eyes as if to warn him to limit the compliments.

"He's grown to be an honorable, smart young man, Buttons. More importantly, he makes good decisions. In Devon's and my tradition, he puts the future of the business and the employees before personal feelings."

High praise for the perpetrator who broke her heart and jacked her company.

"These shares give you an influential stake in Hart Enterprises—the business and the people. With this control, the Harts will be invested in you, too."

"What about Jackson?" He was Cody's quirky missing-in-action brother. He maintained residence under the radar and out of the press. "He could return to stake his claim at any time."

"Haven't you heard? He's a psychic now," her father said. "Whatever he is, he's not engaged in the day-to-day business.

Cody controls his shares, so he keeps a slight edge. Even still, he needs an ally to even up the fight with his sisters."

"He views me as many things, Dad; I promise you an ally isn't one of them. If he does, maybe he shouldn't." She shrugged. "One thing's certain, I'd never vote with the Cruella Twins. And rest assured, they'd never ever side with me. He knows that. So, for my purposes, the shares are all but useless."

"Don't devalue them too soon. You won't know how useful they are until you need them."

"I spoke to Cody before coming here...as you're aware." She exhaled a heavy sigh and bit her lip before saying, "He's going to change my vision for Keep It Real, Dad."

"Really, Buttons? Don't tell me you're afraid of change. Do you think I could build Hart and Sweet Media without it? You're standing in the middle of one of the most significant changes in our professional lives. Sweet Media. It's all about how you respond."

"You didn't give me a choice. When you sold my company, you didn't include me in the decision."

"No, I did not, but how you respond is one-hundred percent under your control. Ten years ago, who would've thought we'd be offering pumpkin lattes, cranberry muffins, and free Wi-Fi in our Ebony stores? Yet, here we are. Businesses evolve and rebrand every day. It's called staying current and relevant to your customers. You'll be fine." He offered a reassuring nod and smile and glanced at his wrist. "Our time's almost up; I've got a business to run. You seem calmer now."

"Oh, I'm calm, all right. Like the quiet space between thunder and a lightning strike. That's where strong women live—a lesson you taught me well." She balled her fingers into a tight knot and allowed the spirit of an overaged hip hop artist to surge through her. "I'm about that life. When the thunder rolls and the lightning strikes, stand back."

He tilted his chin to the heavens. "Lord, help this child."

Tessa stood to make a grand exit on the heels of her self-empowerment speech, but she paused before she left. "Dad, can I ask you something?"

"Anything, Buttons."

"Have you heard what they call Keep It Real in industry circles?"

"An award-winning company?" he replied.

"I mean, behind my back."

"Truth?" he asked.

She nodded.

"Bitter Witch Greetings."

She resumed her trek toward the door and then looked over her shoulder again. "Do you think I'm...that?"

"We who love you realize you're neither of those things." He shook his head. "You, Buttons, are still heartbroken, after all this time. There was no clean break, so you never healed, and you channeled your pain the best way you could. It's okay if hurt and anger are a part of your journey; just don't make them your final destination. If you ask me whether you've extended your stay in the heartbreak part of your journey for a little too long? I think, yes."

She hated to admit it, but he was probably right. The time had come to release the past and the pain that had become central to what remained of her and Cody. Too many challenges lie ahead.

"Some days, I feel like what was supposed to be a quick round-trip became a one-way," she replied.

"You can choose a different path whenever you're ready. You only need to allow it for yourself, your team, and your company."

Miffed though she may be, Tessa couldn't leave without a hug. Losing her mother taught her early that life was too short. She kissed him on the cheek before heading out.

"You're not going to quit, are you?" he asked.

Tessa shrugged. "I'll call you tomorrow."

A new direction. That's exactly what she wanted, what she

needed. She'd devised a plan to salvage what was left of her dream, restore her control over Keep It Real and, rebuild her reputation.

Where would the road lead? Now that was another question altogether.

Chapter Five

C ody

OUT OF CONTROL!

Cody wanted to revel in his new position. He'd ascended to become the chief boss in charge of his father's legacy. But his heart, his mind, they never stood a chance. His father had gotten one thing wrong all those years ago: Tessa was no chicken. Only a full-grown eagle could swoop in his office as if hunting baby goats and put him on the defense when he was winning. Cody's meeting with Tessa ignited a feud that he had no plans to fight.

He didn't expect things to go well, but his abrupt pivot from hunter to hunted caught him off guard. Tessa delivered a tongue-lashing and then practically burned the color off of her red-bottom shoes screeching out of his office, leaving nothing but the scant scent of lavender and jasmine.

Still, he owned Keep It Real; she might not like that fact, but she couldn't deny it. Acquiring Keep It Real Cards was only the first phase of his plan. He needed to work on the next, but she'd robbed him of the opportunity when she made a threat he didn't consider idle.

In the wake of her fury and threat to quit, he leaned forward and banged his head on the acquisition agreement, more as a sign than a coincidence. The monotonous rhythm of the thunks soothed him somehow, even if he'd given himself a migraine. He fumbled through his clouded thoughts, trying to determine his next right move.

That's when a sound from the doorway got his attention.

"Oh-Em-Gee!" a familiar voice called out.

Cody peered up and caught a rare sighting—his brother, Jackson. He watched Cody from the doorway. "What did I tell you about talking to me in Internet?"

The split image of a young Sinbad, the comedian not the sailor, his youngest sibling had appeared dressed as if he'd come fresh off the 18th hole without swinging a club. "Is that any way to talk to your favorite brother?" Jackson flitted into his office and filled the space Tessa had left vacant moments before.

"You're my only brother."

"Potato. Potahto. Listen, I'm not here for the usual small talk. I come bearing words of caution." Something different, maybe even useful. Since Jackson's shift from Hart Publishing to prognosticating, Cody gave little credence to any word his little brother spoke after "hello." He usually came asking for money, not advice. For the first time in ages, Cody wouldn't have to pretend to listen. "I had a dream about you. Look at you—Same tired suit. You sat in that chair, doing exactly what I witnessed when I rolled up to the door."

"What? You mean banging my head against the desk?"

"Exactly," Jackson said. "But—plot twist—in my dream, you'd just made the biggest mistake of your life. You didn't just make the biggest mistake of your life, did you?"

"Well....jury's still out."

"And check this out—there was a four-headed dragon. At some point, you knocked yourself out, but you're still conscious right now, so that's got to be a good sign, right?"

"Jury's still out on that one, too. And?"

"And what?" Jackson replied.

"What's the mistake?"

"I dunno. I woke up—bathroom," he said.

Cody shrugged and rolled his eyes.

Jackson snapped his manicured fingers in a moment of recollection. "But I do remember one thing. On the spot where you banged your head, there was a greeting card with a circle on it—perhaps a square, too, but definitely a circle."

Cody bolted upright. "What'd it say?"

"I dunno. I was about to read it but—"

"Bathroom. Yeah, I got it."

"I've hit on something, haven't I?" He clung to the edge of the silence, waiting for Cody's response. "For someone generally annoyed when I'm in 'psychic mode,'"—he used air quotes —"you seem awfully interested in my visions today."

Cody resisted the urge to feed Jackson's curiosity. "How can I help you, favorite brother?"

"Classic avoidance. Fine, have it your way for now," he said. "Actually, I stopped by to check on you, see how you're doing. Thought you could stand a friendly face with Evilene and Cruella lurking about. Besides, you've been radio-silent since you hooked up with whatsherface, The Chandra."

"I wish you'd stop calling her The Chandra. And we didn't hook up. We're engaged."

"Tomato, tomahto. You and I both know The Chandra is high maintenance like that BMW you drive."

"Quit, man. I love her. She makes me happy. She—"

"Warms the cockles of your hesitant heart, blah, blah blah. Are you trying to convince yourself or me?"

Cody ignored Jackson's jab. His brother never liked Chandra, probably because they were too much alike—demanding and controlling. "Regardless of our disagreement over The Chandra, I appreciate you protecting my interests," Jackson continued.

Cody glanced up from his desk. "I'm thankful you didn't fight me over the shares."

"Hey, I'm a proud trust fund baby. The hustle stops here. As long as you keep the company strong and prosperous, it's a win-win as far as I'm concerned," he said. "Besides, you were the only one of us who ever worked at Hart...well, at least until Dad...you know." Jackson got choked up and turned away. He and Pops were close despite his obvious lack of ambition.

Pops had a unique ability to love all of his kids in their own lanes. He always said that Cody was the only one of the kids who remained loyal to Hart.

"Renee and Regina? They'll want Hart because I didn't give it to them, not because they love it, not because they're committed to the mission or the people," he'd told Cody five years ago on that fateful date. "Jackson wants the stipend, and he's to continue receiving it. You? You love the thrill of solving problems, of finding success, of bringing joy through our greetings. Most of all, you want the best for the people."

Cody wished Pops had more time to grow to love Tessa in the same way. He thought he knew her, but he was wrong.

"She's a flighty hippie who will never adapt to the Hart culture," he'd said. "Moreover, she's the daughter of my opponent. You can't sleep with the enemy, Son. You can't take her where you're going. I will not trust the future of this company with a Sweet at your side."

"Just because you knew her as a child. Doesn't mean she hasn't grown and changed."

"She's the same," he'd replied.

"Maybe I want the same, need the same," Cody had countered.

"Then why haven't you married her?" he'd asked with a

brutal sear in his voice. "I'll tell you why. You asked, and she said no, didn't she"—he paused—"You don't even need to answer. I know the flighty type all too well."

He didn't know anything...at all. Not Cody. Not Tessa. Nothing. And acquiring Keep It Real changed everything...again.

"Anyway, how's it going?" Jackson asked.

"Never a dull moment. I ordered a bulletproof vest online yesterday."

"Nice try. They won't come at you with bullets, and no vest can protect you from catching a knife in the kidney." They let out a loud laugh, and the feeling comforted Cody. He still had an ally.

He'd been warring with his sisters for so long the bonds of family had strained. He wanted, needed to feel connected to people, to his life, like he used to—once upon a wonderful time.

"Bruh! You know it's true." The laughs dissipated, and Jackson turned serious for a moment. "So tell me, what did I walk in on? You were clearly in the middle of a meltdown. If it's not the Devilment Twins, it must be some*thing*...or some*one* else."

"You witnessed the fallout from my confrontation," he said. "The Tessa."

"Woo! Now, there's a name you haven't mentioned in a month of Sundays. I liked that one. She was my favorite. She was good for you, too. Remember that card she made you back in the day. You kept that thing hanging in your office for a long time."

Let's Bee Friends. When the agony subsided, and Cody regained consciousness following the chicken nuggets kick, he rose to find Tessa propped up in the executive chair, doodling on a sheet of paper. She'd drawn him a card covered with flowers and bumblebees. She was more than a boss; she was an artist. Tessa had ascended to the CEO seat as the victor in their "Game of Thrones." However, in a far more gracious gesture than the one he'd offered, she'd left sufficient space for Cody to sit next to her. Even after his shameful display of "authority," she'd still been willing to share the chair with him. That was Tessa's true character, the core of her being, the girl who grew up to become the stunning woman, the force of nature, he'd come to love.

"I've still got it somewhere, maybe in storage. Who knows?"

He knew. It was in his office desk drawer.

"Water under the bridge," Jackson said. "But facts are facts. So, what did you do?"

"I bought Keep It Real yesterday."

"You did what!" His voice hit a soprano unheard in most opera halls. "What in Rhythm Nation were you thinking?"

Jackson overdosed on 80s and 90s pop, daily.

"Okay, the optics look...well, shady. But I thought I'd done the right thing," he said. "Then, in you walk, warning me about making the biggest mistake of my life."

"She and I weren't thieves thick, but you've got to be living with your head all the way in your butt not to understand how much the company meant to her. She invested everything in it—her money, time, heart—especially after you—"

"After I what?" He rubbed the scruff on his chin. "She's over it. So am I."

Everyone had blamed him for the breakup.

"Are you trying to convince me...or yourself?' Jackson said. "It's been five years. Whether you admit it or not, you've got a death grip on something, and it ain't Keep It Real...I mean, if you and I can 'keep it real.'"

Cody cut him with a sideways glance.

"Listen, if there's a right thing to do in this situation, I don't doubt you tried to do it. You can't help yourself," Jackson continued. "The question you need to ask yourself is—the right thing for whom?"

Cody's head fell back against the chair. The truth hit him like a right hook in the lungs. He recalled when his father had said, "You must understand one key principle, Cody. The position of

Hart CEO comes with great responsibility—not only to this company but to our extended family. Our livelihoods, the very financial foundation we leave for future generations, depend on every decision, every choice we make today. Hart Enterprises cannot survive under leadership with split loyalties." When his father later shared his own secret, Cody did the right thing. Maybe his problem had been doing the right thing for the wrong people.

Jackson allowed him the space to linger in the thought before polishing him off.

"I suppose *everyone's* aware of your recent acquisition?" he asked, no doubt referring to the Devilment Twins.

"If they didn't know before the morning edition, they sure do now," Cody replied.

"Did you tell The Chandra?" he asked. "Or have you forgotten how you got sloshed in Punta Cana and blabbed your entire history with Tessa? Guard your Black Card. We don't need a vision to know she'll be angry-shopping before you can say Tessa Sweet?"

He rolled his eyes. "I've told her about the acquisition. She's over it."

"Over it?" Jackson scoffed. "Mmm-hmm, when you left the house this morning, she was still a woman, wasn't she?"

"Of course."

"Then it's never over. The topic may be paused or on a brief hiatus, but over? Never. Trust me on this one. Armor and gird your loins," Jackson said, before snapping his fingers. "That's it! You have created the four-headed dragon. Tessa, The Chandra, and the twins—one, two, three, four." Jackson guffawed. "And you doubt you made the biggest mistake of your life?"

"I don't even know how to respond." Like a sloppy drunk, he slurred his words together. Nausea folded Cody in his seat. "What was I thinking?"

A knock came at the door, and Cody's Chief Operations Officer, Kyle Anderson, entered. The ladies always said he resembled Boris Kodjoe. Cody couldn't see the resemblance, and Kyle was too mellow and chilled to act the part.

"I got your message. Everything okay?" Kyle acknowledged Jackson. "Hey, man! What's up?"

"Me," Jackson replied, standing to his feet. "I've caused enough hate and discontent for one day. I'm out." He sashayed to the door. "Got a date waiting for me at McCormick's and Shmick's." He offered a salute and started for the exit.

"Thanks for everything," Cody said.

"Enjoy!" Kyle said to Jackson as he disappeared.

"I'll call you next week...in case you need a spare kidney," Jackson shot back at Cody.

Cody chuckled loudly and sat up straight at his desk; then, he returned his attention to his semi-panicked COO.

"What's this about a kidney? You all right?"

"I'm fine for now. Listen, I called you because I need you to run point for me—on an integration issue."

"Okay. Which acquisition?"

Cody hesitated and bit his lip before saying, "Keep It Real Cards."

Kyle leaned forward. "What? Wait, Tessa Sweet owns that company, doesn't she?"

Cody nodded. He stood, walked to his picturesque window, and peered across the DC skyline. "You've met her?"

"I don't know her, per se. I've seen her at a few industry events, and she attended the charity gala a couple of weeks back, right?"

"Yes, I think I remember seeing her there," he lied. In fact, he'd never forget seeing her anywhere. She stood across the room, a vision in royal blue turned memory searing on his brain.

"I'm curious. Why'd you make a play for that company? I mean, it's solid and all, but her messaging doesn't exactly fit the *Always and Forever. Our Hart to Yours* image."

"The details are confidential, and the deal is done, so the

debate is over. Now, we need to make the integration as painless as possible and the acquisition successful."

"Right. Well, you know, my managers usually handle integration. You only ask me to step in when there's a problem. So, what's up?"

"Tessa Sweet. She's a little less than thrilled about the move. I caught her off guard. She's now threatened to quit, which would render my investment useless. Help me keep an eye on her operations while I devise a strategy to get her buy-in on the new vision."

"Keep an eye on her? So, you're asking me to do what, exactly?"

Cody steepled his fingers together. "Officially, you'll lead integration efforts, customize an office space for the creative studio. Make sure they have network access, hardware, software, etc."

"And unofficially?"

"Keep an eye on Tessa."

"You mean spy on her?" Kyle's eyes widened; his expression fell somewhere between shock and disbelief.

"It's beneath me to ask you. Yet, I must. I've always been able to trust her in the past, but she's angry and desperate right now. Until she calms down and grows to understand the wisdom of this deal, we've got to protect Hart's interest."

"Well, she's Hart now, correct?"

"Yes. She's Hart. One-hundred percent. Whether she likes it or not. Unfortunately, she hates it."

Cody expected to face some opposition...a tense discussion perhaps. But Tessa, with her tight lips, narrowed eyes, and neck crank all but declared a full-on war against Cody. He understood the reason she'd drawn such a hard line better than anyone else because he'd heard the plot come from the horse's mouth, so to speak.

As the Sweets had guessed, and Cody knew without question, Pops had planned to run Sweet Media and everything that'd spawned from it out of business. He was still angry with Uncle Brian. The audacity of him to leave after working side-by-side with Pops for decades, after helping make Hart an international success. The nerve of him to have ambition, to want a legacy of his own, something bearing the Sweet name.

"He's got a small, boutique publishing company that doesn't compete with us in any market. Why do you hate him when he did as much as you to help you start Hart?" Cody had said.

"Brian may not be in direct competition with us now," his father began, "but that doesn't mean we're not going head-to-head with him."

Cody's brow had scrunched, and his mouth turned down. He could no longer control his expression. "Uncle Brian wouldn't do anything to—"

"You're absolutely correct. Brian wouldn't. And stop calling him uncle. Brian Sweet isn't your blood; he's not related to you," Pops had huffed.

His words left Cody numb. As evidenced by a treasure of pictures, Uncle Brian standing next to Pop at Cody's Christening, at baseball games, at graduations, proms, and every other significant or even insignificant event in his life, who was more family than Uncle Brian?

"In five years, Brian's thing will cease to exist. We will acquire Sweet Media. We'll break it into unrecognizable pieces and sell it off. We will destroy it."

His father 's ambitions had passed on with his body, heaven rest his soul; but, now, Tessa was clinging to ancient history and now bound and determined to make a difficult situation much more challenging than necessary.

Cody, in fact, had envisioned a different future for the company. She may not like the concept, but she'd have to respect it.

By his calculation, Tessa remained the girl in Chuck Taylors, but she had changed, too. The girl he remembered placed business above emotions. Now, she focused so hard on the minutiae of the details; she missed the big picture. Yes, the optics were poor, at best; but she made no attempt even to try to understand his motives, his reasons. She dismissed him without even engaging in a calm, honest conversation. If she'd only get past her stubborn pride and listen.

Chapter Six

T essa

BACK AT KEEP IT REAL CARDS, FOLLOWING THE TÊTE-À-TÊTE WITH her father and Cody, Tessa surveyed her kingdom through the frosted glass of her office window-walls—and prepared to do the unthinkable. She contemplated her clashes—with both of them. They'd left her mind and body heavy; she must now cope with multiple unsettling truths.

The life she'd built had become much like her Spanx—seamlessly smooth on the outside and all cellulite and blubber on the inside. Her life's "Lycra," her fancy Georgetown headquarters and business awards, concealed her profit struggles, all of which paled in comparison to her latest challenge.

She'd awakened as the owner of Keep It Real, which she safely operated under her father's stewardship in Sweet Media. The sun had barely reached its afternoon high before her life's purpose had been sold to the highest bidder, not to just anybody, but her ex-boyfriend and near-fiancé, no less. He appeared poised to take the svelte illusion that was Keep It Real, cut the seams, release the blubber, and leave her with elastic waistbands and ugly ruffles to camouflage the blob that remained.

She plopped in her leather executive chair, leaned forward until her head banged on the desk.

Mabel and Mia blew in like a picnic storm and dashed the iota of hope she had left.

"Um, you do know that your walls are glass, right?" Mia said. "If you want to knock yourself silly, you may want to try the ladies' room."

She and Mabel filled the guest seats in front of Tessa's desk.

They met her feigned optimism with expressions of concern and pity.

"Cody bought"—she clenched her eyes shut—"He bought...he bought Keep It Real." No need to mince words. She slapped them with the news.

For the second time, Cody had used the power of his pen to change the entire trajectory of her life. *Swish!* Another ambushing. The round hole and square peg all over again. Except now, Cody's cowardliness would cost Tessa her company, her staff, her vision, her mission....her heart.

He lacked the backbone to 'Keep It Real,' to tell it like it is with his products and in his life. No, his brand peddled shmoop and idealism.

"I said it three times, and I'm still here," Tessa said in disbelief. "I can't believe it. I just can't believe it."

She shifted her gaze to Mia, who seemed to have a black-market supply of unnatural calm.

"Why aren't you surprised?" she asked Mia. "I'm floored. He made his point abundantly clear five years ago—he didn't want to build Sweet-Hart with me. Now, he's bought my blood, sweat, and a whole lot of tears—at a premium? Doesn't compute. Why?"

Mia shrugged. "I've been around long enough to remember a

time when a dream of Sweet-Hart once belonged to both of you. Maybe he never let go?"

"He's getting married, for goodness sakes. Of course he let go," she replied. "Part of me wants to resign...I've got to quit. I mean, I can't allow him to be the boss of me. He can't really expect me to stay, can he?"

Mia and Mabel nodded. Of course they would say yes. They expected her to be an adult, take this jab on the chin. Perhaps they needed to attend more industry functions and listen to the chatter occurring behind her back.

Bitter Witch Greetings.

"He plans to change my vision to some cotton candy, diabetes-inducing festival of sentiment? That's not what we're about."

"Come on, Tessa. Yes, Cody's move is the definition of shady, at best. But Keep It Real is bigger than cards," Mabel interjected.

Tessa had plucked Mabel from Hart partly due to her sage wisdom. She reluctantly listened to it.

"I left Hart Enterprises to work with you," Mabel continued. "You've got vision and passion. Let's not even get started on your work ethic—insane! And you started this company broker than broke — that is a formula for inevitable success. It's the one your father and Mr. Hart followed. Cody never developed that hunger, not until you two fell in love. This dream you built is alive, evolving. It's going to grow and transform. That's just —life."

"Et tu, Mabel?" Her calm struck Tessa as familiar, like her dad —half of the duo that heaved her into this mess. "How ever, it evolves, I'll work for Hart over my stiff, bedraggled, worm-ridden body."

Mabel offered Tessa an additional two cents. "Judge Judy would say, even in death, there's resurrection."

Tessa sliced Mabel with a jagged glare and changed the subject quick, fast, and in a hurry. She refused to listen, didn't want to hear it. Mable could hang up her take-it-on-the-chin nonsense. "I can't stall any longer. I need to break the news to the team. Where's everyone?"

"Can we clarify which announcement you're going to make?" Mabel asked.

Mia glanced at Mabel and replied, "Last I saw, the writers were still working on the new line."

"I'll round them up and herd them into the auditorium," Tessa said. "You guys grab the rest, and we'll get this party started."

"Just so we're all on the same page, we're not talking about a going-away affair, right? You're not quitting, are you?" Mia asked.

Still conflicted, Tessa replied with a shrug. She'd languished between the proverbial rock and hard place—pride and heartbreak. She'd trusted that when she stood on the Sweet Media stage and faced her team, she'd find the right words to say.

"Cody's media visibility is off the charts." Mia's shoulders slumped. "The nasty litigation between him and his sisters put them under a microscope. Better the staff hear the news from you than from the wire." She stood to her feet and headed out the door. "I'll go turn on the lights—and crank up the heat."

Once Mia disappeared, Mabel turned to Tessa to leave her with a final thought.

"If I may offer one last piece of advice?" she began.

"We both know there'll never be a last..just 'final' for now." Tessa nodded and continued. "Besides, that's why I pay you the one massive buck."

"I realize that, for you, this acquisition means emotional Armageddon. But for them, it's merely change. They'll only perceive this situation in a poor light if you put a negative spin on it," Mabel implored.

Tessa exhaled a long breath as if she'd held it for days.

"Right now, I can barely hear myself over the sound of the rumor mill," Mabel continued. "It's churning like butter at the

Country Crock factory. This team, your team, needs you to step up and guide them through this incredible turmoil."

"I'm not certain I can lead myself, let alone them," Tessa said.

"Sounds as if you've already resolved to give up on your entire dream. My best advice to you is one word: Stay."

"And do what, Mabel? Become Cody's minion? Watch him destroy everything I've built?"

"Plot your next right move. Equip your team to deal with this change by instilling hope. They're here because they trust in Tessa Sweet, in your vision, in Keep It Real. And, frankly, I'm here because I believe in you, too."

Tessa exposed a slight smile and appeared unsure, despite Mabel's call to action. On the one hand, Mabel had pumped her up to march in and motivate her troops. Another part of her was swiftly becoming at one with the idea of deserting and moving to Canada.

"Now." Mabel stood to her feet and patted her bad knee. "Can I offer you a cup of coffee....maybe with a shot of Jack inside? I keep my stash in the bottom desk drawer for emergencies. Your dad gifted me with the bottle last Christmas."

"If this isn't an emergency, I don't know what is." Tessa hesitated for a moment. "How about we save it for after? Stumbling and slurring might diminish the legitimacy of my message. I'll see you guys in the auditorium."

TESSA HEARD WRITERS IN THE STAFF ROOM WHISPERING, SO SHE hovered outside. She wouldn't call it snooping so much as secretly listening to them commiserate over their fate.

"The situation is more urgent than you guys realize." Destiny cleared her throat. The senior editor, she only wore two kinds of clothes—tight and red. After her second marriage, the unwed single mother ascribed to the mantra *better not bitter*. "Everybody grab your cups. I've got the tea, and it's steaming and ready to pour."

With her back against the wall in more ways than one, Tessa leaned in closer, hoping to zero in on the faint whispers.

"You didn't hear this from me," Destiny began, "but my sources tell me Hart Enterprises acquired Keep It Real. Mr. Sweet inked the deal without so much as a warning. The news hit Tessa like fresh bird crap on a clean windshield."

The stone silence told Tessa everything she needed to know. They couldn't believe what happened any more than she.

That's when Destiny added, "I heard the scoop from a friend...with benefits. He works at Hart. After he sent me the W-Y-D text, he broke down the details. Hot mess-dot-com."

With the identity of her source, she converted the disbelievers; gasps replaced their unspoken doubts.

"If we get fired, do we collect unemployment?" Bethany asked in the confusion.

"We're not getting fired," Destiny said. "I'm 89.5 percent certain no one's getting pink-slipped."

A choir of groans filled the room.

"What are y'all moaning about?" said Bethany with her rainbow hair. The resident millennial served as a writer, illustrator, and Jill-of-all-trades. "I'm the one making minimum wage."

"I choose to view this as an opportunity," Judy the judgy churchlady said while sneering at Destiny. She was a senior writer. "Just like a I choose to see your dress as appropriate for the workplace."

Judy was an often foul-mouthed, buttoned-up Christian who specialized in inspirational cards. Destiny's status (divorced and mother) accounted for both of the reasons she and Destiny butted heads all the time.

"I know we're not getting pink slips...so when are we getting our pink slips?" said Dion, a physical specimen, always a workout freak, was mid-transformation. He had arms cut like an Adonis. He reserved his sense of humor and sentimentality for his oddly poignant cards. But he loved animals and cats, he loved baking, and he loved baking with cats...which sometimes curled up in the bowls. "I'd like to receive mine via courier before I get in the rush-hour traffic. No need in me leaving home if I've got biscuits in the oven."

Serving as the resident comic, Zeke was shaped like a Lindor truffle, round in the middle; his civil rights glasses were perfectly suited for his oval face. "I say we stage a revolt...I'm not sure against what. It just feels appropriate."

"Humph," Dion said. "I dare them to fire me. And I'm not writing any of those cavity cards, either."

"C'mon. Who's really surprised? Our sales have been riding on the struggle bus for a minute now. Keep It Real might be revolutionary, but in the greeting card market, we're un-Hart, niche, the independent artists."

"Like Ed Sheeran," Dion said. "I'm a fan, by the way."

"We're the group that rejects Madison Square Garden and instead chooses to appear in the auditorium because we like the intimacy, and art is more important than money," Zeke continued.

"Good point. We need to figure out how to level up without becoming...Hart," Judy said before adding, "but if anyone can do it, Tessa can. As long as she sticks around, she'll protect us and keep us authentic. We'll recover."

Tessa didn't know how, but she understood that the optimal solution to this acquisition problem lies in answering Zeke's question. Could she join her vision with Cody's? Could they remain faithful to the Keep It Real vision under Hart?

She lifted her wrist to check the time, faked heavy footsteps to the door, and poked her head inside.

"Hey, guys!" She'd caught them off guard. The deer in the headlights expressions almost choked her with laughter. Not a single poker face in the room...except perhaps Bethany, who concealed herself behind a Michael B. Jordon magazine cover.

"I need you all to meet me in the auditorium in five minutes. I've got an important announcement to make."

Tessa gulped, sucked in a deep breath, and marched in determined strides through the halls toward the auditorium stage's rear exit. With the curtains closed, she took her place front and center. She bowed her head and said a little prayer for guidance, then reminded herself to force the corners of her mouth upward. When the drapes opened, the brushed-brass Sweet Media logo on the back wall served as a harsh reminder of what had happened...and the trials that lie in the days ahead.

"Good afternoon, everyone. You're all wondering about the reason for this meeting, right? I'm sure the rumors are flying, so let me put them to rest. I have an important message to convey."

Employees bubbled with a chorus of whispers, and a wave of head nods gave way to an awkward silence. She trudged through her hesitation and doubts to continue.

"So, I'll go ahead and rip the Band-Aid—Hart Enterprises has acquired Keep It Real Cards. My father completed the transaction as of this morning, so it's official. We will now operate as part of the Hart Enterprises Greeting Card Division."

After a smattering of murmurs and collective gasps, some genuine and others Oscar-worthy, she swallowed what little was left of her pride and pressed on. "First of all, let me assure you all of one thing—nobody's getting fired. There will be no pink slips, no layoffs, no changes in the leadership structure—at least as far as you're concerned."

An "Amen" bubbled up from the back of the group. She almost wanted to laugh, but she didn't break.

"Your direct line manager today will be the same tomorrow. Furthermore, there will be no change in your pay or benefits. The CEO of Keep It Real will report to Cody Hart, which brings me to what I need to say next."

She allowed the news to settle on them and then prepared for the hardest part.

"I'm not going to lie because I'm not practiced enough to fool you—the news caught me off guard. So, I took some time to consider my role in the future of this company, indeed whether I would remain here. After some careful consideration..." she paused. Choking out the next part required a level of strength she wasn't sure she possessed.

Then just as she prepared to announce her decision, something unexpected happened.

A handsome stranger appeared in the back of the auditorium.

Well, he didn't so much appear as he materialized, as if Scottie beamed him in from Planet Pulchritude. For a moment, a second that felt like an hour, the rest of the room fell away. Only she and he remained. She committed to introducing herself to him, the millisecond she took a break. She questioned whether he was a member of the press nosing around for Hart family drama, but she didn't recognize him from her routine contacts.

More words came. She had no idea from where, but they filled the room with sound that got a definite reaction from her employees, if not the one she expected.

"I'm truly excited about the prospects for Keep It Real. The Hart family purchased our company at a premium, significantly above market value, because they believed in our talent and our vision."

He leaned against the back wall, too far back, and locked eyes with her. She needed him closer so she could savor each detail of this seemingly Mr. Right. The summary of him read scrumptious —ruggedly broad shoulders, a powerful chest, a taut waist, and strong legs, all wrapped in a cut-to-fit suit designed by heaven's seamstress.

"We have achieved so much on our own. Together, with Hart, we'll take Keep It Real and Hart Cards to even greater heights."

A round of applause followed a brief pause. Her consternation dissipated as she filled with relief.

Then the miracle of all miracles happened—Mabel smiled.

She knew then she'd made the correct decision, if not for herself, for them. Still, her heart broke. Moreover, she'd lied so badly, in fact, she could've doused herself in holy water and still wouldn't have come clean.

"We're going to take a short break, and then I'll return to the stage. At that time, I'll answer your questions. Just hang here in your seats for a couple of minutes."

Tessa broke camp the second the period hit the end of her sentence. Outside the auditorium, she turned to the left and right, eventually spinning in circles. With no one in sight, she gave up until...slow claps sounded at her back.

She did an about-face and found him, the specimen for whom she'd been searching. He stood there, in all his gloriousness and splendor, which seemed to spill from his insides out. Three words came to mind: *Good googity moogity!*

"Brilliant speech." His clap dwindled to silence. "Given the less-than-ideal circumstances, you handled the announcement beautifully in my humble opinion." A tall and delicate mix of Boris Kodjoe and Shemar Moore, he was more stardust and magic than mortal, up close. He stood above six feet, looking like a lifetime of snacks.

Tessa's brow scrunched. "Um, I don't believe we've met. Are you—a reporter?"

"No. I'm sorry." He offered his hand. "I'm Kyle. Kyle Anderson. Hart Enterprises. Chief Operations Officer."

"COOhhhh, you work for Cody." She'd seen him before; she was almost sure of it. But for whatever reason, she took full notice of him now. She shook his hand, but she kind of wanted to jab him with a throat punch, given that an order from the Hart C-Suite likely prompted his presence.

"Ah, I see. A pleasure to meet you, Mr. Anderson. I'm Tessa Sweet."

He held her hand for so long, delightful soured to awkward. Even after their hands parted, their eyes remained locked. His were wide, soft, hazel. She pinched her leg to stop herself from getting lost in them. Tessa's new mission began the minute she decided to stay, and common sense overcame her present lust in time to resume it.

"So...tell me something, Mr. Anderson."

"Anything," he said. "And, please, call me Kyle."

"Okay, Kyle." She arched her eyebrow to signal the healthy serving of skepticism she'd be dishing. "Why did Cody send you to spy on me? And, more important than that, why did you agree?"

A disruptive round of coughing stifled his words. Then he smiled—in a devastatingly perfect way.

Chapter Seven

C ody

ONE CLASH IN HIS OFFICE AND THE DAY TOOK A DIFFERENT SPIN than the one Cody imagined. Leave it to Tessa. He didn't believe she'd overflow with gratitude, but he didn't expect her to be so full of rage.

Cody woke up with all the answers, or so he thought. Now, hours later, he hunched over his desk, holding his head, questioning his decision, resolve, sanity...and drug use.

Have I been smoking?

He thanked the heavens that matters couldn't get any worse...and then his phone rang. He glanced at the screen and winced before answering.

"We need to talk," the voice said.

The Chandra.

She spoke the four little words no man in a relationship wanted to hear from his woman, certainly not his fiancée. Each syllable signaled the onset of doom. He ought to know. The last time he used them, he'd said them to Tessa. The present moment felt rife with Karma.

"I'm heading to my car as we speak, Dear," Cody said, trying to diffuse her rancor. "I can't wait—" The cellphone's "END" button eliminated the ability to slam the phone down in anger, but Chandra's echoed so loudly he could yodel to it.

She fumed. Her tone was one-part bark, three-parts bite, and more growl than he could manage without a whole bottle of whiskey. A new panic set in as his mind flashed back to his conversation with Jackson. His brother and his dream—they seemed less ridiculous. A four-headed dragon. He had dismissed the entire idea with a brisk wave of his hand, until now—time for a call.

"Jacks! Hey, what's, uhhh, what's going on?"

"You tell me," he replied. "Let me guess; you're on your way home to The Chandra."

"I will be as soon as I wrap up a couple of things in the office. How'd you know? Did you see a...vision?"

"No visions. I know the sound of unbridled fear when I hear it." He chuckled. "Time to break the news, huh? Can I lend you an ear? A little red corvette? A ticket to paradise? One night in Bangkok?"

"How about a brother who doesn't listen to the ancient pop station? So, let me ask you something. The dragon. It didn't...kill me, did it?"

He laughed too hard for Cody's comfort, given he was next in the line of succession. "Relax. Dreams are seldom literal. Death is almost always symbolic—like the death of an old way of think-ing, an old way of life, or even a relationship. Besides, The Chandra is a neat-freak; she doesn't like messes. She wouldn't shed your blood because red's not in your color wheel."

Cody fell out laughing. His brother said nothing but the truth. Jack's joking at his expense made him feel sufficiently absurd, so he hung up and prepared to face the wrath of The Chandra.

Before he set for home, he'd slay half of the dragon. No doubt his sisters would come rummaging around his office looking for paperwork on the Keep It Real deal. He scurried around, packing and locking up confidential documents, including the acquisition agreement and its terms.

The deal he struck with Sweet Media didn't impact anyone's fortunes but his own. It wasn't his fault they'd mismanaged Hart Publishing, of which they had financial control; it was barely profitable. His dad had so compartmentalized the greeting card business from the publishing side that they functioned as two separate entities.

Unlike the Devilment Twins, Cody had always been more wise than vindictive, even in the face of their constant opposition. He put the people and the business first. Always. They put pettiness first.

Fortunately, he'd remain the CEO for the foreseeable future. He controlled the enterprises with the power of Uncle Brian's shares. As long as Cody maintained Uncle Brian's support, the final vote would end in his favor.

The thought stiffened his backbone as his stepsisters Regina and Renee barged into his office. They stomped in snarling and so fire-angry, smoke emerged from the flowing weaves dangling over their shoulders. They came to a hard stop at the back of his office. With their eyes narrowed into slits and arms crossed over their chests like battle armor, it appeared they'd come to reignite the sibling war.

"May I help you? I'm in a hurry," he snapped.

They assumed flank positions on either side of his desk. He was surrounded.

"I don't know about you, Regina, but I'm not feeling the love," Renee said. "Is that any way to speak to your big sisters?" She was the oldest of the two by five minutes.

He chuckled. "Can we dispense with the small talk? I'm supposed to be halfway home."

"This discussion shouldn't take more than a moment of your

time," Regina said. "Long story short, we're here to verify some news we plucked from the grapevine today. Is it true you've acquired Keep It Real?"

"Remember what Dad always told us?" Cody began. "Don't ask questions to which you already know the answers."

Renee sucked her tongue and rolled her eyes. Her lousy attitude was next-level compared to Regina, but both of them had excess evil to spare.

"Should've figured you wouldn't pay us the respect of a direct answer. Every time I think you couldn't be a bigger disappointment to Dad's legacy, you exceed my expectations. You're back to that ancient Tessa thing, again. How disappointing. We thought you had matured. You can't leave the past in the past," said Renee.

"To think Pops believed you'd picked a side and grown a pair," Regina interjected. "He'd turn over in his grave if he knew you allowed the Sweets back into this company."

The spirit of Tessa dangled off the edge of his tongue, but he managed to hold his silence. There was no need to upset the angry bears when, if he just played possum long enough, they'd find another camp. He needed to save his energy. That's the only way he'd survive his impending confrontation with The Chandra.

"What kind of spell did she put on you? How many years has it been? Five, right?" Regina had the nerve to shake a finger. "Need we remind you that you just proposed to Chandra? She's like family. We love her."

"Please! You barely know her," Cody responded.

"We like her better than that Tessa."

"It's obvious you're probing for answers. But let me make this as clear as country air—I'm not justifying anything. I did what I did."

"Excuse me? We deserve more. We still own part of this company," Regina said.

"Fine, I'll offer this: back off. I didn't conspire with the Sweets to make your lives miserable."

"Of this, I'm sure," Regina continued. "It's clear conspiracies fail miserably in this family."

Fury surged through him. They schemed with Pops. He'd always known what they'd done; he'd never heard them admit it. "Oh, I see you now. You're salty because I've never properly congratulated you. You successfully orchestrated Tessa's and my break up. So permit me to take a minute and give you your due"—he slow clapped—"Bravo!"

He'd have much more preferred a middle-finger salute.

Both of them bowed.

"Since we split," Cody continued, "Tessa and I have spoken exactly zero times. She's as thrilled about the acquisition as you."

Renee and Regina exchanged sinister glances. He could see the cauldron boil. They'd heard opportunity in his explanation. Any attempt to seize it would fail thanks to Uncle Brian's influence on Tessa, and the shares Pops had the wisdom to leave in the Sweet's care.

"If you think you can flip Tessa, please invite me when you ask. I'll bring the popcorn. She can see what side you're on, and she knows it's not hers. Furthermore, as the CEO of this company, I made a business decision, one that was best for Hart Enterprises. End of story. Sayonara. Goodnight!"

He double-checked his briefcase for the paperwork to make sure he left no clues behind.

"This isn't the end. Trust and believe it's only the beginning," Renee warned. "We've been asking for your support to acquire LookBook, the printer for independent publishers."

"I know. And I've refused, not only once, but every single time you've asked. I'm not sure why you're still confused or discussing this issue, for that matter."

"We've researched the business, crunched the numbers, and we've concluded that not only will the company help to expand the Hart Enterprises portfolio, but it will give us a project that we can put our own names on."

"We're traditional publishers," Cody replied. "LookBook doesn't fit within our portfolio. Moreover, it's operating in the red, way too expensive, and it'll go under in a year, mark my words."

"Brilliant insight. Where'd you obtain it? Jackson?" Renee said with a long twist of her neck. "Your fragile male ego just paid ten-point-two million for your ex-girlfriend's company, and you call LookBook expensive?"

"Fragile male ego, huh?" he replied to Renee. "That's ridiculous, especially coming from a woman so shallow she spent seven grand on a dress to wear to a two-hundred-dollar charity event."

"Deflect much? It's clear you used only a fraction of your tiny brain to make this decision. Unfortunately for Hart Enterprises, it's below the belt."

"Whatever."

"Two years ago, your decision would've made sense. Today, it looks a whole lot like an ego trip."

"To someone who doesn't know all the facts, maybe."

"Give me a break, choir boy. Business is business. Keep it Real is in the final throes of its demise, and you acquired it while it's circling the drain."

"The only thing circling the drain is this conversation."

"You didn't pick it up—by the way—at a discount. Oh, no. You paid a premium...for a greeting card company when we already have one. Correct me if I'm wrong, but that's what your baby, Hart Cards, is supposed to be, isn't it?" Renee added.

"I'll admit," Regina interjected. "Keep It Real is quite innovative compared to the stale and tired drivel you release, which begs the question, why'd you buy it? To ruin it? Drag it back into the middle ages with Hart?"

Renee and Regina enjoyed a laugh at his expense.

"At least books are making a comeback," Renee continued. "Cards are going the way of the dinosaur. Everybody's sending e-cards and texts."

"Memes. Don't forget memes," Regina added.

"You want to question my decision. Fine. Debate all you like. But we aren't buying LookBook," he said. "Now, I'm through with this discussion."

He slammed his briefcase shut and loped toward the door. "You know I find this conversation remarkable," Cody continued, "especially given that I can count on one hand the number of hours you spent working at Hart before Pops died." He held up three fingers.

They both huffed.

"Do us all a favor and chalk this up to your last failed power play," Cody added. "If you want to assume the helm of Hart, you'll need to wait until I'm dead and gone because I will not relinquish the reins one moment before."

The edges of Regina's expression hardened at first and then softened as she seemingly shifted tactics mid-thought. "We're not your enemies, Cody. We're family. Dad wouldn't want us to fight. He'd want us to be allies."

"If either of you gave two cents about what Pops wanted, you'd be short two cents instead of being short millions of dollars in wasted litigation and months of lost time. All to get a court to affirm what Pops wrote in his will in plain English. Yet, somehow, we find ourselves here...now, I'm going out there," he said, pointing to the elevator. He pushed his way to the door. "If you'll excuse me."

"Tessa Sweet has no place in this company," Regina barked, sounding like Renee's echo. "Maybe we're stuck with you, but she'll never survive. If you want to go down with her, that's your prerogative."

"If you've got a problem with Tessa, take it up with her. I dare you," said Cody. "And the next time you want to speak to me, make an appointment with my secretary. Or better still—don't."

In his car, Cody shook the steering wheel and expelled a long breath. He'd managed to survive the battle on the first front, but he doubted he'd fare as well on the second.

Chapter Eight

T essa

TESSA COULDN'T TAKE HER EYES OFF OF KYLE ANDERSON. HE STOOD with her at the back of the auditorium as she waited to finish her speech. The sizzle between them thickened to the point that she wished she could wield it like a lasso and wrap and slap him into submission.

Perhaps she'd save that maneuver for a fifth-date mambo, if he ever asked her out, and if he survived that long.

For now, she'd interrogate him. He represented a mystery to solve. Why did Cody send him? And why did he agreed to come?

"Umm, let me try that again in my good English; Cody sent you to spy on me, didn't he?"

"Ah. Straight no chaser. Cody failed to mention your direct-ness." He seemed to be stalling, but compliments and his mildly alarming attractiveness would get him everywhere...after he answered Tessa's question. "As a matter of fact, yes, Cody indeed sent me to spy on you. Well, more so to keep an eye on his business interests."

"Spy," she said.

He shrugged. "Label it what you will; however, given the tenor of the speech you just delivered, I'm almost certain his fears of insurrection are unfounded. Almost."

"I can neither confirm nor deny." Tessa chuckled. Cody feared a mutiny, huh? Maybe he still knew her after all. "Kidding. Sort of," she lied.

"I bet. Listen, just because Cody sent me to keep an eye on his interests doesn't mean that's why I came. You've probably never noticed me, but I've watched your career from the sidelines. It's an honor to meet you."

Meeting him was an honor for her, too. She'd say so if she weren't so choked up with lust.

"I'm an admirer," he continued. "But I'm also leading the integration efforts. It's my job to make your company's acclimation to Hart Enterprises as...pleasurable as possible."

His mind-numbing smile forced drool from the corners of her mouth. She tapped the back of her hand against her lips to sop up the rogue slobber.

"My work will require several meetings with you, you know, to coordinate. You and your team will need Hart equipment, network accesses. We should collaborate on your office space configuration, too." He said before glimpsing her stoic expression.

"You're not going to make this easy, are you?"

"I've got a perfectly good set-up right where I am."

"It's not at Hart. Don't get me wrong; I empathize with you. Here, this is your first home, but you will have to move. Better sooner than later. " He slathered his voice in butter to sweeten the command. "This space is Sweet Media. You're Hart Enterprises now. It's difficult, but you'll adapt. That's what strong leaders do."

Tessa still heard an order, and he repeated it with more bass this time around.

"I'm sorry. You lost me somewhere around admirer. Naturally, I can't deal with this right now." And with those final words, his cuteness faded. "I've got a staff of personnel waiting to ask about issues for which I'm certain I have no firm answers. I need to get back inside."

"Understood," he replied.

"Unless you've got answers."

"I've got answers, but I'm all but positive your team isn't ready for them yet. If you don't mind, I'll listen in."

She shrugged. She might've lingered in his gaze a little longer, but her employees awaited her return.

"Also, given the late hour, maybe we can meet for breakfast?" he asked. "You know, to discuss the logistics...integration."

"I'll check my calendar."

"Done. I spoke to Mabel. She said your schedule is clear. We're good for nine."

Tessa mumbled, "Benedict Arnold," referring to Mabel. She'd encroached into enemy territory. "Fine, then. See you at nine."

"I look forward to it," Kyle said.

"Bring your A-game, Mr. Anderson."

He looked in her eyes and smiled as if he'd been looking for danger and found it. "Should I hire a bodyguard?"

"Look at me, Mr. Anderson. I'm a woman in a suit and heels." She eyed him from head to toe. "If you needed protection, trust me, one bodyguard wouldn't be enough. You may need two."

They parted ways, but a palpable heat and desire lingered between them. Shame. All Tessa wanted to do was flip him the bird, crawl into her corner, find a happy place with a bottle of Xanax, and turn on The Spinners' Greatest Hits or Earth Wind & Fire.

Instead, she did what strong leaders do, returned to calm her staff's fears.

. . .

An hour and a hundred questions later, she exited the stage and entered the zone, her new home. She remained lodged squarely between the proverbial rock and hard place. The whirl of Cody's mass confusion threatened to subsume her, but she maintained a tight focus on two critical next steps: first, protecting Keep It Real from the "*Always and Forever. Our Hart to Yours*" way of thinking and, most importantly, holding on to her staff.

Frustrated, tired, confused, and back home, at last, Tessa called Mia. Her particular brand of misery called for her bestie's company and wine, lots of it. On her scale of red wine days—one bottle being celebratory and four bottles being apocalyptic—today was a two-bottle day, teetering on three.

Mia soon arrived and joined Tessa. She found an adjacent couch and collapsed on it. "I've turned over this situation in my head a million times," Tessa said. "Every time I draw the same conclusion."

"What's that?" Mia replied.

"I've got two options, and both of them are red-button, point-of-no-return nuclear."

Mia peered at her friend as she gulped down a long sip of wine. She expelled an "ahhhhh" of relief before offering Tessa her two cents, twice more than Tessa ever wanted to hear.

"You took a major blow today and adeptly navigated incredibly difficult circumstances." Mia turned toward an adjacent coffee table where a picture frame and a swear jar spilling with fives sat. She picked up a photo frame wrapped in so many layers of toilet paper; she couldn't tell whether to put it on a roller or flush it. "What's this?"

"A picture of...HIM. It was in an old box. Interesting that I'd find it now of all times. I couldn't stand the sight of his stupid face because he's a piece of—"

"Hey!"

"What? I mummified it three days ago. I used generic. He's

not worth my good Charmin—or paying five dollars in the swear jar to curse him out."

"You're not getting off that easily. Pony up."

Tessa jutted her chin toward the overflowing vessel of shame. "I'm fresh out of fives, as you can see. I'm sick of cleaning up my language." She ripped a page from a nearby notepad and scribbled "IOU."

"If you want to see something funny, check out the back of the frame. There's another photo," Tessa said. "Cody snapped it when we got seafood curry at that ThaiPhoon place. You remember the restaurant, right?"

"At DuPont circle? Yep."

"The evening was supposed to be a surprise. I was shocked all right...at the velocity at which the food exploded from my orifices."

"Ew.

"I hate surprises." Tessa snatched the photo from Mia's hand, chucked the memory into the trashcan with a perfect swish, and brushed her hands together. "Trash. The sound of that *thunk* makes me feel better. I'm punch drunk. I've had the crap kicked out of me for two days. Bobbing-and-weaving isn't finessing; it's survival."

"True. But before you veer completely off the reservation, perhaps consider taking a breath. Inhale. Exhale. Separate the business from the emotion. The acquisition may be better for Keep It Real than you think."

"I've got brain damage from the jabs I've taken today, and even I know better than that."

"Before I continue, we need more wine." Mia laughed and trotted off to retrieve the last of Tessa's Cabernet Sauvignon from her newly added basement wine cellar.

Meanwhile, Tessa dripped lavender and jasmine essential oil into her diffuser and tuned her iPod to her father's favorite song selections. Earth, Wind & Fire. She piped them through the Bose sound system wired through her house.

Above the beats, she heard Mia's footsteps approaching.

"Give yourself some mental space. You need to think this thing through." Mia said. "And I can't help but believe there's more to this than business. I sense something between you and Cody."

"Of course there's something. I thought we were soul mates," Tessa said, regretting speaking the words; the sound evaporated from the air.

"He went full coward on you, but you two are made for each other; you're good for each other."

"Whoa. Whoa. Whoa. You're my BFF, so I hear you, but I'm not listening. We both need to pump our brakes." Tessa jerked her head back and narrowed her eyes. She propped up her French-manicured feet and clutched a wine glass large enough to hold a baby head. "First of all, Cody's engaged, and he will be walking down the aisle with whatsherface in a month. Second of all, nothing about Cody or Hart or Cody Hart is good for me or Keep It Real."

"A besties' job is to speak the truth, even when you least want to hear it. Today, the honor goes to this chick right here," Mia pointed a thumb at her chest. "Listen, I feel you, okay? Cody broke your heart, bought your company, and then had the nerve to shack up with a fiancée."

"I'm struggling to see the bright side of all this."

Mia set down her wine glass and focused her full attention on Tessa, who winced in anticipation of what she'd say next.

"But, would working with Cody be so bad? Yes, he may be a jackass, but he's a savvy one. Maybe he could help solve the profit problems. Furthermore, the man is easy like Sunday morning on the eyes. I mean, he puts the 'ine' in 'fine.'"

"Really? You had to go there. Not that you're exaggerating, but the kicker is," Tessa began, "when it comes to fine, Cody's got nothing on the COO. Have mercy!" Tessa fanned herself as they giggled themselves silly. The wine had officially kicked in.

"Is this situation ideal?" Mia continued. "No. It sucks. Royally.

I know you'd rather meet Cody again in a position of strength. But let's think of Hart Enterprises as a parking spot for Keep It Real, not a permanent destination. In time, you'll figure out a profit plan and save enough money to buy him out."

"With anyone else, I might agree. But he's like the paid hitman who missed his target the first time. He's my Achilles heel, my blind spot, my weakness. I trusted and believed in him —and when he left, he meant to take me out."

"Mmmm...take you out? Or move on with life?" Mia said, see-sawing her hands.

"He broke it off with a card, for goodness sake. And now I'm supposed to smile while politely eating the bull crap because he bought my company?" Tessa shook her head. "Humph. I wish I would. He didn't want the company when we could've led it as equals. Now, he still can't share the chair." She had a flashback to their game of Big Business.

"Share the...what are we talking about, again?"

Mia didn't understand the history, and Tessa possessed not an ounce of energy to explain.

"Power. I'm not ceding mine to him. I refuse to be collocated with him. I was a good woman and friend to him. And did I stalk him when he broke it off, cyber or otherwise? I think not. I left him alone. He should've done the same for me. I don't deserve this, and I won't accept it."

"You're right about one thing. I mean, the way he ended your relationship was shady at best."

"Let's not forget cowardly...and spineless."

"No arguments there. But how often would you see one another, anyway? Certainly, not every day. He's running an entire enterprise. Keep It Real will be a small fraction of it."

"It may be a small part, but you don't really believe he's paid ten-point-two million to ignore it, do you? Oh, he'll be very hands-on, condescendingly picking apart every decision I've ever made. Trust me, you weren't at our first meeting. You didn't see his smug, fat, arrogant, fat, smug face," Tessa said.

"You said smug and fat twice," Mia said. "Just pointing that out."

"The worst part is, every time I see him, I'm reminded that Hart Cards is the manifestation of my plan for Sweet-Hart Cards. The business plan, the concept - all from right here." Tessa tapped her temple. "He took my original plan and then used it to compete with me. What kind of man does that? Hart Enterprises intended to destroy Sweet Media and Keep It Real Cards right along with it. At least Cody's father did."

"I had no idea." Mia's mouth fell open, and she flattened her hand against her A&T sweatshirt. "I mean, I knew about the bad blood, but destroy?"

"I don't dredge it up. But I'll never forget what he did. I mean, after that, how am I supposed to trust him to do right by my business, let alone dating someone new?"

"You've dated plenty...although it's been a while since you allowed yourself to get lost in a serious relationship."

"What can I say? I doubt myself. If I could be so wrong about Cody, how could I tell the difference? To me, it's insurmountable. Even if I want to forgive him, how can I?"

"Forgiveness isn't for him, Tessa. It's for you. So, you can let go and move on. I suppose, if this situation is that untenable, you could always negotiate a golden parachute and then use the buyout to seed your next big thing."

"Abandon my company? Reward my team's loyalty by skittering into the night like some kind of coward? That's what Cody does, not me."

"They'd follow you...we'd all follow you."

Tessa released a deep sigh and peered out of her palatial window into her idyllic neighborhood. She considered the notion of starting over and relished in one fact: she was a miracle.

She had been set up to fail, yet she succeeded. What would he do if she asked for a buy-out?

"He'd never allow me to walk away clean," Tessa concluded.

"If he's not destroying me, he's fixing me. He's also got a savior complex."

"He should know by now you're not Lois Lane; you're Wonder Woman."

"Precisely. He won't let go of Keep It Real unless we become a liability. He hates to lose. Why do you think the court battle with his sisters went on for so long?"

"Renee and Regina. They must be thrilled about this acquisition," Mia said sarcastically. "Why's there so much bad blood?"

"Girl, Papa was a rolling stone, and most of their turmoil is rooted in that fact. At his fairytale, upscale wedding to Renée's and Regina's mother, Devon Hart fell in love at first sight with Cody's mom, who was sitting on the groom's side. A few years down the line, she got pregnant...before the divorce. Let's just say the math didn't add up."

"Wow. Any chance they'll help you?"

"Over the short ledge of a steep bridge, maybe." She grabbed a notebook from the table and started scribbling.

"Didn't I read in the paper that the acquisition isn't truly complete until the final shareholder vote?"

"That's true. It's a few weeks away, and I've got my dad's votes. Cody and his sisters are fully aware of that fact...or soon will be."

"Is there any way to stop the vote...or influence it?"

"I don't have any ideas right now. Collaborating with Cody could risk our jobs, Keep It Real, everything—and strategizing with the sisters could destroy Hart Enterprises...and Keep It Real Cards along with it."

"What happens if you hold your nose and...stay?"

With a melancholy expression, Tessa fell back against the sofa. "That is the one move that could destroy *me*."

Keep It Real Cards

You Got the Promotion.
Surprising? Nope!
Deserving? Well...

Let's Keep It Real—Judging from the trail of dead bodies you snatched off of the ladder of success to get ahead, probably not. Congratulations, anyway!

Chapter Nine

C ody

THE CHANDRA HAD BARKED THE WORDS, "WE NEED TO TALK," causing the rush-hour ride home to fill Cody with dread. Not only did he have to resist leaning into bouts of road rage during the slog home, but he also braced himself for a confrontation with his fiancée over his ex.

Once home, he crept up to his penthouse door, lugging his briefcase and love offerings, along with a load of panic and emotional baggage.

Regret overcame him like the swine flu. He usually trusted his instincts and never second-guessed himself. For the first time since he took the company helm, he'd given second and third thoughts to a business strategy that perhaps deserved fourth and fifth.

Still in the hallway, he emptied his arms on the floor beside his feet and stuck his key in the lock. Before he could wrap his hand around the cold brushed nickel knob, the door flung open.

Chandra stood there; her angelic face was tightened and she breathed like a charging bull. Her snarled expression doused him, like with a bucket of ice water.

He handed her the Tiffany's gift.

"Diamonds?" Her smile was as fake as his sentiment. He barely inhaled a full breath before she snatched the bag out of his hand and the life out of his lungs. Then, ungraciously, she slammed it into a nearby trashcan. "Original."

Truth be told, they were both guilty of shorting one another in the communication and intimacy departments. He'd practiced daily since she moved in.

"Don't you dare. Don't even think about pulling one over on me. I can see the lie written across your face. Just explain to me why you didn't tell me all the facts this morning. How about you lead with the truth this time?"

He dropped his belongings and reached out to her, but she yanked back, shuddering at the prospect of his touch.

"Please, sit down," he pleaded.

She crossed her arms over her chest, stomped toward the ample leather sectional, and plopped down in a hard thunk.

"It's not what you think." He'd always thought men sounded ridiculous, saying those words. It was usually exactly what we think, and this was his second time pulling this card. "This morning, when you and I spoke about the deal with Uncle...Mr. Sweet, I skipped a few details. *Erm*, Hart Enterprises acquired Keep It Real today. Tessa's company is integrating with Hart Cards."

He dropped the bomb; now, he awaited the explosion.

"First of all, how can you nonchalantly tell me Hart bought Tessa's company as if that is somehow disconnected from you?"

"The company made the—"

"You are the CEO and owner of Hart Enterprises. The company didn't buy Tessa's company; you did," she said.

"Yes. True, but—"

"And before you even attempt to Jedi Mind Trick me, let me

be clear about one thing. I'm a Realtor, so I may not be savvy about acquisitions and mergers, but I know how to Google and read. It doesn't take a Wharton graduate to figure this out. The questions regarding your motives become deafening when we consider you two were one proposal away from marriage."

Cody's stomach curled.

Volcano Chandra might've erupted if he'd confessed the entire story. He and Tessa were less than a proposal from marriage; they were a "yes" away. He dared not speak that truth.

"She and I haven't spoken a single word to one another in five years. This wasn't about her. Ever."

"Five years, five days, five minutes. Zero words, a million words. The number of words you speak or the length of time between them doesn't matter if you're still in love with her."

"But—"

"No, let me finish. Your motives are murky, at best."

"Chandra..."

"Cody. You've always warned me not to ask questions I didn't want the answer to. Now I'm asking. Before I commit my life to you, I want to know. Straight up. What's happening?"

"You deserve a reply, a truthful one." He tried to move closer to her, to hold her, but she strong-armed him, kept him at a literal arm's length.

"And trust me, I can smell BS a hundred miles away with clogged sinuses in a snowstorm," she added. "So, reach into the depths of your soul, find the truth, and speak it, or I swear by the Holy Maker of Heaven and Earth, I will make my exit from your home with a swiftness that'll give you chronic whiplash."

He heard the desperate ultimatum of a woman who'd once believed in him—but he also saw an exit strategy; did he really want out? If he did indeed love Tessa, the choice was his to make, and the time to make it was now. Unfortunately, all the turbulence had blurred his emotions.

"Okay, brace yourself. Here's the whole truth," said Cody. "I acquired Keep It Real for many reasons, the majority of which have zilch to do with Tessa Sweet. Her father called me."

"Wait a minute," she said. "He. Called you?"

"Yes. And despite this ridiculous feud, I listened because, in my heart, he's my family. He chewed his nails in the waiting room on the day my mom gave birth to me; she had some complications. Dad said he was more nervous than even he had been. He's been there with me, beside me, watching, guiding me for each and every milestone in my life. He and my father pledged Omega in college, so he was a part of my father's life long before my own mother."

"This is all touching, but how does this sentimental tale pertain to me and you?" she asked in her usual disaffected way.

"Blood didn't make them brothers; love did. Business tore them apart, not betrayal. Now I've helped bring them back together."

"You're a good person, but I still don't understand. You don't owe anything to that woman or that family. Why put yourself at odds with your sisters? With me?"

"If you're asking me, then you don't even comprehend the kind of man I am. It's not about what I owe anyone. It's about doing the right thing. You've agreed to marry me, and you don't even know who I am."

Now she moved to him, and he jerked back. He'd peeled back an unsettling layer of their relationship.

"I'd offer you more detail if a non-disclosure agreement with Sweet Media didn't legally prevent it. But I won't breach it. If you don't trust me, we need to reconsider what we're doing here."

"Okay." She offered only a blank expression, clearly expecting a different response. "What about Tessa? How does she factor into this equation?"

"I'd like to tell you I don't care about her, but I can't."

Her face screwed into a sour pucker, and she increased the distance between them.

"She and I were raised in separate households, but we grew up at Hart. Since we were ten years old, at least," he continued. "Of course, I care for her; what kind of man would I be if I didn't? But you're the woman wearing my ring, who shares my life, my heart, and soon my home. This deal is business and nothing more. You can live with that, or you can't. The decision is yours."

"Well, I know one thing for certain," Chandra said.

"What's that?"

"You told me the truth because that's not what I wanted to hear."

"Then you're really going to believe this because I'll be honest, you matter to me, but I'm done talking about this. If you want to walk out the door, I understand. But this is me. Take me or leave me." He hadn't planned to make his own ultimatum. His stomach lurched, leaving a pit.

"Is that final?" she asked.

Cody only nodded in reply.

"Fine," she disappeared into the kitchen, and plastic bags began to crinkle. "I bought groceries. What do you say to a candlelight dinner and a hot bath?" she called out.

He should've smiled. He should've been giddy with the anticipation of the relaxing evening to come. He wasn't. "Sounds perfect."

He removed his jacket and loosened his tie, relieved that he'd negotiated peace successfully. Then he strolled to the patio. He beheld the skyline, the ocean of lights. Not even the scent of the grilling porterhouse distracted him from thinking about the question that had plagued him for five years.

Who's loving Tessa tonight?

Chapter Ten

C ody

A CRUEL BEAM OF SUNLIGHT BROKE THROUGH CODY'S MAHOGANY wood blinds. The universe had not taken mercy on him overnight. After a sleepless night on The Chandra's art deco couch, he was still alive and now was forced to face post-acquisition day one with The Tessa. With greatness of forethought, he'd delegated the heavy work of her handling to his COO, Kyle.

Usually, cooling Chandra off meant heating her up, but Tessa had left him too conflicted to indulge. He opted for another solution—escalating the argument until she banished him from the bedroom. He held refuge on the oversized and overpriced sofa.

Someday, he may feel guilty about weaseling his way out of making up—not today. Instead, he turned his attention to a more critical mission: hit the road early to deal with another head of the dragon.

Cody entered Hart's offices, expecting to breeze past Kyle's empty office and grab a hot cup of his favorite Ethiopian blend.

To his surprise, Kyle had arrived before opening hours and now sat hunched over his desk with his fingers dancing across his keyboard in furious beats. Cody took his cracked door as an invitation to barge in and then helped himself to a seat.

"Well, you're in early this morning," Cody remembered Kyle's meeting with Tessa. He had no doubt his COO could handle himself with her during their get-together, but he'd warn him anyway. "I just wanted to make sure you still had a pulse after your encounter with Tessa yesterday, but I don't want to interrupt. Need any help?"

"Nah." Kyle shook his head and looked as if he could've melted in his chair. "My clash with Tessa went, well, as expected."

Cody chuckled.

"Now, I'm making some notes to prepare for the actual meeting."

"There isn't enough typing in the world," Cody said.

"You're telling me?" Kyle replied. "She's no joke. We met because she caught me listening in on her speech. She accused me of being a reporter. When she found out I'm your COO, she went full-tilt." Kyle smirked. "I chalked up my brush-with-death to an absurdly rough day. She's not usually that bad, is she?"

"No, she's worse." Cody's hard stare dissolved into a hearty laugh. He propped his feet up on a nearby coffee table. "I'm kidding. Sort of. Dealing with her can be like chewing broken glass, but she's all heart, and it's almost always in the right place."

"I'm not sure about her heart, but she's...spunky."

"She wants to do the best thing for all concerned even if she goes about it the wrong way. She's ambitious, yes, but she's also committed. If you work for her, you're family. If you work with her, you're blessed." The beauty of her spirit began to flourish in his mind, but he needed to put a stopper in his mouth. This was business, not love. "Don't get it twisted, though. With her kind heart comes a stubbornness that'll drive you to drink if you let it.

I mean, she possesses a mule-headed determination that could compete with any jackass."

Kyle's eyebrows arched. "Sounds like you know her well."

"I used to." Cody deliberately concealed the depth and breadth of his relationship with Tessa. Enough people in his circle questioned his motivation. He didn't need to add his COO and best friend to the list. "We grew up in the same circles. My father started Hart but, together, our fathers partnered to build the enterprise."

"Oh, right. And then Mr. Sweet left, the root of the big feud."

"Exactly," he said. "But I can't imagine she's changed very much since then."

"I know a few people in creative and marketing over there. This industry is small. I've reignited some old relationships to get ahead of her next move. Rumors are crawling through the grapevine. I've heard everything from her plotting a major move to her tendering her resignation. Lots of subtle and not-so-subtle whispers but nothing rock-solid."

"I'm not surprised," Cody replied.

"Everyone closest to her, the ones who know the ground truth, stay locked down," Kyle said. "It's like maneuvering a shield of secrecy. I've been in business for a long time. You can't buy or bully your staff into this kind of allegiance. You can only earn it."

"Can't say I'm surprised about that, either," Cody replied. "Her team is next-level. Uncle Brian and I understood going into this deal that she wouldn't concede without a fight. The only question remaining is how hard she's willing to buck against me...I mean, the acquisition."

Kyle shot him the side-eye. "One thing is clear: she'd like nothing more than to find a comfortable spot under your skin and make camp."

"Then she should think better of it. I respect her, but I'm only willing to tolerate so much. If she pushes me too far, she'll regret it. Best she lean into my plan sooner than later."

"If I may ask, what's the plan?"

"Good question. I'll increase her market share and profits by knocking some of the edginess off of her messaging. She's never going to reach her goals, financial or otherwise, if consumers view *Keep It Real* as *Bitter Witch Greetings*. Furthermore, that's not the kind of person she is—it's who she became after...well, the point is that Keep It Real was never her plan."

"Visions change, don't they?"

"Yes, but her first approach is more profitable, and this business is about the mass appeal and the dollars. She'll come to realize the truth if she gets past her pride and ego. I'm going to ask her to oversee a Hart project, one better aligned to her original strategy. She'll do what she does best; she can't help herself. That'll be the baby step we need to expand Keep It Real's messaging, to make us a stronger company."

"So, you're really not going to ax it."

"Not today," Cody replied. "And if this plan works, not ever."

"Do you have a Hart Card project in mind?"

"Still chewing on it," Cody said. "However, you've got a critical mission if you choose to accept it."

"What's that?"

"Help her believe she's still in charge while keeping an eye on her. The more control she believes she has, the sooner we can make the kind of progress that will benefit Keep It Real and Hart."

Kyle nodded. "I think I can handle that."

"And let me add one incentive to your motivation. My ascension to the CEO leaves my Executive Vice President position vacant. If you successfully manage Tessa, you're a shoo-in."

"Are you serious?" He bolted upright, and his eyes brightened.

Cody's appeal to Kyle's ambitions would help keep him on task.

"Of course. But I'm pitting you against a lioness. If you survive, you'll deserve to be Hart's number two."

"Only one thing left to do." Kyle glanced at his watch and stood up. "Head into the den."

HE LEFT KYLE'S OFFICE, TOOK A BREATH, AND PAUSED TO WEIGH HIS thoughts. Ms. Dee had packed his schedule. The day would begin with a series of long, drawn-out, and unnecessary meetings, which he'd blow off. He felt like a hypocrite. His smugness over her "new" business strategy gave way to regret as he recalled the cards she created for him, starting with *Let's Bee Friends*; Hart cards wouldn't exist without her vision for Sweet-Hart Cards. Who was he to push Tessa to embrace the woman she used to be, especially when he'd long abandoned the version of himself that he once was?

For years, Cody suppressed the single insatiable craving he had outside of loving Tessa—creating Hart Cards. After they parted ways, he buried his inner artist and embraced the businessman. Why?

One reason surfaced above all others: art reminded him of the love he shared with her. With her gone, his dream drifted away. He lost the best part of himself to the company. Perhaps Tessa wasn't the only one who needed to reevaluate aspirations.

Maybe that's the reason he'd grown so comfortable in his relationship with Chandra. Being around Tessa always stirred up internal unrest, forced him to face his dissatisfaction with the status quo, made him want more...want it all.

Chandra embraced contentment. Tessa craved evolution, and with the Keep It Real acquisition behind him, he felt a shift.

He tightened his lips and gave into an urge, one he was done fighting. One that had evaded him for five years. He maundered to the creative studio, greeting the friendly double-takes from his staff with waves and nods. He had not descended below the Executive floor in far too long. Once upon a time, before he took Hart's helm, he avoided the C-Suites. He preferred to learn Hart operations in the trenches—from the ground up.

When Pops passed, Cody abandoned his own shoes for his father's. Hart needed the continuity at the time, so he neglected the woman and dream he wanted and accepted his duty to his father's legacy. He never regretted the choice until now.

He slipped into his original space where he and Tessa had spent many summers. He said a quick hello to its lone resident.

"Haven't seen you down here in a month of Sundays," Rice said. His hair was more white than silver, hence the nickname. He had every single color of Docker and polo shirt known to man. This day, he wore a navy and beige combination.

Rice McHugh, his father's hand-picked senior graphic artist, was an old head, a Hart purist. He'd refused to move to the modernized creative studio claiming the intense light interfered with the energy. He resisted change. He preferred the dark. Rice still produced some of their best-selling collections of all time. Cody took a seat next to him, grabbed a hand full of colored pencils, and paused.

"I came downstairs to soak up some of your energy." Cody pulled out a sheet of paper, folded it in half, and positioned a pencil at the top. For a few moments, he froze, paralyzed by too many thoughts; a flurry of ideas bum-rushed his mind, over-whelmed him. Soon, Cody's hand found the color blue, a stroke, and then a rhythm.

"Glad to see you. It's been too long," Rice said, watching the motion of Cody's pencil. "When life gets crazy, we naturally gravitate to our creative sides. I hoped to see you sooner than later"—he paused—"Like riding a bike, isn't it? After so many years, you're scared to fall, forgetting about how you once popped wheelies."

Cody acknowledged the truth with a smile and a series of nods. He closed his eyes and let his hand lead, allowing his instinct to take him places where his mind refused to tread. When he opened his eyes, a slight grin disappeared quickly. He'd drawn a heart with a break.

Above his sketch, he wrote, "It's all my fault." Below, "I'm sorry."

The longer he stared at his creation, the more the words blurred. He lost himself in a time long passed, at least until a voice crept up from behind him and yanked him out of his thoughts.

"Cody? ... Cody?... Cody?"

He clutched his chest and looked over his shoulder. He soon realized Ms. Dee hovered near the door.

"I've been looking for you everywhere. Haven't seen you down here in forever," she said with a smile. "Not a bad look on you. Not bad at all."

"Did you need something?" he asked, hoping to hasten her departure so he could return to his craft, his thoughts.

"The focus group? You asked me to set up one for today. The research for Hart and Keep It Real Cards?"

"Aw, man! I completely forgot."

"Took me a half hour to find you. They started about twenty minutes ago. Thought you might want to head to marketing. They're in room four."

Cody took off running.

"Hurry," she said, calling after him. "You don't want to miss anything important."

Huffing and puffing, he clambered up three flights of stairs and arrived in record time. He slipped into an entrance that led him behind the one-way glass in the conference room. He took a quick note of the participant demographics—three diverse women; three generations; he only recognized the facilitator. Cody leaned back and listened with interest.

Susan, a familiar face, said, "Now that you've all had a chance to review and read the selection of graduation messages from Hart Cards and Keep It Real, I'll pose a few questions, and you tell me what you think about the messaging? Would you buy them? Would you give them to your family members and friends? Do they speak to you, for you? Let's start with the Hart Cards and our Gen X'er, Marie."

"What can I say?" Marie wore a Nirvana T-shirt and drank a kale smoothie. "When I need cards, I buy Hart. They're my favorites. To me, a graduation card to a loved one should convey sentiment, love, acknowledgment, and appreciation." She opened her sample and read. "Today, we celebrate your hard work, perseverance, and commitment. That's what it's all about, isn't it? I choose Hart. Yes, I said the word heart too many times, but you get the picture."

"I agree." Alyssa, the youngest woman, flipped her pink-streaked hair over her shoulder and glanced at her constantly buzzing cellphone before shuffling through her pile of samples. "Hart always leaves a smile on my face. It's a paper hug; plus, mine almost always arrive filled with money. I prefer money over hugs."

"I've been mailing these to my family for thirty years," the baby boomer, Leona, said. She looked queenly with her silver hair and bifocals perched on the end of her nose. "When I want to express messages of happiness, love, and hope, joy, or some-times even 'I'm sorry' or 'I'm here for you,' I buy Hart. I mean, it's the perfect expression, right?"

They all looked around the table and nodded in agreement.

"Thank you all so much for the thought and energy that you've brought to the process," Susan said. "Is that all you'd like to offer about the Hart product?"

Everyone agreed with a nod or a thumbs-up.

"Okay, let's move on to Keep It Real. What did you think about their congratulations or graduation offering? Anyone have any thoughts?"

Marie raised her hand. "I love them, myself. I mean, some-times you want to send sentiment, and other times you want to tell it like it is. Some members of my family need straight talk, no beating around the bush. Depending on the receiver, a card with humor can be even more meaningful.

"Let's take my nephew, for example. I swear, he took seven and a half years to finish college. Not because he struggled with the work, rather he refused to apply himself. This boy par-tayed. Okay? Stayed in the streets with his frat brothers. He rolled into class late, hungover. The evidence is a YouTube video some-where, recorded by one of his classmates. If anyone in my family told you they believed he'd graduate, I'd advise you to take two steps to the left because the lightning's coming to take you out."

The room erupted with laughter.

"Yet, somehow, he got his act together—finally. Anyway, I went looking for a Hart card, and the 'Congratulations, We Knew You Could Do It" card didn't capture the spirit of his colle-giate struggles. I bought it, regardless. However, if I had seen this Keep It Real card. *It's about time!"* She said. "Now, that's what I really wanted to say. I'd have been all over that like flies on a dog...well, you know."

Another round of chuckles followed.

"Hey, I'm *keeping it real.* See what I did there?" Marie contin-ued. "Listen, he was driving the struggle bus. The whole family knew it, and he would've appreciated the humor, especially given he did graduate...eventually."

"I agree," the millennial said with a shrug. "Obviously, these cards aren't for everyone, but I can imagine a market exists for them. Some people will buy and appreciate them."

"Well, I disagree," the baby boomer said with her face screwed into a frown. "My mama always said, if you can't say something nice, keep your mouth shut. Just because you say something hurtful with a smile and a little bit of humor doesn't make it any less mean. You could have the best of intentions, but you never know what someone is thinking or feeling. You never know what might push people over the edge."

"A little deep for a graduation card, isn't it, Ma'am?" Marie asked.

Leona glared at her as if to say *I said what I said.*

"We'll just have to agree to disagree," Marie said. "As for me and my money, Keep It Real Cards can take me to the bank. Some of these cards gave me my whole life. Right now."

The millennial nodded. "Agreed. They can't have all of my money, but they can surely get some with the right message."

"And that, I think, will conclude this spirited but respectful discussion," Susan said. "Thank you all for your participation. We won't take up much more of your time. I'd like to wrap up with my first question. I asked you all to think about a time when you wanted to buy a card and couldn't find it. What would that card have said?"

The room grew silent before Alyssa spoke. "I have a friend, and she's in a wheelchair. She was paralyzed after a car accident. She always tells me she'd love to see herself represented on a card. I think some of the messaging can be similar to what exists now, but what about changing the images to make diverse the new normal, like a differently abled girl in a wheelchair? Maybe for a kid with Autism, you could change the message to something that doesn't rely on sentiment for them to understand."

Cody perked up in his seat and muttered, "Hmmm...a special needs...no specially abled line." He leaned back in his chair and allowed the thought to fester and then grow. Pulling off a collection so significant would require artists and writers with wells of kindness and heart. And this team would need the right leader, someone to nurture, motivate, and drive the employees and the direction of this new collection.

He clapped his hands and punched his fist in the air. "Perfect," he cheered. "Absolutely perfect."

Chapter Eleven

T essa

DESPITE AN UNCONSCIOUS WISH FOR THE NIGHT TO TAKE HER, SHE'D survived. Now, her first day as part of Hart Enterprises lurked ahead of her, a day that would begin with a meeting with Kyle.

The struggle was real, too real.

Thick clouds stifled all but a few rays of sunlight, which mirrored her life. Cody owned Keep It Real, and her employees feared for their futures and paychecks. Her hope to begin a turn-around started in a few hours. She felt like the golden beam of light in her room had ridden out an ugly battle through the murky grays to find a home and easer her mind.

Finding the right outfit proved to be as challenging as accepting her fate, but ogling Kyle Anderson just might make up for the adversity.

In her closet, she pushed the hangers aside, suit after suit, until she finally settled on her royal blue Jackie-O-inspired number, a timeless favorite. The asymmetrical neckline and curve-hugging cut would raise Kyle's eyebrows—and a few among her team. Usually, Tessa and dresses didn't mix. When experiencing upheaval, she paced a lot, a habit better performed in pants. Then, again, she'd never met a man like Kyle Anderson.

The mere thought of seeing him again made her stomach flitter.

She spent part of the night stewing over her plan for their discussion. She'd strategized a way to reclaim full ownership of Keep It Real; she lacked one key ingredient to survive Hart Enterprises—an ally. She needed a "friendly" on her side, and then she'd position herself as an annoying distraction to keep Cody and Kyle off-balance while she plotted her way back to power. Tessa decided to present herself to Kyle as honey to a fly. Thanks to Cody, she'd handled men of his ilk, fancy COOs, all her life. Plus, a man like him had raised her.

On her way to work, her idea for Mr. Anderson materialized.

Once in the office, she searched the credenza behind her desk for the Keep It Real design plans that would help put her strategy into action. She'd use drawings to stall the move. She'd refuse to leave her headquarters until they implemented her ideas, and that demand may give her enough time to recruit her target and find a way out of this deal. She'd need to be strong, sharp, and on her guard. Tessa drummed her fingers on the desk as she waited impatiently for Kyle.

"Is it safe?" Tessa nearly jumped out of her skin when, through her brain fog, she heard the question along with a tap on the threshold.

"What in the—what is this?" she exclaimed.

She grasped her chest and crumbled with laughter.

On her guard? Not so much.

Kyle lurked at the door wearing protective headgear with a face shield and ear protection. "You look like a Storm Trooper. I felt my soul leave my body when you popped up."

He joined in the laughter. "Well, you said a bodyguard

wouldn't do the trick, so I needed to do something to safeguard myself."

Her chuckles tapered off. "Well, unless you're expecting to defeat the Rebel Alliance, this get-up isn't going to do you much good, either." She gestured her hand toward a chair and offered him a seat. "Please, I promise not to hurt you...much."

With the tension broken, he obeyed her command. In his seat, he gave her a generous once-over before kicking off the integration discussions.

"Our conversation yesterday didn't end on a positive note," he said. "So I stopped by Home Depot on the way in and dropped fifty bucks on this contraption, hoping for a better start to this one. Based on the width of your smile, I'd say it was money well spent."

She hated herself for blushing. It happened so quickly she couldn't stop the cheesy grin. She felt outed and a little naked and then comfortable again. That's when she realized the universe had listened and delivered. "You're funny, not cheap, and prompt. If it were after six, you'd make a perfect date."

"Well, it's before nine a.m., and I'm just getting started." He flashed a smile for the ages, and the mere sight gave her a double-espresso rush.

"Shall we begin?" she said. "I thought about avoiding this meeting, but something told me if I didn't show up, you'd come back." Her effort to regain all the cool points she'd lost with her blush failed when another smile made her face warm all over again.

"I'm often accused of dogged persistence," he said.

"Good strategy. Paralyze resistance with insistence," she replied. "Heard the quote somewhere. Fits you well. But don't get beside yourself, I got started at four a.m. I've put considerable thought into our discussion, and I will amaze and confound you with my awesomeness."

Did I just flirt? She wanted to sound like she was on her game, not playing 'the dating' one. *Ugh.*

"Before we begin, can I offer you a doughnut, a bagel, some coffee?" *Hot butt-naked sex?* "I'm fully stacked...I mean, stocked."

Stacked? Blushing once more, she thanked her brown skin for not betraying her.

"Hmm. I could stand a bite," he said. His smile disappeared. "Maybe I'll take you up on your offer, but...later." He crossed his legs and eyed her from toes to nose, letting his gaze linger in the mid-range. "Right now, I've got everything I need." He held up his leather portfolio and pen as if that's what he really meant.

Please!

Then he snickered and offered a sultry look that suggested the only snack he wanted was sitting in front of him. Unfortunately for him, she wasn't on the menu, and the kitchen stock was all she'd planned to offer...for now.

He'd thoroughly checked her out, and whether or not he paid attention, she returned the favor—tenfold—from the moment he stepped in her office to this.

"Good. Shall we begin," she asked, moving into business mode.

"First, I'd like to preface this discussion by admitting some apprehension. Cody suggested you might be tough to handle...his words, not mine."

"Is that right?" She phased through reactions, first tilting her head to the side and then narrowing her eyes and pursing her lips. The nerve. She welcomed Kyle's transparency, though. Since he'd opted to "keep it real," she'd reward his honesty.

"First of all, I'd recommend you take anything Mr. Hart says about me with a grain of salt. His statement presumes an untruth—that he'd been among the privileged few who could, as you say, handle me. Trust me; he was never fortunate enough to make that list."

"Ouch." He'd tried to stifle his laugh, but a little spilled through.

"Anyway, time is short. Let's get down to this integration

discussion. I'd like to start with the fact that we'll need a new creative studio."

She passed Keep It Real's architectural layout drawings to Kyle as he explained his master plan. The lilt in his voice, a crisp, soothing tenor, consumed her thoughts. Their conversation forced her into a constant battle between business and distraction.

She heard his proposal, but she struggled to listen. The details became muddled and lost as her eyes roamed him, feasting on every visible part. She paid just enough attention to nod at appropriate intervals while keeping her eyes trained on his dreaminess.

His caramel skin popped against her black leather office seating. His eyes were problematic, round and hazel, and his lashes curled. His nose, more pointed than curved, betrayed his mixed heritage. With a steady gaze, she traced the line of his broad shoulders down across his sculpted chest into the "V" of his taut waist. Her eyes continued their delicious journey down his juicy, muscular thighs, snaking around his tailored slacks, which hugged his muscles in every right and perfect place.

He continued speaking, and she kept nodding. Her eyes meandered up to his lips, which, in the most serendipitous timing, she witnessed him glossing with his tongue. The gesture seemed more an unconscious habit than a calculated attempt to exude sexiness. He naturally and with ease achieved what would be a challenge for most men.

He played magnet to her metal, a state that left her drawn to him in a way she wanted to control but couldn't. Her only defense against his irresistible wiles was recalling the hard-learned lessons from mixing pleasure with Cody and work.

Don't.

Her dreams depended on it.

"So, your team should have access to the networks within the week," Kyle continued.

She'd suffered enough disappointment to last her three lifetimes. Seeing Kyle, perhaps desiring him, served as a stark reminder that even though five years had passed since her last tangle with love, she remained unable and unwilling to risk another heartbreak.

Not yet.

"Everyone should receive Hart Enterprises' email addresses and passwords via their existing accounts," he continued as she nodded. "They can use those to sign in to our collaboration site."

The reality of their situation allowed her to refocus her attention from his lips and eyes and thighs to his words. Unfortunately, most of what he told her for an hour remained a mystery. She found herself in a predicament, needing to maintain the appearance of professionalism while somehow asking him to repeat every word he'd just spoken.

This would be tricky.

"Sounds perfect," she replied. "With my busy schedule over the next few days, it would be great if you could send all these details to Mabel so she can help keep me straight."

"Completely understandable. Provide all the details to Mabel." He spoke the words aloud while jotting them on his notepad.

Mission accomplished, but she did bring up one final and substantive issue—the cornerstone of her stall tactics. "I know I mentioned this earlier, but I spent a year developing the proposal for our creative studio; it's warm and bright. It optimizes staff productivity—obviously, the antithesis of everything they've got over at Hart."

His brow furrowed. "Uh, well, I wouldn't say—"

"I know your business is—business. But, for creatives, the environment is critical. We spend a lot of long days and late nights working in our space. Sticking us in some dank cubicles over at Hart won't suffice."

"When's the last time you visited Hart?"

She shrugged.

He stood up, moved toward her glass wall, and surveyed her

kingdom, giving her the perfect opportunity to take in his rearview.

"I see," he said. "Well, obviously, you've put a tremendous amount of effort into building Keep It Real. No doubt. The design is innovative. Coffee shop-inspired, right?"

"Exactly." She smiled at his perceptiveness. He may be a weasel, but he was a charming one. "I need my team here, though. Not at Starbucks...although it helps to work outside of the office every now and again."

"The influence is undeniable. Tall counter-height tables and open seating to encourage collaboration. But also, comfortable, quiet stations along the periphery because sometimes you've got to live with your work in your own head."

Now her eyebrows furrowed. "Sounds like you speak from experience."

He didn't offer a direct response, just revealed that dangerous smile, causing her stomach to flutter. "I also like conference rooms equipped with interactive, digital whiteboards and iPads. Brilliant use of technology."

"What can I say? I'm a tech junkie. Sometimes the tools make the work more fun."

"I think you'll be pleasantly surprised by what we can do with this at Hart. Now that I've actually taken in what you've got here, I'll start the ball rolling. How about I return in a couple of days with my facilities team to conduct an initial site survey and baseline connectivity assessment?" He jotted more notes in his portfolio. "After that, I'll work up a set of plans...for your approval, of course. It may take a few weeks, but, speaking for myself, I'm looking forward to your relocation."

"Please, take all the time you need." *Humph*. My approval. Cody wasn't slick. She could see though this tactic as if she had X-ray vision; he'd used Kyle to make it seem as if she had some authority when she didn't. No matter. She still chalked up a score in her column as she'd achieved both of her goals—stalled the move and wooed an ally.

Still, the beginning of a life at Hart meant the end of the Keep It Real she'd built and loved, the thought of which seared through her like hot steel. But Tessa could do nothing but smile at Kyle, at the expression he gifted her, at the man he was, at the way he made her feel for that brief time. He helped her remember something she thought she'd forgotten, even if they were only meant to share stolen glances.

She drew herself back from fantasy to reality and shook off the afterglow from her time spent with him to focus on the real prize. If all went according to plan, his attempt to replicate her design would take months. By the time he completed renovations on her Hart office space, she'd have regained ownership of her company, and she'd tell Cody where he could shove his integration.

She glanced at her watch. "Wow, just under an hour. I guess you can head back to school and report to the principal that I remained on my best behavior."

"Indeed, you did." Kyle chuckled, rose to his feet, and glided toward the door. "I'm sure he'll be disappointed. I wasn't. Although, I don't think I'd mind seeing you misbehave."

Wait. What? Did he just flirt?

"In fact, would you consider dinner? You and me? I promise I'll be on my best behavior...unless you request otherwise."

Why, yes, he did!

Her knees nearly buckled from the shock. Her heartbeat skipped, stomach butterflies fluttered, and her eyelashes batted. "Dinner?" Her voice sounded coyer than she intended.

"Yes. You know, food, drinks...dessert," he replied.

"Mmm. I'm not sure this is a good time. I've got so much to do."

"Sometimes, you have to set the work aside and put yourself first. Let me help you do that. It's all aboveboard and legal, and certainly not against company rules. After all, we don't report to one another."

"Sounds like you've thought of everything. How can I resist?"

"You can't. I'll pick you up here. Six?"

She smiled and nodded. "You're on." She sent her sweetness into overdrive with a flirtatious, wiggle-finger wave as he strolled away. She kept her eyes peeled on the back of him until he disappeared.

"Mhm. Mhm. Mhm," she muttered. "Well, what do you know? I've got a date!"

She'd gone out with men since Cody, but they weren't "Kyle" by any stretch of the imagination.

Mia appeared from nowhere, disrupting her line of sight. She glanced back over her shoulder to see what Tessa was looking at and shot her a suspicious smirk. "Oh, you are so cold busted. Drool much?"

Tessa chuckled and swatted the air.

"Can't say I blame you," Mia continued. "That man is fiiiiiine. Woo-wee!"

Tessa refused to offer Mia the reaction she wanted but mentally acknowledged she hadn't been anything but honest. "Before you allow the thought of him to set your drawers ablaze," Tessa said, "remember he's in the enemy camp, explicitly sent here to spy on me...us."

"You don't know that."

"Oh, yes, I do. He confessed...through both of those very shapely lips."

Mia gasped and covered her mouth.

"Oh, yeah," Tessa continued. "And while he may try to play Mr. Nice, don't forget that he receives his orders from Dr. Evil. Sometimes, you've got to keep your enemies close. That's why I accepted his invitation to dinner."

"Dinner? Whaaaat?" she replied. "*Humph*. Keeping your enemies close has its advantages...and with a man that fine, you should enjoy it immensely."

"I can only hope so."

"We're supposed to meet the writers now. Should I tell them you're on the way?"

"Five minutes."

Tessa retrieved her Moleskine notebook from her desk and flipped to the page on which she'd drafted ideas for the new line. One, a breakup card inspired by Cody's sayonara, had bitter witch written all over it. She tucked it in her notebook, thanking the heavens that the remnants of her poison pen would never see the light of an Ebony Bookstore.

Then she left her office with a little extra bounce in her step. With a date on deck, this night would be better than the last, one way or another.

Her team posted around the table in the conference room, appearing slightly shell-shocked since the big announcement.

The truth is until they were forced to change office space, the acquisition would have minimal impact on their daily routines. Also, as CEO and creator, she bore the brunt of the hit. That's why she hoped her plan, however risky in the short-term, delivered the results best for everyone involved in the long term.

"Good morning, all. So just a few things," she began. "First, I met with Kyle Anderson this morning regarding the plans for integration."

A choir of groans filled the room; the group was led by Destiny. "Integration is code for say goodbye to your office and hello to a cramped cubicle."

"We'll have none of that. One positive development was that he decided the move will be phased, a slow-peel Band-Aid approach rather than a rip. I provided him with the designs for our offices, so I'm hoping they'll provide near-identical space when he's done. Also, you should receive your Hart Enterprise system accesses within a week or so. Any questions so far?"

"We won't have to swap out computers, will we?" Dion asked. "I've had this one for a year, and I just figured out how to use all the features."

Tessa cleared her throat. "*Ahem.* To be honest, I'm not certain. My mind might have wandered once or twice during the conversation. You know, with him droning on."

She pretended to roll her eyes; in truth, she'd been anything and everything but bored.

Mia gave her the stink eye.

"But nobody's coming for your MacBooks if that's what you're worried about. I'll make sure you retain them, even if you receive the Surfaces they use."

There was a collective sigh of relief.

"Any other questions?" she paused for a moment, and when no one responded, she continued. "Good. Zeke and Destiny, your revised copy for the special occasion graduation and divorce cards have been submitted to the artists, so congratulations. They will be included in the current line."

There was a short round of applause.

"Dion, I actually think your marriage copy would be an ideal starting point for Keep It Real's new line—or at least one of them."

"One of them?" he asked.

Tessa wrote the words "kinder" and gentler" on the white-board. "Yes, one of the new big ideas. Cody Hart wants Keep It Real to evolve to this: kinder, gentler. That way, we can expand our market share and boost our profits."

Another wave of groans echoed through the room.

"My sentiments exactly," Tessa said.

Zeke pushed his glasses back on the bridge of his nose and raised his pencil in the air. "I don't mean any harm, but we're not Hart. Frankly, the thought of pink flowers, sugar, spice, and everything nice sends me into an allergic shock."

"Preach, brother," a voice said. She couldn't tell whom.

"Come on. I came to work for you so I wouldn't have to write that kind of stuff. I chose you; I didn't choose Hart. I say we go hard or go home."

Go home?

"Wait a minute. You guys aren't thinking about quitting, are you?" She scanned the room, gauging their reactions.

No one spoke a word, but everyone answered with the

angst in their expressions. For the first time, she genuinely feared losing not only her company but also her team. How could she blame them? They didn't sign up for this acquisition or the results of it. And they were invested in Keep It Real, not Hart.

The thought of coming to work, and being greeted by resignation letters made her shudder inside. Saving her staff meant doing something drastic—clearly Cody's "kinder" and "gentler" wouldn't do the trick. She pitched her other concept on the fly and hoped it would they'd bite.

"I agree with you. That's why I've got another idea. We must change without being a parody of Hart. So, if we want to shake ourselves out of the sales rut, we've got to go hard."

"Harder?" Mia asked. "I don't mean any harm, but if our messages go any harder, our consumers will need therapy...and some hugs." Then she muttered, "Mailbags."

"I, for one, am with Tessa. Everything she touches turns to gold...or green, as it were," Judge Judy said. "What's your idea?"

Mia narrowed her eyes at Tessa because she knew something the rest of the team didn't—focus group research indicated that "go-hard" was too insensitive and would fail miserably out of the gate.

"Let's face it, guys,"—Tessa paced the room—"The world has gotten a lot meaner and colder. Some people believe you should counter the negativity with love and kindness. But sometimes, when someone's negativity is consistently cold and lacking empathy, you've got to give it right back. And eye for an eye, a tooth for a tooth."

"Can that really work?" Mia asked. "I mean, is that what we really want to be? Is that the vision?"

The answer in Tessa's heart was no. She didn't want to go harder. She certainly didn't want to send anyone to therapy.

But she couldn't risk losing *everyone*...in addition to *everything*.

She'd handpicked this well-oiled machine. Rather than lose

them, she decided to distract them with this rogue project. Once she regained control of Keep It Real, she'd put an end to it.

"If any team is capable of leaning into this vision without going overboard, it's you. So, here's what I want"—Tessa paused to watch their reactions—"For the next few weeks, I want you to work on this line. Instead of hardcore, let's call it plain talk or something along those lines."

"Ooh, that's not bad," Zeke said, his idea lightbulb switched in the full-on position. "Plain Talk...no, no, Real Talk. That's it. Real Talk."

"Yep, Zeke. I'm picking up what you're putting down," Tessa said. "The copy should read like something you would say to a friend, but only after a shot and a few glasses of chardonnay."

Everyone's eyes widened, and a few team members chuckled.

"So, um, question," Bethany began. "Will we be able to distribute these in stores?"

She nodded. "Our distribution remains unchanged. In the short term, let's not worry about sales. Let's appease Cody Hart and buy ourselves some space to do what we really want. Thus, your charge also is to come up with a few Hart card concepts, 'kinder and gentler'" —she used air quotes—"while quietly developing Real Talk," she said directly to Destiny. The latter's lips routinely loosened under the influence of a mojito or three.

"No limits for the Hart Cards. If you can squeeze some love out of your cold hearts, let your mush muses fly free. Everybody clear?"

Everyone chuckled and nodded.

"Great. Let's adjourn for now and take this up in a couple of days. I want ideas for both product lines and some sample copy. Now go forth and prosper."

The room emptied quickly. While Zeke appeared eager to tackle the assignment, the others remained firmly on the fence.

Mia's icy glare frosted Tessa over. She was vehemently opposed to the idea of the line. She trudged toward Tessa, her face scrunched in a grumble, and whispered, "Tessa, what are you doing? I gave you the data for the same collection three months ago the first time you concocted it out of desperation."

"I know, but—"

"You may not remember because you haven't actually read it yet. The projections said this idea is not only bad; it's unprofitable. And numbers don't lie."

"You summarized the data for me, but what could I do?" she asked with a shrug paired with frustration. "They were gonna—"

"You saw that, too, huh?"

"I had to give them something," said Tessa. "I couldn't—"

"I get it. No one wants the team to quit," Mia said. "But this— if you go with Real Talk, you risk tanking the business and losing what little market foothold we have."

Tessa clenched her eyes shut and took a cleansing breath. "You know I respect your opinion, Mia. But this is my company, my brainchild. Not a single one of us would be standing here if I ever played it safe."

"Agreed," she said. "But...this tactic could mean—Cody's gonna flip."

"He won't find out. But if he does, I sure as heck hope he flips. Getting a rise out of him, throwing him off his game— that's when he makes mistakes."

As Tessa offered Mia a comforting pat on the shoulder, Cody approached, appearing out of nowhere. "Speak of the devil, and he shall appear."

Mia turned and grumbled. "Talk about timing. Grab me when you're done."

"Fine, fine," Tessa said to Mia. Then she turned her attention to her visitor. He strolled into the conference room and scanned the board, then her.

"Kinder. Gentler." Cody's smile, which revealed at least thirty of his teeth, was that of a man who'd just made a critical blunder. He read the words on the whiteboard and assumed he'd won all the battles and the war. "You've taken my message to heart, no pun intended."

"Uh, well, uh," She clammed up to avoid lying but wait until he found out the truth. "I'm doing what's best for the company."

After some small talk and idle chit chat to break the tension, Tessa asked. "What brings you here?"

"A couple of critical issues related to the integration...and, to be honest, I could use your help on a new project."

"A new project...for Hart Cards?" She jerked her head back. "Do I really want to hear this?"

Chapter Twelve

C ody

THE FOCUS GROUP HAD SERVED CODY THE ANSWER TO HIS TROUBLES like a snack on a platter. Of course, if the idea failed, he'd choke on this mistake.

He'd need to sell Tessa on a concept that would pique her creative interest and appeal to her heart. He questioned whether the idea would do the trick, but he'd give it a shot, anyway.

He arrived at Keep It Real without announcement or fanfare, and used the opportunity to scope the layout. He rambled through the halls, noting familiar touches from his memories of Tessa, only half following the instructions Mabel gave him. As the room numbers drew closer to the one marking his destination, he grew more jittery. The thought of seeing her...she still made his stomach flutter.

Through her office's frosted glass wall, he caught sight of Tessa's silhouette as Mia lingered in the doorway. His breath stopped in his chest, like it did when he saw her in that blue dress with the butterflies and flowers. Nothing had changed, yet everything was different.

The office door opened and Mia exited. He passed her and stepped inside first looking at Tessa and then behind her.

"Kinder and gentler." He read the words aloud from the whiteboard but scarcely believed them. He recognized them as his own. When he first pitched her the ideas for the "pivot" messaging, he thought the message had fallen on deaf ears. But now, in this rare occasion, he believed Tessa had heard him, that she listened, that she respected him as he did her. He congratulated himself for coaxing the mountain toward Muhammad, and then approached Tessa with cautious optimism.

"You've taken my words to heart...no pun intended." He smiled and jutted his chin toward the board. "I love the scent of miracles in the morning."

Once upon a time, they lived in synch, moved in the same strides, breathed in the same rhythm. Before Keep It Real and Hart Enterprises, nothing in the world existed except them, cold Ramen noodles, a compact apartment, and their art. Those times were as close as he'd ever come to living his ideal life. He questioned the wisdom of clinging to some faint hope that they could ever return to a place so right...in light of...The Chandra and The Tessa.

"Oh, yeah. The scent of something's strong in here," she said. "Smells like smug spirit."

He chuckled and wagged his finger. "I would really adore your sense of humor, if you were funny," he deadpanned before continuing. "But I'm glad you're moving forward with such enthusiasm." He gestured to the board. "I suppose this means you've just finished briefing your team on the marketing pivot. Right?"

"Umm, yes, we're pivoting. You're exactly right. I explained your direction, and then provided them with some instruction to follow."

"How'd it go over? Is everybody sold on the new direction?"

"Hmm. Well. It's interesting you should ask that question. It's safe to say that after some initial resistance, I corralled the team, and they're mostly excited about the new concept."

"Mostly?"

"Well, obviously, there was some well-founded pessimism. Keep It Real didn't make its bones on kinder and gentler."

"No, you did not. But I really believe—"

She gave him the hand. "But we...all of us realize that if we are to survive in this sluggish market, we need a new strategy, perhaps even a drastic one. If nothing else, they are consummate professionals. I've no question we're going to be successful as we shift into this new direction. But I could've told you all of this over the phone. What brings you here?"

"A couple of critical issues related to the integration...and, to be honest, I could use your help on a new project."

"A project?" She jerked her head back. "Do I want to hear this?"

"It's business."

"Just business, huh? After everything that's transpired between us, you drove all the way here to discuss business."

He knew a loaded question when he heard one. That one weighed about a ton. Her query contained with more truth than he wished to acknowledge. He'd thrust himself back into her life and had offered zero acknowledgement of the way he'd broken off their relationship. Nor would he, at least not in a way that would satisfy Tessa. So, he allowed her a moment to vent.

"Go ahead and talk about your little project as if we have no history, as if you acquired a stranger's company, as if we parted ways on good terms. Really, you could've spared us both the face-to-face, especially since you designated Kyle as your point-man to keep me in check."

"Keep you in check? I'm not sure what you mean."

"Don't play coy. You directed him to come to Sweet Media, serve as your watchdog, and spy on me."

He maintained a stoic expression and refused to react.

"C'mon, Cody. I've done my time at Hart Enterprises. I probably know that campus as well as you do."

His jaw clenched.

"And Keep It Real shouldn't be much of a stranger to you given you were by my side as I planned Sweet-Hart. Well, you in your own Benedict Arnold way."

She'd spoken the truth, but he couldn't give her the satisfaction of acknowledging it. So, he did what any red-blooded man would do in a similar situation—deny, deny, deny. "I have no idea what you're talking about. Kyle is the COO and the enterprise operations manager. With Keep It Real being *so small*"—he dealt a low blow—"you may not understand the complexities of integrating two companies, especially when it comes to technology and communications. That's why he works for me. That's the job I pay him to execute on my behalf."

"So, the invitation to dinner was all his idea?"

Cody jerked his head back. A fiery surge burned through him so fast he couldn't restrain it. He could feel his eyes flush with jealousy before his whole expression betrayed him.

"Whoa. You really had no idea, did you?"

"I'm a publishing magnate not a pimp. And, quite honestly, I'm offended by the accusation," he said, half lying and half trying to force back his real reaction.

"I apologize for being presumptive. Besides, you're in a relationship with whatsherface."

"Chandra. Yes. And I'm taking her to dinner tonight, so I honestly couldn't care less who you date." He lied, but he would make it true.

"Under the circumstances, I had to ask. Now, I'm certain I made the right decision."

"You turned him down?"

"Of course not. That's why we need to wrap up early. Since we're avoiding the past, let's talk future. What's this project you want to speak to me about?"

He cleared his throat. The woman before him was not the one

he remembered. Once upon a time, she'd never have accepted a dinner invitation from a coworker at any level. Now?

He scanned her office searching for the words he needed to divert the conversation. He'd gather the nerve to say what he really meant, a difficult feat because she knew him like no other person on the planet. "I like the set up you've got here."

"Should be familiar. I figured one of us should get some use out of it."

"You'll have to give this up once your Hart space is complete."

"Yes, Kyle made that quite clear. He also indicated we could move after he completed the reconfiguration."

Cody nodded. "We can replicate it. You think you can handle working in the office with me every day without things getting awkward?"

"Awkward? But, why?" She pursed her burgundy lips and placed her a hand on her hip. "Let see, you broke off our relationship with a handmade Dear Jane card. You've avoided all contact with me for five years, except when you acquired my company without so much as a white flag or an olive branch. Hate to break it to you, but we took a hard left past uncomfortable and now sit squarely in Awkwardville."

"True."

"But we're professionals. We'll do what we have to do, right?" She rolled her eyes so completely he wondered if they'd ever return forward. "Anyway, you were saying?"

"I want to expand the Hart line."

"A new line? You've got cotton candy, puppies, and roses covered. Let me guess. You're adding fluffy white clouds and rainbows? Nobody does that better than you."

His plan to ignore her little outburst and tolerate her temper tantrum was about to fail. She could do many things at Hart, but he would never allow her to belittle his company after everything he'd done for Madam Ungrateful.

"Agreed. At least as far as Hart goes. That's how we've

become the number three supplier of greeting cards in the country. How's Keep It Real doing these days?"

"Still going for the jugular, I see." She swallowed hard and her eyebrows pinched together. "Maybe after this meeting you'll write that in a card and send it to me. It'd be just like old times."

"This conversation is not going the way I imagined it."

"Oh, really? And how did you imagine it?"

He rubbed the scruff on his chin and grimaced. "I pictured myself apologizing for any hurt I've caused you. I saw myself telling you that you're one of the most talented writers and artists I know. Your experience in building Keep It Real is exactly the kind of know-how and leadership the Hart team requires to create a long-planned new line of cards and make it successful. I would've made sure you know what an honor it would be if you, in addition to your duties in running Keep It Real, accepted the lead consulting role for my new specially abled line."

Her shroud of anger disappeared in an instant and a twinkle of light once again flickered in her eyes. "Maybe we ought to schedule all future meetings in your head." She tapped her lip with her finger. "But...specially abled. Wow. That sounds like an interesting challenge. It's certainly an underserved niche market, and I love targeting those. Do you have a vision for it?"

"You're the one with the vision, remember? I'm the previous visual art—now—business guy, and I try to stay in my lane...mostly."

She locked eyes with him and smiled. "Hmmm. The line really lends itself to multiple approaches. Who's on the team?"

"Well, that's the catch. It's not a seasoned group—at all."

"And by not seasoned you mean, junior? Two to three years of experience?"

"No, I mean former interns. New graduates, fresh out of college. The idea actually emerged from a focus group we held, you know, a while back," he said, squeezing out the lie. "One of the participants spoke of a girl paralyzed from the waist down following a car accident."

"Oh, no."

"She wanted to see herself represented on a card. As African Americans, who could better relate?"

She revealed a sliver of a smile. "I confess. I'm intrigued."

"Does that mean you're on board?" he asked.

"I'll meet with your team." She turned to gaze at him, a look he'd seen many times before; her eyes sparkled with life and energy. He was thankful for the welcomed sight, one he could never see enough. "We'll see how it goes from there."

"Great, uh...well, I think we're done for now"— he glanced at his watch—"How do you feel about lunch?"

"It's one of my favorite six meals of the day," Tessa replied.

"I mean, with me. You know, maybe we can discuss your initial thoughts on the line, hash out some preliminary concepts and a rough schedule."

"We survived this meeting with all of our appendages intact —barely," she replied. "Perhaps we shouldn't push our luck."

He chuckled. "You're probably right. Next time."

"Next time," she said as he offered his goodbyes and turned to walk away. "You know what? On second thought, lunch might be a nice idea. It's been five years. We've built some goodwill here. This may be an opportunity to capitalize on it and put an end to the dissension forever."

"Excuse me?" he said. "Did I hear you correctly?"

"You'd prefer I turn you down?"

"No, no. I'm just surprised. I've got a quick stop to make, but how about we meet in an hour, at say, the District Chophouse? Used to be your favorite."

"Still is." She smiled demurely. "You still remember."

"How could I forget?"

"You should hurry along," she said. "Grab a table so I don't have to wait. You know what I'm like when I'm hangry."

"See you in an hour."

Rarely had any man, woman, or child left him speechless, but Tessa had managed to do the impossible.

When hurt, Tessa was akin to a wounded African buffalo, the Africans nicknamed the beasts "black death." Watching them graze on dried grass, they seemed relatively harmless. But when threatened or injured, they didn't cower. No. Instead, a ton of muscle, fat, and horns barreled directly toward the perceived threat at thirty-five-miles an hour. Death on contact.

Tessa.

He'd braced himself for a full-force African buffalo attack, but she'd accepted his invitation to lunch. He hoped her acceptance signaled their relationship had survived the worst, and they could erase the pain of the past to achieve greatness—together.

The sounds of midday chatter and clanking dishes greeted Cody as he entered the District Chophouse for lunch with Tessa.

He arrived fifteen minutes early to secure a booth in the back corner. He anticipated her fashionably late arrival and a spirited conversation that would escalate from a simmer to a boil. But he truly believed a truce would ensue once they aired out their frustrations and emptied the emotional baggage they'd lugged for five years.

With their differences resolved, they'd ease into a new normal. At least that's how he saw the afternoon playing out.

It wouldn't be long before he found out Tessa had envisioned something quite different.

"Here's your seat," the waitress said, as she laid out a couple of menus. "Would you like something to drink while you wait?"

"A whiskey sour, please," he replied. "No, actually, make that two. One for my guest."

The last time he felt such anticipation waiting for Tessa, she'd tried on fifty-eleven dresses before dinner with Pops. She wore a blue dress with a low-cut back and emerged from the bathroom and offered him a little hip wiggle as she asked him how she looked.

"Like warm bread and honey butter," he replied. His smile had oozed through his frustration and her reflection brightened his mood.

"You, okay? Why so tense?" she had asked. "It's the dress, isn't it? I promise I'm wearing this one. You owe me Jiffy Pop and movie night if we survive this."

The problem wasn't the dress; it was the dinner. His commitment to Tessa wouldn't change no matter what his father attempted to dictate later that night. He'd kept her in the dark for her benefit more than for his own.

"When he sees how perfect we are together, he'll not only accept us, he'll finance Sweet-Hart Cards. Our dream will become reality. Mark my words. He's changing."

"Yeah, like the pre-acid vat joker he's changing. With all due respect, we can do this on our own. We don't need our fathers, and I only want you."

She meant every word. So did Pops. At dinner, while Tessa was in the ladies' room cleaning up after they traipsed through a monsoon to arrive on time for dinner, Cody's father whispered five words that changed his life forever.

Perhaps now the time had come to confess the truth to Tessa.

"Fantastic. I'll be right back with your order," he heard the waiter say. Tessa still had not appeared.

He tugged at his collar and adjusted his cufflinks just so. Then he watched the door.

An hour and a half later, Cody pinched his lips into thin slits as he glanced at his wrist for the umpteenth time. Heat rose up into his neck and burned his ears.

When the waitress passed him in the distance, he waved and signed an air-check on his hand.

Minutes later, she bubbled back to his table with an unexpected delivery, an envelope. "Sir, a young lady left this with the maître d' moments ago."

After she left, he found a handmade card inside.

She'd covered the front with a picture of a broken clock. The copy read, "Did I keep you waiting?" The inside read, "Sorry. Not sorry." She'd signed it, "Petty, Bitter Witch."

So, that's how it's gonna be?

He slapped a twenty on the table when the waiter returned. "Another whiskey sour, please. Make it a double."

As the server nodded and walked away, Cody glanced at Tessa's delivery once more. *Black Death.* He began to believe his brother's warning was more premonition than vision. Acquiring Keep It Real may yet prove to be the biggest mistake of his life.

Chapter Thirteen

T essa

THE FROST ON HER WINDOWS PALED IN COMPARISON TO THE CHILL on her heart. She'd sent Cody a card instead of showing up to their lunch date, mild in contrast to the heartbreak he delivered, but still effective. She embraced the well of pettiness bubbling within her, as her eyes locked on the leaves tumbling across the ground under the force of the frosty early-winter winds. The twists blew the final remains of autumn, rust and bronze leaves, into tornado-like cones until they dissipated and scattered into the streets.

Tessa welcomed her sense of smugness as she stared out of her office window. She tried to picture Cody's reaction when he received the card. She would've sworn under oath that she'd fully recovered from Cody's betrayal. Now, she wondered if the deep wounds inflicted were less impactful than the years of scarring they left behind.

Was her card to Cody beneath her? Wrong? Probably.

Thankfully, she didn't have time to linger in her thoughts. Mia stuck her head into Tessa's office to remind her that creative was waiting for her in the writing studio. She'd braced herself for the first round of Real Talk ideas.

"So, how'd your meeting with the boss man go?"

"You mean the jerk who bought my company?" She'd hedged. Her voice sounded fake and she responded in a sing-songy way. "It was civil. Mostly."

"Mostly? What does that mean?"

"It means, we talked, he offered a backhanded apology, and he invited me to lunch."

"Lunch. Hmm." Mia glanced at her watch. "You mean, today?"

She nodded. "Right now, this minute as a matter of fact."

Fury, revenge, spitting anger —for years, she refused to lean in to the Molotov cocktail of emotions after the break-up, but she invited them with open arms right now. She let her bitter witch fly free and forgave herself for the petty moment, with nary a pang of guilt.

Mia snorted. "And you were supposed to be there..."

"An hour ago," she sang.

Tessa sneered at the thought of Cody arriving at the restaurant and waiting for a lunch date that would never arrive. He went low during his cowardly break-up, leaving her devastated. Now, too many years later in direct response, she'd swan-dived off the high road and seized the opportunity to deal a crippling blow.

Not only did she wallow in the muck, she basked in it like a hot pig in cold mud.

"Now, let's beat it. I'm prepared and ready for the next meeting."

Mia hung her hand on her hips and wagged her finger. "Wait a minute. You stood him up? Tessa, call me crazy, but this is a bass-ackward way of endearing yourself to our new CEO. And, no matter how long you wade in the pool of your denial, he is your boss."

"First of all, owning Keep It Real does not make him the boss of me."

"Uh, no. I beg to differ. Buying your company means he is, by definition and in fact, the boss of you."

Tessa sucked her tongue and rolled her eyes like a grade school girl. Without realizing it, she was slowly turning into *The Wiz* witch, Evilene, who didn't want any bad news. "Second of all, you're supposed to treat others the way they treat you."

"Mmm...no. That's not how that works," Mia said with a jagged-edged glare. "You treat others the way you want to be treated. You hear the difference? Want to be treated."

"Potato, potahto. I've got the gist, and I promise you this: this minor inconvenience and embarrassment that I subjected him to pales in comparison to what he did to me."

And, yet, the minuscule trace of pleasure she'd derived from the swipe at Cody's ego slowly melted away and her shame mushroomed. In the end, what had she proven except that she'd become the thing that everyone believed her to be—petty and bitter.

There was no honor in that.

"I hear you, but it would behoove you to remember one thing," Mia said, "while we can debate whether or not he is the boss of you, you are, in fact, the boss of us. That means we, all of us in Keep It Real, have a stake in your ability to build a positive relationship with Mr. Hart."

She deflated, and her shoulders slumped. She'd been so consumed with effecting her own brand of revenge against her ex that she had scarcely considered the impact her behavior would have on her staff.

She used to prioritize their needs above her own, understanding that they, more than any grand idea she concocted, were core to her success. The corporate drama had begun to change her for the worse in more ways than one—the card, the lunch, the new fake collection. These were not her finest moments.

"You know what? You're absolutely right. What am I doing?" She raised her hands in the air and released a heavy sigh. She couldn't crawl in the bed and drown herself beneath a weighted blanket with a bottle of Grey Goose like she so longed to do. No, there was only one way out.

"The sooner I restore this company's independence, the sooner I regain my sanity. Then I can focus my energies on doing the right things."

"You know what you've got to do now, don't you?"

Tessa clenched her eyes shut. "Absolutely not. Not in a million years."

"This is non-negotiable," Mia declared. "From what you've told me about him, and what I know about you, any tit-for-tat war between you can only end up bloody for the rest of us."

Tessa vigorously shook her head no, but under the glare of Mia's stare, she wavered. "Don't give me that look. You're not going to make me. It won't work." She diverted her gaze to another part of her office. "You're still looking at me, aren't you?"

"Can't you feel your weave burning?"

Tessa laughed and fluffed her hair at the shoulder. "It's mine. I paid for every inch." She spun around. "Fine. I won't like it, but I'll take one for the team."

"If you can't do it because it's the right thing to do, then, fine, take one for the team. Now, let's go to the meeting."

Two hours and five presentations later, the team had used her sample "break-up" card to build the entire concept for the new Real Talk line. They'd progressed much faster than she anticipated.

Fear overcame the pride.

She banked on tortoise-pace workers and she got hares. Too many hares. She didn't tell them to slow roll the design effort, but she didn't think she needed to. They dragged their butts on everything else. She figured that by the time they finalized the initial designs, she'd have regained control of her company.

She meant the project as a temporary distraction from the acquisition nightmare, not a permanent collection. How could she stall them now that they'd finished so much? She'd think of something—and fast.

"Guys! I can't tell you enough how completely fantastic this is. You really nailed it. Not hard core but real talk. It's politically incorrect. It's real. It's funny. It's straight no chaser."

"You don't think we've gone over the line?"

Tessa guffawed on the outside while cringing on the inside. "There is no such place. Like it or not, these cards represent the world we're living in right now. You can't be faint of heart today. Better to listen to the truth than live with blinders on, and I think this card line represents authenticity."

Mia stepped in to bring some welcomed interference, even if for reasons opposed to hers. "These ideas are quite diverse. To give a line any chance at survival, we probably need to narrow down the offering, don't you think?"

Tessa embraced the subsequent silence and paced the room. If she was honest with herself, she hadn't given the market as much thought as she should've. The collection was never meant for the shelves. She only wanted to keep the team from leaving. But since Mia brought up the issue, Tessa decided to use the oversight to stall the line.

"Good question. I'll give it back to the team and let you all narrow down the selection. Dion, I've got to tell you. That 'Fronting on Facebook' idea is so cold it hurt my feelings—and I don't even check my account."

"Thank you. Thank you. It was a stroke of brilliance if I do say so myself," he said without an ounce of humility. "How many times have we been inundated with posts from people who brag about their lives and significant others one day and then post a GoFundMe for the divorce the next. Whatever happened to..."

"Real talk?" Zeke asked with a shoulder shrug.

"Exactly. Telling it like it is," Dion said. "There's no shame in pain."

"Ooh...that's a tag line if I've ever heard one. We need to use it," Zeke said.

Destiny waited for a break in the chatter to confess her thoughts. "I can't even lie. Every day I scroll through my timeline feeling like an utter and complete failure. My longest relationship over the past three years was a Marvel marathon during Netflix and chill."

The team laughed and someone said, "T-M-I."

"You know I'm not lying. Shoot, every time I scan my feed somebody's celebrating an anniversary, saying yes to the dress, or taking 'ussies' and parading around as if they've met the last good man on earth."

"Tell it!" Bethany called out from her spot on the couch.

"No sooner than they get boo'ed up we learn the awful truth —it's all fake! Come to find out Bae spent the anniversary with the side piece. Now, home girl has sliced the ussie in half with a machete on Facebook Live. Then, while burning up his side of the picture, she accidentally set the house on fire."

Laughter erupted with a few knee slaps and head nods. Destiny could stretch the heck out of a story, which is what made her so good at her job.

"Next came the go-fund-me account to pay for the damage. Turns out, she used the insurance money to buy Bae the new Jordans. Now, she's calling me on the phone in the middle of the night singing a song of woe, dragging him like a bag of steaming dog crap. All I can think is why didn't you tell that half of the story on Facebook? So, do I plan to buy these cards to air my grievances? Trust and believe, I'll be first in line."

"For this collection, we need to push web sales," Tessa said.

"What about Hart's existing market? Traditionalists still want puppies and cotton candy," Zeke said. "Keep It Real took tradi-tional to the left with snarky. This new line, whatever we call it, goes to the left, up the street and around the corner to the liquor store."

"Exactly," Destiny piped in.

"We won't attract well-meaning consumers," Mia warned, "which is most consumers. These are almost mean...almost. Let's just pray no one takes this all the way to the left and causes someone emotional pain they can't recover from." Mia sucked some of the oxygen from the room. She'd kept her lips tight and listened ... until now. "I dunno. I'm listening, and uh, we're way off the reservation," Mia continued. "The messaging is polariz-ing. People are gonna love it or hate it. There's no grey here. Only black or white."

Tessa stood up and moved front and center. "I agree. This is a risk...and a sizable one."

"If it's a success, it may pull up the sales on the other card lines," Mia interrupted. "My fear, no offense, is it'll pull down the other lines. We could cede our existing market share to the Hart Enterprises of the rest of the world."

"On paper, Real Talk isn't workable, but that's what everyone told me about Keep It Real," Tessa said. "I learned that revolu-tionary ideas cause radical shifts. To escape this sales rut and build some momentum, we've got to try something even more innovative and edgy. This fits the bill."

"What about kinder and gentler. You know, cotton candy, roses, and puppies?" Zeke said.

"Going that route would be inauthentic. Don't you think?" Tessa glanced around the room to gauge the level of support. The team was on board. A few questioned her sanity and motives, as well they should.

Bethany rarely talked during creative meetings, although her work was superb. Her general silence was the reason everyone listened when she spoke up. "I think we're all forgetting one key factor—our new boss, Cody Hart. The soul of Hart Cards will never agree to release the Real Talk line. Not in a million years. Just go to the local CVS and pick up their collection. What we're proposing is the opposite of everything he stands for."

Tessa's back stiffened. "First of all, he's not in charge of our operations. I still maintain full control over our creative vision." This was among her greatest fears, that her own team would constantly question her authority. "Next of all, he's already aware that we're cooking up a new line and he's onboard," she said, before mumbling, *sort of.*

She hadn't lied...entirely.

This idea might take a little getting used to...oh, who was she kidding? She didn't want Cody to love the idea. She needed to save her relationship with her team, not with him.

She checked her watch, the five o'clock hour had almost arrived. The time had come for dinner with Kyle. "Let's adjourn for today," Tessa said. "How about we stick a pin in this discussion until we develop a few mockups. Destiny, Zeke, Dion, and Judy, send me your copy and I'll pass it on to Bethany for graphic design. When we've got some artwork, we'll finalize the Real Talk concepts."

The meeting broke, and everyone dispersed except Mia. Tessa braced herself to receive the serving of truth her bestie would offer, but she didn't want to hear it. Turned out Tessa was wrong. Mia's only goal was to dish on Tessa's date with Kyle. "So, what time are you leaving?" she asked.

"I plan to arrive fashionably late."

"Mmm-hmm. Riiiight. Meaning you'll get there a half hour early, stalk the doorway from a distance, and walk in five minutes after him."

"Exactly."

Chapter Fourteen

C ody

TESSA STOOD HIM UP FOR THEIR LUNCH DATE AND LEFT HIM WITH A card. Deja vu. Except this time he'd received rather than delivered it. Maybe he deserved this Karma—he didn't have to like it.

"Ms. Dee, please find Kyle for me?" Cody ambled around the halls still brooding over the fact that he'd fallen victim to Tessa's special brand of petty. She'd infuriated him. He couldn't think straight.

He'd invited her to lunch to offer her an olive branch, and instead of grateful acceptance of his charity, she stripped the leaves and beat him over the head with the entire tree. Then she left him with a bitter card and nothing resembling dignity.

While stewing over his cold lunch and warm cocktail, he plotted and schemed to exact revenge for her bitter, witchy act of war. No more Mr. Nice Guy. He vowed to become a tick burrowed beneath her skin.

Game on.

Caving to family pressures, he'd hurt her in immeasurable ways, ways from which she'd not fully recovered. But had she not gotten over their break up—or him?

Didn't matter. Now, he was petty and bitter.

Kyle had a date with Tessa, and Cody planned to be Tessa's tick.

If she wanted to play tit-for-tat, she'd get more than she bargained for. The acquisition had placed Cody in a position of power, and he'd wield it any way he chose.

Bright sun rays and oncoming whiskey-sour headache proved to be too much for Cody's eyes as he trekked through the corridor area leading to his office. The glare obstructed his vision so much he bumped into Kyle and knocked himself off balance. His friend, foe for the moment, whistled with more cheer than Cody could stand.

"Hey, excuse me," Cody said before he reached his door.

"You all right?" Kyle said. "Ms. Dee said you're looking for me. How'd lunch go?"

Cody had no desire to tell the truth, a stark contrast from their routine. On friend- time, he shared all the details. Before Chandra, women considered him to be a catch. Tessa wasn't normal. "Well, let's say Tessa's never short on surprises."

Cody adjusted the blinds in his office as Kyle took his usual seat.

"Did you need me for something?" Cody continued.

"It's Tessa..." Kyle began.

"What's going on?" Cody braced himself to hear the date news...again.

Kyle's expression was happy...and yet not. "A couple of things," he said. "First, be forewarned. Word's seeping out that Keep It Real's working on a new collection."

Cody smiled to himself, knowing what Kyle had said was true. He'd seen the evidence of it himself. The team was hard at work on the "kinder and gentler" messaging he'd proposed to Tessa, the only suggestion from him she'd ever followed. "Yeah,

I'm aware. I walked in on Tessa's planning session with her team. I'm on board. Actually, it's a good idea. One might even say I played a small part in developing the creative vision for the new direction."

"Wait a minute. You're cool with it? I mean, you support what she's doing...as part of Hart Cards?"

Cody's brow crinkled from confusion. He didn't quite understand Kyle's reaction. "Absolutely! Like I said, the pivot was practically my idea."

"Yours? Wow. Okay."

Cody jerked his head back, tilted it to the side, and shrugged. "In the original plan I developed with Tessa, back when we were kids, I was the artist."

"Original plan? You mean Tessa worked for Hart before the acquisition?"

He nodded and shifted his gaze to his hands to avoid the true confession: Hart Cards should've been Sweet-Hart Cards. "Something like that."

"Ah. Light dawns on Marblehead. I'd suspected you two had a little history, but I didn't realize...why didn't you ever tell me about her?"

"Well, it's not a best-kept secret. Besides, you and I met after Tessa and I broke up, so I had no reason to mention our ancient history. At least until now. Unfortunately, our relationship remains complex, to put it mildly."

"Wish you had told me sooner." Kyle's lips pressed together with consternation. "I mean about your involvement."

"Why?" he asked deceptively. Tessa had already informed him about their little date. He wanted to find out whether Kyle would confess the truth.

"I invited Tessa to dinner," he said, keeping his eyes trained on Cody, studying him as if trying to catch changes in his expression. "From what you're saying, that's not a problem, right? I mean, as you say, ancient history. Besides, Chandra's amazing and you're marrying her in a matter of weeks."

Cody nodded.

"I've known you longer than her. Maintaining this here,"—Kyle pointed toward Cody and then himself—"is my priority. We're boys."

Cody shrugged, forcing his mouth into a straight line, burying his jealousy below the surface, far below. The thought of Kyle dating and kissing Tessa made his stomach curl into a massive knot. The thought of him sleeping with Tessa made him borderline murderous, but he and Chandra were a tuxedo rental and an aisle away from marriage.

"Awkward? Please. I can literally count the number of years since we were together on one hand"—he holds his palm in the air— "And I broke it off. Now that I think about it, she may have mentioned your dinner in passing this afternoon. No issues here at all."

Kyle's lips stretched into a broad smile, and he breathed a sigh. He swiped the back of his hand across his forehead, and said, "That's a relief. Since we're all Hart now, I thought I should ensure there was no conflict of interest. Once the integration's over, there's no issue, whatsoever."

Cody offered Kyle a salute. Why? He didn't know. Maybe it saved him from choking Kyle...or flipping him the bird. Truth be told he wished he could molly-whop Kyle, but he'd need to keep his hands and opinions to himself for fear of exposing his lingering feelings for Tessa. Fighting Kyle because his friend fell for Tessa would serve as an admission of Cody's painful the truth—and he preferred to dwell in denial. "It's all good. Really, you're overdue for a night on the town. You haven't been out since whatsherface. So, where are you two kids eating?"

Kyle stared into space for a moment and then shrugged. "I hadn't had much time to think about it. Honestly, I thought she'd turn me down flat. I can't believe she's still on the market. A woman like that should have a man—or at least be in a committed relationship."

Cody coughed...hacked was more like it. Choked on the

whole truth and nothing but the truth. "*Ahem*. Sorry. Swallowed down the wrong pipe," he said. "Yeah, Tessa's quite the catch, but, as you said, I'm practically married to Chandra. So, how many men does she have cooking in her oven? Who knows. I do remember one thing about dating her, though. She'll let you shoot your shot, but you only get one. She remembers bad dates like family vendettas. If she hates it, you'll never live it down, and never is a mighty long time."

Cody hoped to spark Kyle's curiosity, provoke him ask the question only a tick trying to get under her skin could answer.

Kyle chewed on the thought for a moment too long for Cody's comfort. Then came a reversal of fortune.

"Honestly, I'd planned to keep the evening simple, so we'd have time to talk, get to know one another. McCormick's and Schmick's? Maybe Ruth Chris's."

Cody's stomach tanked. Ruth Chris's. Hell would freeze over before he ever allowed Kyle to take her there.

Anywhere but there.

His friend's dinner plan was a nonstarter. Cody didn't respond verbally, rather allowed his face to pucker long enough for Kyle to react. "What? Something wrong with Ruth's?"

"No, not unless you want to be completely forgettable or bore her to death, take your pick. She may not even remember your name."

"Really?" Kyle believed him for all of thirty seconds. His pursed lips suggested it lasted only that long. "Man, try again. Sounds like sabotage to me. You need to quit messing around."

"Hey, you don't have to listen to me. Enjoy your steak and potatoes. They pair well with loneliness and blue balls."

After a hard laugh, Kyle prepared to leave and blow off Cody's snarky comments. A second before he reached the door he did an about-face. "Okay. What do you suggest?"

"No, you didn't want my advice. Go on and order your little filet. That'll excite her into sedation."

"Cody, man..."

"Fine. She's addicted to Thai...seafood curry. If you want to ride the expressway to her heart, you've got to go through Thai-Phoon. It's not far from Chandra's and my place on S Street. She loves that restaurant," he lied. She'd remember the place, but not in a good way. "Surprise her. The only thing she likes more than ThaiPhoon is big surprises. Trust me. This is fool-proof."

"You better not be B-S-ing me."

"Me? B-S you?" He replied with a question to avoid the outright lie. "I promise, after tonight, she'll only ask you one thing: how soon can we go out on our second date?"

Kyle smiled and stroked his chin. "Until this moment, I suspected you had feelings for her. Glad I'm wrong. I really appreciate the advice."

Somewhere in the dark crevices of his soul, Cody wanted to feel guilty about leading Kyle into the disaster. He should've, but remorse wasn't in his vocabulary. A quick flashback to his miserable lunch removed all guilt and all doubt. His only hint of regret stemmed from his inability to witness her misery himself with his own two eyes.

NIGHTFALL BROUGHT BROODING CLOUDS, THE DISTANT ROLL OF thunder, and chilled winter winds, but no storm would stop Cody from his latest mission.

Chandra balked at walking in bad weather and despised the way the untamed winds whipped her sleek black hair into a frenzy. Hat hair would never do for The Chandra, not in a quasi-posh public setting where she could be spotted. After all, she was the lone daughter of Dr. and Mrs. Barrington.

After an hour of her droning protests, he threatened to go alone. Only then did she concede. She accompanied him, grousing the whole way. He needed her presence, more for the optics than the company. Otherwise he'd have spared himself and left her at home.

At six p.m., he and Chandra entered ThaiPhoon, a rare midweek date that took a lot of convincing on his part. In the foyer, she charmed the maître de who zipped off to find their seats shortly thereafter. Meanwhile, he craned his neck inside the nearly packed dining room, admiring the quirky design. The colorful modern Asian decor glowed under the recessed fixtures. The open floor-plan made it a cinch to spot Tessa and Kyle sitting in a cozy corner overlooking S Street. The expression on Tessa's face was everything he hoped it would be—nauseated, even though there were no plates on the table.

He leaned into the petty, reveled in the moment. He now understood how Tessa so excelled at it.

In truth, he regretted coaxing her into trying the Thai shrimp dish at ThaiPhoon all those years ago. How could he know the contents of her stomach would shoot out of her ends like propane flames from a blowtorch? He witnessed her transform from a beautiful brown to Godzilla green and snapped a photo for posterity before rescuing her from her fate.

So, Cody knew the only thing Tessa hated more than Thai food was surprises. To Cody's delight, Kyle had followed his advice to the letter, and now Cody could watch the fallout in the flesh.

He donned a self-satisfied smile as Chandra turned toward him to grouse. "Seriously, Cody? Why were you so pressed to eat out tonight? I'm exhausted. I'd rather be in bed than standing in this lobby."

"If we stay home, you're cranky. You complain that we never go out enough. If we go out, you fuss and say we should have stayed home. A brother can't win for losing." Inside of an hour, his part in the impending fiasco would end. He'd make it up to Chandra when they arrived home, perhaps with a massage and foot rub. But now he needed her for his ruse.

She huffed for a moment and shrugged. "What can I say? When you're right, you're right. Forgive my grumble wumble, Codykins." She'd reduced herself to baby talk. Apparently, she was more sorry than he thought.

She stalked the waiter through narrowed slits, impatient to be seated. He must've felt the hole burning through him because he locked eyes with her and approached.

"Here he comes. Thank goodness. Five more minutes and I might've considered eating Cody-fricasseed," she said.

He chuckled. "Did you ask for a table with a view?"

"As you wished."

They followed the waiter, weaving through a maze of dining patrons on a collision course with Kyle and Tessa who were so engrossed in conversation they never saw him and The Chandra coming. He wondered what magic words Kyle had spoken to keep Tessa so entranced in their conversation. Her perfect baby browns glazed over as if she was hypnotized. He couldn't remember her gazing at him with such adoration and affection. Then again so much time had passed, he wouldn't.

Conveniently, Cody's targets took up two adjacent seat at a table for four. As he reached them, he slammed on the brakes and performed an exaggerated double-take that could've won him an Oscar.

"Well, hello, there," Cody sang to Tessa and Kyle. "Imagine meeting you two here."

Keep It Real Cards

Always the bridesmaid, Never the bride.
Now your special Wedding Day is just around the corner.

Let's Keep It Real—It took a bottle of brown liquor and a pole in your bedroom, but you bagged that loser. It's about time. Congratulations!

Chapter Fifteen

C ody

WITH KYLE AND TESSA IN HIS SIGHTS, CODY GAVE A GENTLE TUG TO Chandra's elbow to stop her at their table.

"Kyle, Tessa, how wonderful to see you both." Cody was *on one* as he played the lead in a performance as phony as a six-dollar bill.

He'd never pass up the opportunity to get front-row seats to Tessa's misery. Chandra stepped back toward him and the table, but not without a cost for which he'd pay later. She flashed a wisp of anger at Cody but seemed to recognize the couple, at least Tessa. They were introduced via Tessa's "About Me" page.

Didn't matter.

He ignored everyone's reaction except one.

"Oh, please, meet my girlfriend, Chandra. Chandra, this is Tessa and Kyle. We all work together, at least we do since Hart obtained its latest acquisition."

"Good evening," Chandra said, greeting Kyle and Tessa with a slight bow.

Tessa's eyes turned so deadly he feared they may spew venom. Her horrified expression made enduring Chandra's aggravation worth every second.

His gaze shifted toward Kyle, whose bottom jaw slammed on the table. Cody shrugged, faking confusion, but he well understood the drama unfolding—with pure, unadulterated clarity. "Always nice to see you, Kyle."

"Yes," Chandra said to him. "What a surprise! It's great to see you here...and with Tessa." Always a gentleman, Kyle stood and greeted Chandra with a kiss on each cheek and a brotherly embrace.

After a quick calculation, Chandra perked up, seemingly relieved to see Cody's ex on a date. She excitedly volleyed her glance to Kyle then Tessa. "We've never been formally introduced. I've seen you...in passing at some industry events, but it's a pleasure to meet you in the flesh."

"Same here. I've heard so much. All good things, of course." Tessa reached out her hand to Chandra in a gracious follow-up to Kyle's lead. "What, uh, what brings you two out to ThaiPhoon tonight?" Tessa shifted her gaze between Cody and Chandra.

Chandra jutted her thumb toward Cody, placing all the blame on him.

Tessa used to tell him he could've earned a doctorate for his execution of one single skill: burying his head in the sand. His willful disdain for reality even astounded him, and her words felt a whole lot like the truth in that moment...especially looking at Kyle's deadly stink eye. It was potent enough to make Cody shrivel up and die; after glimpsing it, he ignored that, too.

"I'd been planning to bring my Chandra here for some time. The food is fantastic, especially the seafood curry dishes." He emphasized the latter part as if Tessa needed more of a reminder. Cody grabbed Chandra's hand and threaded his fingers with hers. "So, when my lunch plans took an unexpected turn this afternoon, I figured tonight would be the perfect occasion to share this experience with my sweetheart. Our condo's right up the street and around the corner."

"Yes, indeed," Chandra said in a sing-song voice. If he won an Oscar for lead actor, she'd win supporting actress in his comedy. Chandra had caught on to his game and apparently opted to play along. "It's close by and I've been hearing such wonderful things,"—she shrugged—"and, of course, what my Codykins wants, my Codykins gets."

The Codykins bit drew eye rolls from all present, including him.

While everyone else was distracted with a round of chuckles, Tessa faked a stomach heave when she thought no one was looking.

Cody noticed.

He turned his attention back to his fiancée and waited for the consequences. Chandra's anger would present itself as a tight smile or a Kung Fu death grip around his arm. Tessa, on the other hand, would've taken him out at the jugular with Ginsu glares when she discovered his true motive for date night.

Kyle, oblivious to Cody's impending plot, waved down a server. "Our waiter's heading over," Kyle said to Tessa. "We can finally put in our orders, and I'm sure you two would like to get to your seats."

Nice try.

Maybe he hoped Cody would take the hint and leave. Where's the fun in that?

"Yes, I'm absolutely famished," Tessa said. She took the signal and made her play. "Looks like your server's on his way, too. Shame. It's been such a pleasure chatting. We'd love to have you guys join us, but—"

"Well, don't mind if we do." Cody pounced on the opportunity with a smugness so thick it could choke a whale.

"Oh, no," Chandra said. She had other plans. "We wouldn't want to interrupt—,"

"It's such a kind and generous offer, we can't refuse, can we, Chandra?" Cody said, swooping in with a deft response. He didn't even wait for her reply. "Thanks so much for asking. I, for one, would never want to deny anyone the pleasure of your company."

Oh, the bull. Molasses-thick and knee-deep.

He wasted no time pulling out a seat for Chandra, who cut him a hard side eye before pasting on a fake smile.

She flaunted a cheerful mask even if she secretly wished to slap him into the New Year.

In a similar situation, Tessa would've turned her inner-witch on full tilt and, with barely a swish of her broom, embarrassed the heck out of everyone within a fifty-mile radius.

"That's fine, Sweetie. You know what I always say."

"Let me guess," Tessa piped in. "What your Codykins wants, your Codykins gets."

While Chandra tossed her head back with a giggle, Tessa's eyes rolled out of the restaurant and back inside.

During their honeymoon phase, he thought Chandra's laugh angelic and cute. Now the squeal had the same effect as fingernails dragging across a chalkboard.

"Cody, it's good you snapped this one off the market before she got away," Tessa said. The smirk she wore was less than subtle. "I couldn't have engineered a more ideal match for you. Absolutely perfect."

Now, Cody felt *his eyes* roll out of the restaurant and back. He knew exactly what she meant, and it was nothing nice.

"You are too kind. And I appreciate you allowing us to join you for this wonderful, *damp* evening," Chandra added.

During an uncomfortable, brief lull in the conversation, Chandra leaned over and rubbed her fiancé's arm.

"Well," Cody said, looking at Tessa. "I'm sure we're all famished, right? My stomach is growling since my lunch plans changed, abruptly."

"You don't say." Tessa tilted her head toward him and feigned a pitying expression. "I hate it when that happens. I'm a bear when I miss a meal. What happened? Do tell."

"I won't bore anyone with the details." To Cody's relief, they were saved by the bell, or the server, as it were. "Time to put in our orders." He glanced over the menu and then at Chandra.

"Everything looks so delicious. What do you have an appetite for?" he asked his future bride. "The shrimp curry is heaven. I can't recommend that one enough." Cody shifted his gaze from Chandra to Tessa, whose hostile squint greeted him like stink on a skunk.

"Red curry chicken," Chandra said. "It's one of my favorite dishes."

Kyle rubbed his hands together. "Mmm. Sounds perfect." He looked at Cody. "I can't thank you enough for recommending this place...this afternoon."

Snitch.

"Yes, I recommended it," Cody said, trying to hedge, "but I had no idea you'd take me up on it so quickly."

Cody would be sure to "thank" Kyle for blabbering later. Chandra wouldn't miss that beat. He'd be sleeping with one eye open—and on the couch. The look she flashed confirmed his suspicions.

Meanwhile, Tessa showed uncharacteristic restraint at the revelation, but Cody knew that her head would've spun off her neck had they been alone. At last, she placed her order. "Curry chicken and a whiskey sour—double, please."

The waiter disappeared and the awkwardness was so palpable it took a fifth seat at the table. Cody had prepared to fill the uncomfortable silence, but Tessa beat him to the punch.

"Kyle, you know," she leaned into him. "I never get to watch TV anymore. Everything's so crazy with the business. But I caught an episode of Jeopardy the other day, and I finally got a question right." Cody watched Kyle slightly lean in, inhale her scent. Had to be lavender and jasmine. He could never forget it.

"Jeopardy? What was it?"

"Who is a coward? I'll bet you'll never guess the right answer," she said. As the waiter returned with her drink, her eyes sparkled with joy and relief.

Kyle chewed on the question not realizing she'd taken a nasty swipe at Cody.

Cody growled inside but remained visibly cool. If he retaliated, he'd bring their simmering tension to the surface. He'd already earned a spot on the couch. No need to shoot for the moon...literally.

"The lion on the *Wizard of Oz*?" Kyle eventually replied.

"Ooh! So close! You almost nailed it." With her glass turned up as she gulped down the whiskey sour, she hacked Cody with a lethal glare.

Cody seethed. He should've returned to the high road to keep the peace, but he didn't—refused to contain his tongue.

"What a coincidence. You know, I saw that episode. Must've been the *Wizard of Oz* Category. I got one about a bitter witch right, too. My answer was: who is petty?" He sucked down a long sip and hacked her with a squint of his own. "Wait, no. Maybe I overheard someone discussing that at lunch today. Oh, never mind."

Cody glared at Tessa as her jaw clenched. The veins in her neck popped into her skin. She tried to suppress her anger by folding her napkin across her lap and steepling her fingers, but she reached the point of eruption. "Excuse me. I'm going to the ladies' room. Another minute and we'll have some serious problems at this table."

Without regard for the optics, Cody bolted up and followed on her heels. He caught her in the lobby and stopped her with a gentle elbow tug. She spun around bearing her teeth, waiting for one wrong syllable. She extended her claws and stood ready to strike.

"What was that all about? Coward?" Cody asked. Breathless with anger, he noticed curious onlookers and lowered his voice to a whisper. "Jeopardy? Really?"

"Well, if the question fits," she replied, mirroring his hushed, angry tones.

"How many times do I have to apologize for what I did *five years ago*? I was a different man, then. I'm sorry, okay?"

"You've got that right, you're sorry." She folded her arms over her chest. " So, what now? You think that's it? That you can just pat me on the head, say I'm sorry and like magic. *Poof*!"—she snapped her fingers—"you erase the hurt you caused, the betrayal? The loss? You've known me for most of my life. You couldn't actually believe you could pacify me that easily, could you?"

He opened his mouth to speak but no words came.

She pressed her voice into a scary whisper. He almost wanted to take a step back. "You left me in ashes and Keep It Real saved my life. You didn't really expect to ambush me, and I'd march along like an obedient little soldier, did you? Please tell me your fancy little CEO position affords you better medication than that."

"Sending you the card was the hardest thing I had to do."

"*Had to do*, huh?"

Again, he had no words.

"The only thing we ever have to do in this life is die. That's it. Devastating me, destroying us, you made choices. Maybe I'd respect you if, for once in your life, you owned up to them. But, no, admitting you're a pile of cow dung is too much like right. And then you don't stop there. *Oh, no!* You use a lovely date to make Kyle an accessory to murder by food poisoning. What did I ever do to you, except receive the pain you inflicted on me and survive? Are you *so small* that you didn't even want to see me survive?"

"I was angry."

"Therein lies the difference between you and me." She pressed her lips together and nodded. "When you hurt me, I channeled my pain and energy into building my company. When I hurt you, you channeled your energy into *hurting me*. I've never intentionally caused you pain. Oh, but I will now. And this slick move you pulled right here, tonight? You declared war. Now watch me bring the fight to your doorstep."

"Tessa—"

"Oh, no. It's on! Now, if you'll excuse me, I'm going to take my date and leave. With this weather, it's the perfect night for Kyle and me to snuggle up and take things to the next level."

Cody grunted and stormed into the bathroom where he paced until his hostility subsided. By the time, he returned to his seat, Kyle and Tessa had disappeared.

Only a frighteningly calm and cool Chandra remained. She didn't often allow her anger to get the best of her, but if she'd been an alley cat, his body would be fully mauled and half eaten.

"Tessa treated for dinner," she said with an eerie calm. "She insisted before she took off with Kyle. Quite kind of her given the circumstances, don't you think?"

"Chandra..." He took a seat beside her and grabbed her hand, but she pulled it away.

"Help me understand this—exactly what did you expect to happen, huh?" She asked sweetly, leaning her cheek toward him to request a kiss. The daughter of Dr. Barrington believed in keeping up appearances. "What did you think?" She didn't speak with a scowl in her tone. Rather, she squeezed each word through a tight smile and gritted teeth. "Did you really believe she'd revere you as the hero in this scenario? That she'd somehow obey you like some trained Yorkie? These are the mysteries perplexing me right this minute. What did you think?" The sugar in her voice was coated with deadly venom.

"I didn't."

"Now that's the first truthful thing you've said in days. You didn't think about her—and you sure didn't think about me—or us, which makes me question everything about our relationship." Despite the height of her anger, she still spoke with a steady tight grin. "And, unlike your little ex-girlfriend, I'm a woman. When it comes to us, I don't play games or *Jeopardy*. Frankly, I despise questions."

Cody wanted to do right by her and their relationship, but, at that moment, he didn't know if appeasing her was the right answer for either of them. She didn't like questions, but he lacked answers.

"Now"—she grabbed her purse— "I'm going home. I have no idea where you're going to sleep tonight, but I promise that you will not rest soundly anywhere within a close vicinity of me." She warned, "Don't you dare follow me" in the final kiss she left on his cheek with nary a syllable spoken. "Enjoy the rest of your dinner, Hon, and thank Tessa for her generosity when you see her at work tomorrow."

He didn't chase her. He didn't have the energy to feign regret. She was no more perfect than he, but she deserved his honesty. He couldn't speak the truth without causing a massive scene. She hated scenes more than questions. So, he grinned and waved as he watched her walk out of the restaurant and, for all he knew, out of his life forever.

Two servers returned prepared to fill the table. "Looks like a few of your guests are missing," one said.

"And they won't be returning. I'll need some to-go boxes. Leave the drinks to me."

He grabbed Tessa's whiskey sour, chucked it down, and stewed in the mess he'd made.

CODY CURSED THE MORNING SUN AS HE WRIGGLED HIS BODY IN THE squeaky leather couch cushions; his back creaked and his butt sunk into the springs. The previous night's cocktails hung over his head like a cement hat. Tessa first crossed his mind, then Chandra. The order of his regret wasn't lost on him. He had some wrongs to right, and he knew exactly where to start.

He let out a long yawn and flipped to his side so he could roll off the office sofa. The position offered a city view which held his focus while he cleaned the crud from his eyes...then Kyle entered. Cody braced himself for hostility, but the greeting was unexpected.

"Well. Morning, Sunshine." He spoke with neither a smile in his voice nor his face, and dropped a pile of files on his desk. "Looks like your evening ended as I expected."

Cody struggled to sit up, but he was determined to own up to his behavior the night before. Upright, he buried his face in his hands. "Man, I apologize. I stepped completely out of bounds."

"You don't say."

"I don't even know what came over me. Five years ago, I broke up with Tessa, and the woman still makes me crazy."

"Thanks for the recap, Captain Obvious. But we're boys. We'll be cool again...eventually," Kyle said with a bit of bite in his voice. "You've got some thinking to do. You need to figure out why she still has this effect on you. Neither Chandra nor I deserved your performance. Neither did Tessa."

Chapter Sixteen

***

T essa

I DE-CLARE. WAR.

By the time the blowout ended, Tessa and Cody had abandoned all semblance of civility. He crossed a red line—actually, all of them—with his ThaiPhoon dinner antics, so Tessa jumped in his butt with both stilettos, paid the tab, and stormed outside.

Now, fat raindrops plopped against Tessa's tense jaw as Kyle took forever to return with the jacket she left. She felt thankful for the reprieve, a moment to simmer down and cool off. She resolved to unleash her fury on Cody tomorrow. Now, more than ever the night belonged to her and Kyle.

"Here, I've got you." Kyle's sweet words made butterflies flitter in her Tummy. She stepped backward out of the rain and into the vestibule. He held up her jacket so she could slip her arms into the sleeves.

"I'm sorry about the scene," she said to him. "What looked

like a petty argument over dinner was, in fact, five years of regret paired with frustration, spite, and resentment."

"It's okay. Really. I can relate." He chuckled. "Put me and my ex in a room, and you'd need a parka and ski mask to survive the chill. Are you sure you want to hang out tonight...I mean, after everything that's happened?"

"Kyle, I'm starving." She sucked her tongue and cranked her neck. "If you think the display in the restaurant was something to behold, you don't want to see the destruction and discontent I'll unleash upon the earth if you don't feed me. I take hangry to unseen levels." Her eyes zoomed in on a protrusion coming from his coat pocket. "Is that an umbrella—or are you happy to see me?"

At first there was silence. Then he folded over laughing which proved to be contagious as they both curled at the stomach.

"You have a warped mind...and I like it. A lot."

"Trust me. You have yet to glimpse a fraction of my debauchery."

He opened the umbrella with ease. The problem came when trying to figure out how they fit together beneath the undersized canopy. "You're going to have to put your arm around my waist," he said. "I mean, for us to both stay dry. It's starting to pour, unless you want it all to yourself."

"No," Tessa said. "I want to share...with you." She wanted to be close to him...as close as possible, to inhale his scent, to feel his warmth, to forget her pain.

Heavy clouds emptied onto the hard ground, but the sound dissipated into soothing muffled pitter-pats. She slipped her arm around Kyle's waist and allowed her hand to rest on his six-pack. Her heart skipped so many beats, she thought she had a minor stroke.

His arm found her shoulder, and he snuggled her tightly to keep her dry. Thank heavens for the rain, for the security of his arms around her; he shielded her, and she felt protected. Even outside in the chilly fall mix, he warmed her with his man-magnificence. The delicious leathery scent that peppered his skin might induce her to devour him if they were in private quarters. For the first time in a long time, she realized she missed the closeness.

To think she once loved Cody, a man she now wanted to annihilate. A time existed when the passion between them consumed her mind and body. They had a rhythm better than clockwork. They'd survived the depths of hell and despair, leaning on one another as they endured the losses of grandparents and a mother. They were connected through love and survival. They were balms to each other in times of trouble. They were everything to one another...and then nothing.

Cody had moved on to a new someone, and now so should she.

Except Kyle was no ordinary someone, no ordinary man. He displayed old school mannerisms in a modern time.

He exposed his brand of gentleman in the little things. He cared about the details, like maneuvering her around puddles to spare her feet the sloshing soaks, saving her from sniffles and colds. He also kept post on her street side to protect her from the splash of passing vehicles.

During their revealing and chatty stroll, the rain, the pangs in her stomach, even Cody became inconsequential. She was hungry but not for anything she'd order from a menu.

Her resistance to the possibility of a future with Kyle weakened as she ceded control and allowed him to lead them along the cobblestone walkway to their next location. With every step they took, tiny breaches formed in the barriers she'd built around her heart forced her fortress to crumble and tumble. But she realized she'd forgotten to ask one very important question.

"Uh, exactly where are we going?"

"We're going to eat. Food," he replied with a wink. "I want to spoil you, if that's okay. I've watched you from afar for years, always taking care of others, always putting your team first. I'd like to be the one who helps you put yourself first," he said with a wink.

Me first. That's something new and different.

She wondered how he could deliver such knee-shaking sexy winks. Must've been the lashes. Also, he'd said nothing but the truth. She'd prioritized everyone else's needs over her own. Kyle helped her see what she really wanted: dinner and Keep It Real Cards, in that order.

"The perfect spot's up the block."

"I can't wait."

A few steps later, Tessa wish they'd arrived someplace else. Anywhere but here. Her panic set in—hard and fast. All the air left her lungs as she gasped. "This is...this is Ruth Chris."

"Wow. That's not quite the reaction I expected. I was aiming for something more along the lines of yum or a thumbs-up," Kyle said. He stopped in his tracks and peered into her eyes. "It's not the prime rib, is it?" She didn't see him or hear his voice. "Hello? You hate it. Who doesn't love steak and potatoes?"

"Potatoes." She'd drifted off but snapped back to the present. "Oh, I'm sorry. Here is fine, exactly what I needed. Something to stick to my ribs."

In her peripheral vision, she caught him leaning to catch a glance of her backside, as they entered the vestibule. He allowed her to enter first. "And hopefully those hips," he mumbled in a sexy tone, continuing from her *stick to my rib* comment. Then he added a lustful grunt. "Mhm!"

Her ears warmed and, from the inside out, she glowed red from blushing. Ruth's posh, modern decor appeared dark under the low, iridescent lighting. Polished cherry wood tables covered in linen and topped with china and mini lamps flanked the bar, but her eyes searched for one spot—*the spot*.

Just walking inside required more strength than she believed she possessed.

She managed the feat by convincing herself that of all the

seats in the entire restaurant chances were slim that they'd wind up at *"the"* table.

Yet, here they were—headed straight toward it, the one with the perfect view of the city lights, the spot where it all happened.

The one spot she hoped never to see again. The place she would always remember but wished she could forget.

"Is this okay?" the waitress asked. Kyle echoed her server's question, probably sensing her reticence.

"It's okay." She stretched her tightened lips into a thin smile and lied, "This will be fine."

It wasn't, and the end of dinner couldn't come soon enough. Only then would she be fine again. She had a dragon to slay to build any semblance of a relationship with Kyle. There was no better place, she supposed.

Tessa had barely breathed in the scent of au jus before the waitress returned bearing hot crusty bread and took their orders. Kyle kept a watchful eye on her, the gentleman he was.

"Are you sure you want to stay here for dinner? This night hasn't gone as planned, certainly not as I planned. I can take you home if you'd like."

She struggled to pull herself from the past that surrounded her. She stormed away from Cody at ThaiPhoon only to find him here, again—the best of him and the worst of him. A vision of Chandra snapped her out of her thoughts, and Kyle's voice broke through the fog.

"I want to stay here. *You* couldn't be more perfect tonight. I just wasn't expecting Cody to show up."

"Me, either. He told me you guys have some history."

"The acquisition scraped the scab off of an old wound. Rest assured, in this case, history will not repeat," she said. "I'm a bit loopy because I'm famished. I'll recover quickly after I scarf a basket of bread and enjoy a nice bottle of wine."

"My superpowers are limited, but they can handle that."

"Just don't use 'the Force' to feed me," she said with a chuckle, calling back to his Storm Trooper outfit. The laugh broke the ice and eased them back into the comfort zone. So did Kyle's next move: placing the order for more bread and wine before excusing himself to the bathroom.

After taking in the beauty of his rear view, she turned her focus to the city lights. In the slit of silence, her mind drifted to her last visit to Ruth Chris's, the moment everything changed between Cody and her.

The night had begun in pure perfection, starting with a night sky as clear as Tessa's love for Cody. With immense pride and anticipation, she had entered Ruth Chris on his arm.

For months, he'd promised to treat her to a pricey meal. He requested she dress in her Sunday's best. The time had come to celebrate. He'd received his first real paycheck from Hart after completing the first of many acquisition deals. The small companies would later combine to make Hart a publishing giant.

After plying her with prime rib and Patrón, he was ready to celebrate something bigger than the sale, unbeknownst to her.

"Now that I've got you right where I want you—"

"Where's that? Drunk and too fat to run?" she had asked.

"I was going to say satisfied. But, yes, I had to square you away first. You know how you are when you're hangry"—he'd begun—"anyway, what I wanted to say is that...we, you and I, we've been through so much together. You mean everything to me...the world."

Tessa assumed the syrupy speech was from a man trying to get lucky later. She wondered if she should tell him he could've stopped at the Patrón. He held his palm open like an invitation and she placed hers inside his to accept.

"As you know, we had a big win this week."

"We? No, baby. That was all you," Tessa had said.

"I couldn't do it without you by my side. You make me feel like Superman, as if I can do anything, achieve anything. That's why I want you with me on the next leg of my journey."

"I'm sorry...*my*?'" Tessa asked. The conversation started with *"we"* and then shifted to *"my"* without so much as a pause or stammer. She continued, "I realize it's taken me some time to accept your whole commitment is more important than marriage concept, but—I thought we were in this journey together."

"We are...maybe my words aren't coming out right, but I'm hoping we can *pivot a little*," he'd said. "The thing is...after I sealed the deal on the acquisition, I accepted a new position—Senior Vice President of Hart Enterprises."

"Senior Vice...wow. That's...not exactly what we planned but —wow." She stumbled to find the right words to say. Only months ago, he groaned that he'd rather clean gum off the floors at Hart headquarters than accept a senior position. So, she didn't quite grasp the meaning of his speech. She squeezed his hand and forced a smile. "That's a little more than a pivot. That's like a full one-eighty. But I'm happy for you, I mean if you are. I guess, I dunno, what does this mean for Sweet-Hard Cards?"

"Oh, we'll develop Sweet-Hart...eventually. As Senior VP, I'll have the power to establish a greeting card division, as we always dreamed."

"Well, yes, but...it won't be *ours*. It'll be Hart's. I'm not a Hart. I'm a Sweet."

He tightened his lips before exposing a thin smile. "See, that's what I want to talk to you about." He scooted his chair closer to hers and squeezed her hand. "My father, my entire family knows you're the most important person in my life, no matter how hard they try to pull us apart. If Uncle Brian hadn't started Sweet Media, we wouldn't be facing so much resistance from them. Sweet Media is the problem, not you."

"So, you're blaming *him*?" she'd asked.

"No, that's not it at all."

"Then what're you saying?"

Frankly, Tessa didn't need to know. Devon Hart held sway over his son to a degree that not even Cody yet realized.

Sweet Media wasn't the problem, either.

The righteous Devon Hart couldn't breathe if he didn't control his family, especially his eldest son. Mr. Hart had suppressed her father under his thumb and now Cody had succumbed to the same pressure. Only Cody seemed to forget their dream and embraced this new direction—or he'd been too blinded by money and power to recognize his father's manipulation.

Her heart broke a little. His love for her had given way to ambition.

He eased out of his seat, onto one knee, and pulled out a box. She'd never forget the Tiffany blue. Then he popped the top to reveal the heart-shaped diamond in a platinum setting.

She should've been elated, exploded from her chair and into his arms as she shouted a string of excited yesses.

But he'd spent a year convincing her they didn't need or want the commitment of marriage. The reversal not only shocked but confused her. What had motivated him to switch so abruptly? Furthermore, his whole "my journey" spiel excluded her and her dreams.

"Tessa, I need you to join me on my journey."

There he went again.

"I can't become the man I'm destined to be without you beside me, supporting me, and loving me. Spend the rest of your life with me. Please, give me the honor and privilege of being my wife."

His journey.

His life.

His wife?

A tiny taste of success had exposed his expectations and transformed the man she adored. How could she marry this stranger? Someone she no longer recognized? What would a big taste of success do to him? To them?

He offered his hand in marriage as a gift to her, as if inviting her to take a VIP seat in his cheerleading section. He made an offer he didn't believe she could refuse, but she viewed it as one that would force her round life into his square one.

She might accept a plan—how could she accept this plan?

A voice drew her out of her thoughts, the past, and back to where she needed to be—with possibility for the future.

"Hey!" Kyle said, waving his hand in her face in circular motion, jarring her out of her thoughts.

He startled her, made her jump. "There he is!" She forced some cheer into her voice, but she felt less than convincing. The warmth in his gaze said he viewed her differently.

"Didn't mean to scare you," Kyle said. "Looked like you were deep in thought. Anything you want to talk about? I'm a great listener."

She skirted that conversation like a rack in Prada.

"Don't you just love rainy nights? I never smile more than when I'm watching the drops fall," she said with a shrug. "My grandma used to have a country house with a tin roof. Rain showers poured music all over the house, like a lullaby. And she used to make these heavy quilts. Man, talk about some delicious sleep." She quieted. "Can you hear the music?"

"It's our song. I've heard it since the moment we met," he replied.

She wanted to hold his hand, but something kept her from reaching for it.

"Raindrops cleanse, renew somehow." She smiled and her eyes brightened, both at the sight of him, and what was approaching from behind. "Ooh, the carbs and booze are here."

He poured her wine and served her several slices of bread slathered in butter. "Keep this up and you may just sell me on this Prince Charming act."

"It's not an act. And I'm only a prince when I visit Wakanda," he said with a chuckle.

He could be her Black Panther, anytime. *Rawr!*

"Here, with you, I'm just a man crushing on a pretty lady." His deep, sexy laugh played like rain on a tin roof. She could listen to him all night.

"Now, let's toast"—he continued—"to many more rainy nights...together."

Back in Georgetown, Tessa pushed the key in the lock of her townhome. She could feel the heat from Kyle's presence behind her. She opened the door and turned to her knight, a kind man who'd used charm and humor to transform a grim evening into a glorious reprieve from the madness.

"So, I had a wonderful time," she said.

"Wonderful?"

"Okay, well, eventful at the start. But then the rain and music...and then pretty amazing," she replied. "You sure know how to spoil a girl."

He pushed his body closer to hers and looked deeply into her eyes, keeping steady contact. He released an appreciative smile and winked. He'd gotten her attention, holding her hostage to his smoldering eyes and irresistible lips.

Her heartbeat quickened as he leaned in. She stood to her tiptoes and edged closer to allow him to cover her mouth with his, leaving her breathless, alive. Each body-part tingling, wanting.

This was the beginning of something wonderful.

She just wasn't quite sure what it was.

As they slowly parted, his warm gaze pierced her, and he left her with one final offering. "Amazing. Yes...you are."

Keep It Real Cards

A new job.
Congratulations!
Let us not become weary in doing good, for at the proper time, we will reap if we do not give up. Galatians 6:9.

Let's Keep It Real—Whether it was your twerk or your werk, you finally earned a new title.
At least you'll be working in the *upright position* from now on.
Cheers to you!

Chapter Seventeen

✦❧✦

C ody

CODY HAD DECLARED A SILENT WAR AGAINST TESSA AND, USING ALL of her words, she returned the favor. Hungover from the dinner debacle, Cody calculated his next move with her. He resisted his inclination to escalate the battle and wield his CEO powers to crush her, but the faint smell of defeat reminded him that if he'd made better choices they wouldn't have reached these contentious levels.

Cody approached Tessa's office door, tucking away the guns, and instead came bearing a proverbial olive branch. He'd braced himself for Tornado Tessa, but hoped her violent winds and rain had passed. They'd endured too many storms over the years. The time had come to recover and rebuild.

"Knock, knock." Holding a makeshift white flag—a #2 pencil, a sheet of copy-paper and a sloppy tape job—Cody pushed his hand through Tessa's door; she'd left it slightly ajar. He waved the peace signal from side to side hoping to catch her attention and maybe a chuckle.

As he waited for a sign of safe passage, he clenched his eyes shut. His murky actions and choices were his own, but he could've handled things better...differently.

He could've minded his business. He could've dismissed Uncle Brian's call, perhaps never picked up. He could have refused to write the check and kept his money in the bank. He could've convinced himself to be content with Chandra, the growing monotony of their routine, and her passive-aggressive bossiness.

He could've done all those things, but he didn't.

Despite the poor optics, he heeded the call, drained his cash flow, and acquired the company, knowing he'd need to appease the ungrateful owner who would curse him to the south side of hell for it.

Cody peered inside in time to catch Tessa snorting at his peace offering. He couldn't tell whether she'd snickered or grunted like an angry bull. He took his chances and widened the gap until she acknowledged him.

Without a word or a smile, she waved him in and gave him "the hand" the second he cracked open his mouth.

"Door, please," she barked. Her tight-faced expression suggested she'd rather giftwrap her company in a pink bow than entertain his nonsense.

He closed the door and tipped to her guest chair, taking careful quiet steps.

"So you're surrendering before I have an opportunity to lob my first shot—a classic Cody tactic." She smirked at the flag. "That strategy won't win you any battles with me."

"If I were the coward you believe me to be, I'd be barricaded in the safety of my own office, not standing within right-hook distance inside yours."

"My right hook. At least you remember the important things."

"Yes, your right hook and your Chuck Taylors. How could I forget?"

"Are you here to finish the job?" She huffed and nodded. "Your latest attempt to murder me in cold blood failed."

He let out a frustrated breath and shook his head no. "First of all, maim, not murder. Second of all, not so much maim as get your attention."

"Congratulations. Mission accomplished. I'm short on time. Let's get to it. Chop. Chop."

"Listen, the last thing in this world that I want to do is to hurt you...or go to war."

"ThaiPhoon? That was a guided missile if I ever saw one. Lucky for me I learned what not to order."

"Okay. Yes, I was dead wrong for recommending ThaiPhoon to Kyle. But you had a slight case of food poisoning back then, you weren't going to die."

"You ever had food poisoning? There's no such thing as a slight case. It's the grim reaper's appetizer."

Cody burst out laughing. Only one person could make him lose it at a time like this. He quickly pulled himself together.

"So maybe you exploded...everywhere. I'm sorry. I didn't know you were allergic to shrimp. In my defense, I only recommended ThaiPhoon after he mentioned his plan to take you to Ruth Chris. It's...you know. Impulse overcame reason, I suppose."

"You suppose." The viciousness of the side-eye she delivered could've crippled him for life.

"I apologize for ruining things between you and Kyle. Furthermore, I promise heretofore to butt out, mind my own business, and try hard to be the best boss in the world."

"Anything else?" she asked.

"That's not enough?"

She expelled a long breath tempered by a groan of concession. Then she leaned back in her seat, and weaved her fingers together.

"You caught me off-guard with the acquisition, okay? If I had the slightest inkling that anyone had an interest in buying my company—and I could choose from any name in the world—I'd list the last name...and yours would fall beneath that one."

"I understand what you're saying, but that's not exactly how it—"

"Cody, you didn't want this when it belonged to us. You abandoned me, the dream, which is your prerogative."

"I didn't exactly—"

"Through a lot of hard work and a small side of nepotism, you achieved every goal you wanted to reach. You got the girl— Chandra; the position— CEO of Hart Enterprises. You got the money, the status, the notoriety. You got everything."

"I didn't exactly get every—"

"And everything wasn't enough to satisfy your ambitions. Did you really need this little thing of mine, too?"

For all his effort to bridge the gap, there couldn't be more distance between them. Now silence filled it.

His eyes froze on hers as they lingered in a hush. A million thoughts flooded his mind, all versions of the same truth, none of which he could speak. Not right now. Before he had a chance to piece his reasons together, she broke the stalemate.

"I guess the truth is what's done is done. We can't go back. We're in the here and now, and the acquisition is a fait accompli. We're in the thick of it, at least for a little while longer."

"A little while longer? What does that mean? You're not resigning, are you?"

"Wasn't that your strategy all along?" Her head tilted to the side. "I mean, if not making me quit, what exactly did you expect of me?"

"I can't change your perception. All I can tell you, promise you, is that no matter what you believe, I'm Cody. You know me, maybe better than anyone on this planet. You don't have to believe in me, all I ask is for you to trust your own mind. If you do that, you'll know what I want you to do."

She shrugged. "Well, if what you need is mind reading, I foresee an epic failure on the horizon."

"Fine. You want me to be more explicit?" He glanced down to check the time and pointed toward the door. "What I expect you to do...is come with me. Now."

"Now...as in *now* now?"

"No, the 5th of Nevuary. Yes, *now*. And hustle or we'll be late."

In a refreshing twist, Tessa didn't argue. She didn't balk. She trusted herself and followed him. He gave her time to grab her jacket and purse and whisked her downstairs to an awaiting car. Then he took her on the ride he wished would change...everything.

CODY STUDIED TESSA'S EXPRESSION AS THEY TREKKED THROUGH THE renovated Hart creative studios. As he always hoped, she moved in wonder and awe, her mouth gaped open as wide as her eyes.

He'd evolved and modernized the area, to the point it barely resembled the building of their childhood.

She remained suspended in disbelief as they wandered through the transformed workspace largely based on her early drawings for Sweet-Hart studios. He had the resources to elevate her original vision. "Whoa! You've made a few changes," Tessa said.

"The leading edge is where success lives, right? Isn't that what you always said?" He led her into a large room that anchored a conference suite. There, more awaited her than she ever expected.

～

TESSA

Inside the soul of Hart's new division, Tessa's lips curled into a smile genuine and wide as she greeted the eager group of youngsters. Cody outpaced her to the chair, but this time was different from that summer so long ago. Instead of competing against her, he pulled it out for her to take a seat. Then he found a seat beside her. Tessa took note.

Cody had strolled in like a boss and transformed, like Clark Kent stripping down to his super onesie. Tessa sat in awe of his authoritative vibe, one-part commanding, two parts sexy. Something about crossing the threshold from the outside world into Hart Enterprises altered him. An air of positivity oozed through the threads weaved into his million-dollar outfit. He wore power like his suit. It was tailored to fit him like a glove. He emanated a kind of glow. He was something new, a different man from the one she fought the night before. This version of him reminded her of the man she fell in love with.

From that point forward, the universe shifted. Something changed. She was impressed by the man he'd become.

"Hey, team! Welcome to the kick-off. Our new project begins today," Cody began before explaining Tessa's presence. He commanded his audience in the best way with every word spoken and every moment that passed. She respected his leadership, didn't recoil at the thought of him leading her. Perhaps Mr. Hart had seen a quality in him that she missed. Clearly the acorn did not roll far from the oak.

"As promised, Tessa Sweet, the creator and CEO of Keep It Real Cards joins us, today. She has graciously agreed to serve as your consulting manager, at least during project initiation." He glanced at her. "But I'm truly hoping we can all convince her to stay longer."

A wave of hellos and excited mumbles rippled across the room. Tessa avoided acknowledging his last statement, the one about supporting the team longer. She embraced the apparent delightfulness of the crew but made no promises about staying on full-time. Despite her revelations about Cody and his intentions, her eyes remained fixed on a single prize, wresting her company away from Hart Enterprises as quickly as possible.

Now that he'd offered her a path to arrive at her desired destination, she'd do it.

"My invitation to this meeting was a little last minute, so I'm afraid I'm not fully prepared. Maybe we can start with portfolios? If you all have them, I'd love to take a quick peek, see how deep the talent runs in the Hart organization." She gave a thumbs-up.

A choir of yesses followed.

"Perfect. Then I'll start with a very brief introduction of—me. Very brief. After that, I'd like to go around the room, learn a little bit more about you, and flip through each of your portfolios. Everyone good with that?"

Tessa practically smelled the Enfamil dripping from the groups' cherub cheeks. Generation Z. Her first inclination was to blame the youth factor, but she soon realized that none of them seemed to take for granted the opportunity to work for Hart or be graced with the audience of its CEO.

Tessa stuck to the basics when discussing herself—a BA in Communications from North Carolina A&T, Aggie Pride, and the schools of all Sweets and Harts. Then she, with the thinnest layer of detail possible, and under Cody's watchful gaze, described what inspired her to create Keep It Real Cards. "I would describe my life as a series of setbacks, signs, and decision points. Unexpected life events have a way of sending you into a tailspin. But I truly believe that in the space between the rocks and the hard places is where you find out not only who you are, but who you're meant to be.

"Signs. You have to believe in them and watch for them. Then you have to be brave enough to choose the direction in which the signs point. Courage and persistence will be the difference between reaching your next goal or languishing in a plateau. I discovered Keep It Real in the space between the rock and the hard place, and I had the courage to follow the signs. I received a spark of inspiration which led me to design my first card. It hangs on my wall today."

Cody released a sigh of relief that was barely audible. He knew enough of her honesty to appreciate her ability to speak it without saying the words.

"I've never desired to walk in someone else's path, not that there's anything wrong with following a trail someone has left for you. You can go as far as you want to make it your own. For me, I needed something of my own. Keep It Real took off because I achieved what most successful start-ups do—tapped an underserved niche market of consumers and served them."

Tessa deserved a pat on the back for deftly navigating the high road when she could've gone low. With her part over, she proceeded around the table, greeted each new face with a smile, and welcomed each attendant to offer their own introduction.

First in the line-up was Calvin, the cute kid if one liked the Pharrell type—artsy, nerdy. He wore a hat with a weird zigzag and seemed a little stiff with his dark-rimmed glasses and bowtie. Tessa couldn't help but think he'd be highly suited for two jobs in this world—greeting card writing and playing Urkel when Family Matters rebooted.

"Graduated in May," he began after a quick hello. "Majored in music with a minor in computer science. I guess you could call me an undercover poet. I participated in some spoken word events in school."

Her head jerked back at the thought of him having the nerve to speak on stage in front of an audience. There was more to him than she'd given him credit for.

"I've been writing verses and lyrics, practically since I was old enough to hold a pencil. The master plan was to become a rapper. Don't ask me my rap name. My mother, who is my biggest fan, told me I can't wrap a gift." Everyone laughed. "She suggested I find another outlet for my art. Hey, she's like you. She believes in 'keeping it real'." He used air quotes and faced Tessa dead on, and a wave of chuckles filled the silence. "I got into music because I like to make people happy. Unfortunately, it seems making people happy and rapping are mutually exclusive in my world," he said to another round of chuckles. "So, I figured I'd give greeting cards a try. Turns out I'm good at it. But I'm a copy guy. I don't do art."

"You're preaching to the choir, brother," Tessa said, flipping the pages of his portfolio and then glancing at Cody. "I like your stuff. Very upbeat cards. These don't contain a lot of verse, but I like your themes. Not cheesy. Really good work. Next."

Everyone, especially Calvin, turned to the lone mousy girl in the group, Joya. In fact, the starry-eyed Calvin couldn't take his eyes off of the pre-ball Cinderella.

A brief trip to the MAC counter and junior's dress section at Lord & Taylor would expose her as a fraud.

Beyond Joya's striking features, Tessa sensed a humbleness with a quiet strength; she'd probably be the last person to ever speak of herself that way.

He crushed on her big time.

"You look like you'd rather skin a snake than speak today," Tessa commented.

"Is that an option?" Joya asked in a voice somewhere between dead serious and joking. Everybody laughed which seemed to loosen her up a bit. "Yeah, I'm not much of a speaker. Writing is my jam."

Whatever her present "before" state, Calvin only saw the "after." She seemed more introverted than shy. She wore glasses and a long ponytail as a cloak, a failed effort to hide an outer beauty that couldn't be hidden.

Tessa sensed that Joya was Tessa before Cody, and Calvin was Cody before Tessa. Cody dragged Tessa kicking and screaming out of her shell. They brought the best out in each other, at least they did once upon a time.

"I so can relate." Tessa wanted to say more, assure Joya that the more successful she became, the more she would evolve, but Joya was just fine as she was. "Can I take a peek at your portfolio?"

Intentionally or unintentionally, Joya had rested it under her elbow to keep it at close guard. Hesitantly, Joya lifted her arm so Tessa could slide the leather binder from the table. One look inside and Tessa's eyes bulged. She jerked her head backward in shock. "This artwork is...amazing. Who's the artist?"

Joya raised her hand weakly and tightened her lips.

"You?" Tessa's eyebrows arched.

"That would be me. Turns out between dodging the paparazzi and escaping crazed fans, I've got a lot of free time."

Everyone laughed again. Her sense of humor, driven by a dry, self-deprecating wit, struck everyone's funny bone.

"Oh, this one is very Keep It Real." Tessa read aloud. "This is weird. I'm thinking of you, again."—she flipped to the inside copy—"I'd rather be doing yoga. I hate yoga."

Tessa laughed...hard. Maybe too much so. She related to that message. Heck, she used to be that message. "Very relatable message here. I like this a lot."

Joya's "voice" aligned perfectly with the Keep It Real vision. Despite the brave front, Tessa detected something else behind the glasses. A melancholy vibe, perhaps. She couldn't put her finger on it.

Next up—Max. A Notre Dame graduate, she looked like the Addams' family's lost sister. She was goth and tatted. From the outside, she seemed dark, like the spirit of a serial killer dwelled within her, but her portfolio nearly stunned Tessa silent.

"Cody, you would love these," she said holding them up for him to review. "That's funny. I never would've pegged you as the hearts and bunnies member of this group."

"Excellent stuff, Max," Cody said.

"What can I say? I'm complex," she said, without breaking a grin. Everyone else glanced at each other unsure of whether it was safe to laugh, so remained silent, until she cracked up. Then they all followed her lead.

There were only two girls left. The next to last looked like a twenty-something Diana Ross if she knitted and baked banana bread.

"Guess I'll go next. I'm Denesha, the middle daughter of a thrifty mother. We made everything, especially around the holidays. Our own soaps and bath salts; every gift for all occasions, lots of baked goods and quilts. So, I guess it stands to reason that we created every greeting card. I was one of four children who went to Howard."

"Awww, I'm so sorry about the school. Are you still angry with your parents?" Tessa teased. "Aggie pride." They both laughed.

"My parents said that we may have appeared cheap and broke, but that's how they saved enough money to send all of us to school."

"Wow. Looking at your portfolio, I can see the evolution of your style. You've been writing cards for every occasion since you were a kid."

She nodded. "We didn't get store-bought gifts until we graduated high school—even then we each got a business suit, a set of suitcases, and a watch. Mom wasn't one for subtle messages: Get out of my house, get a job, and wherever you're going, be on time."

Another round of laughs. The more they introduced themselves, the more Tessa forgot about the acquisition and remembered what made her love the business and building her team. They sparked in her a nostalgic bliss.

The longer they spoke, the more Tessa began to embrace the idea of serving as a consultant for the new line. With everything she'd gained in building her company, her brand, she realized she'd lost one thing—her joy.

Finally, TiTi spoke. With her blonde wig, voluptuous boobs (tastefully covered), strong square, jaw line and Adam's apple, she wasn't hiding any secrets, not that she was attempting. The beautiful thing about the room is nobody cared, including Cody. She didn't even wait for Tessa to reach out for her portfolio, just jammed it in her face.

Tessa flipped it open and smiled. "Wow. These are fantastic.

Lots of women's empowerment. Uplifting. They'd make for a great addition to an any-occasion line."

"Honey, black girl magic is real. Humph, got all of my melanin, poppin'!" She flipped her waist-length weave over her shoulder and snapped, startling Max out of her daze.

Tessa wished she could bottle TiTi's energy and drink it before struggle yoga.

"Girl power is not only the theme of my art. It's my life. All women, but especially women of color, need to be reminded of how exquisite we are every day. I think spreading some of this love around the world would make this a better place. Oh, I could write these cards for days!"

"I bet you could. And the universe could use more of them."

After introductions concluded, Tessa spent another half hour discussing the specially abled line, ensuring everyone understood their assignments. Then she glanced at her watch. Two hours had passed, and, to her disappointment, the time had come to leave.

"I'm going to wrap this up, but we'll meet in three weeks. I should be finished with my integration duties by then. Based on your portfolios, I've got a lot of faith in this group. I look forward to seeing what everyone comes up with. Now, go get to work."

They rewarded her presence with an applause she wasn't sure she deserved.

After everyone dispersed, Tessa and Cody stood alone. "So, what did you think?" he asked.

"Oh, my gosh. They're better than amazing," she said. "And Joya. She's got to remind you of me, right?"

"How'd you guess?"

"The snark was strong with that one," she said with a loud chuckle. "I hate to admit it, but I couldn't have selected a more perfect group. It's almost as if you know me or something." She flashed a wide smile, which he returned.

"So, you're in?"

She nodded. "All in."

"Perfect." He glanced at his iWatch. "Now before I return to work, you're treating me to lunch."

"Excuse me?"

"Boss's orders."

"Um, I believe that's illegal." She chuckled and capitulated quickly. "Okay, I'll meet you in an hour."

"Oh, no. Fool me once, shame on you. Fool me twice, shame on me. This time, you're coming with me."

Chapter Eighteen

C ody

WATCHING TESSA INTERACT WITH THE TEAM REMINDED CODY OF the moment he abandoned the woman he loved, a time he tried to forget. She had a way with people, a way with life, that never manifested in the way he lived without her. And now, here it was, in front of him once more, just beyond his reach.

He departed the Enterprises impervious to the chill in the air, warmed by the remnants of the days, hours, minutes spent with her. He couldn't stop time, but he wasn't ready to let their time together end. The impromptu lunch invitation escaped his heart and his mouth before his head had a chance to stop it. It was an unexpected gesture on his part given she'd ditched him for a lunch date only days ago.

He secured her inside his sleek, black stretch corporate Mercedes. As they drove away from Hart headquarters, the windshield met a few frozen flakes released from the wintery clouds. He turned his attention from the outside to the inside, just in time to watch her slide her tongue across her sultry lips leaving a gloss he wanted to kiss.

"Well, now you've got your captive audience," she said. "Which Michelin-rated slop joint shall we grace with our presence today? Marcel's? Pineapple and Pearls? Or will we be dining at the Four Seasons?" The woman he knew would give the world and a ham sandwich to be home in her pajamas, reading a book next to her fireplace instead of minding her etiquette in some stuffy restaurant.

The woman he knew had not a single crap to give about his longing to show her how far he'd evolved from their Ramen noodle and butter pecan nights. She'd have zero desire to put thought into the correct fork to use with the right dish or in which direction to face her cutlery on her plate when she stepped away to the ladies' room.

That's the reason, in this moment, there was no other place he'd rather be—and no one else he'd rather be with.

"This may shock and surprise you, but none of the above."

She grinned a little. She was relieved.

"I thought we'd take a trip down memory lane," he continued. "What do you think about Di'Angelo's?"

"You mean to tell me you still eat pizza?" She snapped her head in his direction and looked at him with a bemused expression. "Chandra looks more like the green, gluten-free ice water and kale type."

He laughed at the factualness. She was as perceptive as always. "I want to say you're wrong about Chandra, but I ate here last week. Alone."

"Call me crazy, but it's hard to picture you in your tailored pinstripe, folding a slice over a frosted mug of beer." She looked into the distance. "I wonder if they still have that jukebox?"

He nodded. "Sure do. As a matter of fact, I don't think they've changed the music in a hundred years. Still the same," he said. "Remember K4?"

She turned toward him, and her eyes seemed to shine. With

every fiber of his being, he wanted to erase the distance between them and kiss her.

"Mmm. K4. The memories. I think we single handedly kept Di'Angelo's in business with the money we spent in that jukebox —and on that pizza. It's amazing we haven't died of heart failure with all that greasy cheese, pepperoni, and sausage."

"I've probably had a couple of near misses, heart-wise, but no permanent failures. For better or worse, I'm still kicking."

They pulled up to the quaint little hole-in-the-wall tucked into a quiet, tree-lined street on Capitol Hill, not far from Union Station. Di'Angelo's hadn't changed a bit, although everything around it had evolved. It remained a blast from D.C.'s 1950s past. Inside, the crowd (mostly local) was sparse, no doubt hindered by the weather. "Their table" sat empty in the cozy corner, so Cody requested it.

"Wow," Tessa said. "Back down memory lane." Cody helped her off with her coat and she slipped into the booth, the red vinyl remained a throwback to a time long gone.

"Hope you don't mind. I texted our order ahead. I figured you'd want the usual."

"Mmmmm," she moaned, briskly rubbing her hands together. The sound made his stomach flutter.

"Sounds perfect."

Her eyes roamed, seemed to sparkle with their memories as Cody concocted a strategy to keep their afternoon as enjoyable as it had begun.

"Why don't we strike a bargain for today, huh?" Cody said. "No business talk. Just for an hour. We can rile each other on the way back to the office. Truce?" He offered her a hand and waited for her to shake in agreement.

When she took his hand in hers, a pulse surged into his fingers and his arm and then through his entire body. He froze as she shook on the deal, but at the time they should've let go, they held on. Both of them.

"Your hands are cold." Cody sandwiched her icy hands in the

warmth of his. He blew his toasty breath on them. Part of him wished he could do more; most of him was glad he couldn't. "Is that better?" he asked.

Tessa hesitantly pulled away.

"Yes, much. Thank you." Now her eyes laser-focused on him; they were at once innocent, fierce, and wicked. His insides twisted and curled with excitement. Her mere presence made him feel intoxicated, high. He hated that she still had this effect on him.

"So, let's catch up. Tell me something about you, something non-work related," Cody said.

"Not much to tell. You want me to bore you to death? I'm the same workaholic. If I'm honest, I need more substance in my life, but Keep It Real is a hand full. A few more movie nights with Jiffy Pop wouldn't hurt a bit."

"You still make Jiffy?"

"Is there any other way to enjoy movie night? Well, when I make time, that is. It's been a minute."

"What else haven't you made time for?" He couldn't conceal the mischievousness in his voice. He asked with the hope of hearing the answer he wanted and with the fear of her saying the opposite.

She let him stew, taking a sip from a water glass. "My life includes everything I need to make time for...at least for now. Thank you very much."

"Point well made," he said. "Present company excepted, any regrets?"

"Contrary to what you believe, I don't regret you. How could I? You brought me to my decision point. Because of you, I heeded the sign." She shrugged. "I've made mistakes, but I've also focused on making the next right decision. And someone once said we don't learn from successes but from failures which means I've learned far more than the average human."

Cody chuckled. "Impressive. Impressive, indeed." He bit his

bottom lip, something he only did when deep in thought. "Don't get me wrong, I've got a great life. The right girl, the right job, picture perfect by all accounts. Under my father's watchful eye, there wasn't room for mistakes. My decisions impacted so many lives."

"Thirteen thousand, five-hundred, seventy-seven. The number of people you employ, globally."

His eyes brightened, surprised that she knew. "See? Truth is, I wish I had chosen a path that allowed me to stray, to fail. I probably couldn't admit that to anyone but you."

"We always fought as hard as we loved." She focused her gaze on her finger which traced a nick in the table cloth. "I guess, in some small way, we will always find a piece of home in each other. A place where we can say the things we can't say to anyone else."

"A seat to share after a kick in the family jewels," he said. "I don't mean to sound ungrateful. I'm...content."

"But not happy?" she asked.

He glanced away, probably because a truthful reply would've been damning.

"I'll be right back." He slipped out of the booth and strolled over to the jukebox. He beamed and, by the time he returned, a smile spilled into her lips. She heard it. "K4."

He stopped short of his seat and extended his hand in a familiar gesture. "May I have this dance?"

Perplexed by the offer, she glanced over each shoulder and peered up at him with a wrinkled brow. "Here? In front of everyone?"

"It's funny you should mention that because from the moment we took our seats, I forgot anyone else was here. You can't leave me hanging now. Dance?" He pleaded with his eyes, waiting for her to accept.

The sad puppy face proved effective, moving her out of her chair and into his arms. They danced and swayed to K4. An oldie but a goodie. The falsetto harmonies, the rhythm, the lyrical honesty took him back to another place, another time, the best of both.

Her body puddled in his warm embrace as her hands roamed from the middle to the small of his back, sending waves of chills through his toenails.

His eyes drifted close as the chorus played; he could feel the song's beat pound in rhythm with his heart. Once again, they were in sync; dancing with her felt as natural as breathing.

The sound of K4 dissipated, but they didn't part when the jukebox fell silent. Maybe all they had left was K4. Maybe they couldn't let go of the song, of each other...at least until the server arrived with a pizza pie so enormous it would make a Brooklyner jealous.

The double extra-large covered much of the checkered linen beneath it.

"Holy mackerel," she exclaimed. "No wonder you called ahead. We'd have been here through the New Year waiting on this to finish cooking."

"Note the toppings."

"Mmm...pepperoni and sausage."

"Any more would ruin it," they said in unison.

After sharing a round of chuckles, they each grabbed a slice, halved it, and touched the tips in a toast. "To K4," Cody said.

Tessa smiled. "To K4."

TESSA FLITTERED INSIDE KEEP IT REAL'S CREATIVE SUITE NEARLY hyperventilating from the onset of a panic attack. "Whatever you ate for lunch, don't ever order that again," Mia warned her flustered friend who stood in her office door.

She'd tried, without success, to ground herself after lunch with Cody. Instead, she floated into her car, high atop cloud nine, desperate to hear K4 once more. The past had become the present.

She and Cody traveled through time, not back to a moment, rather to the feelings, the emotions they'd invested in one another. She returned to her office elated and was mowed over by their unfortunate reality, one she'd have to face sooner or later.

Chandra? Kyle? Real talk? What am I gonna do now? Tessa mumbled to herself.

Staying away from Cody, letting him go five years before, meant allowing herself to believe he'd transformed into the worst of men. In one afternoon, he obliterated the notion. He reverted to the familiar man, the soul mate, who once consumed every fiber of her being, her body, and her mind. In a span of mere hours, he rejoined the broken parts of her heart she'd long thought beyond repair.

"I think I'm making a mistake," Tessa said.

"With what?"

One listen to K4 reconnected her to the Cody she fell in love with, a love he couldn't return, a love that kept her from facing the new horizon where Kyle stood waiting and available with open arms. Bitter witch behaviors were easy to embrace in the midst of anger and fury, but impossible in this...whatever she was feeling.

With every sincere apology he offered, however egregious his offense, he chipped away at the barrier she'd constructed to keep herself safe from him. With K4, Cody caught her with her defenses low. The breach that remained after their dance, filled with confusion, indecision, and uncertainty. She dashed inside Mia's office and shut the door. Mia paused to absorb Tessa's disturbed demeanor.

"The new line. Real Talk. I'm having second thoughts," she said. "Maybe...I dunno. Maybe it's not such a good idea."

Mia stood up, placed her hand against Tessa's forehead to check her temperature. Then she leaned against the front of her desk.

"Mmm-hmm. You must've forgotten who I am. You and I

both know your change of heart has nothing to do with the line. So, tell me what this is really about."

Tessa scraped her fingers across her scalp and expelled an audible, throaty groan.

"He fed me pizza and beer. We danced, too. Okay, perhaps I misjudged him."

"Who—him?"

"Cody. I thought he bought Keep It Real to prove I failed, to rub my struggles in my face. I thought he saved the company so that he could lord it over me for the rest of my life. I never suspected..."

"What?"

"I never conceived that he valued the company. I certainly never believed he valued...*me*. And, today, let's just say I learned that, well, I might be an idiot."

"First of all, I've known you were an idiot for"—she counted on her fingers on both hands which made them laugh.

"Tessa. For real? How about I can't believe we're having this conversation? How about I went on a date to the movies with a man that debated whether I was entitled to Twizzlers with my freaking popcorn."

"Aye aye aye."

"You spent lunch with a man who not only paid for the meal, but bought your company at a multi-million-dollar premium, and sent your valuation through the roof. I'm trying to figure out what reasonably intelligent man would pay millions more for a company he believed to be worthless? To quote my Southern mama, may she rest in peace, 'where they do that at?'"

Tessa found a snicker inside of a sigh. "I might've seen that if I hadn't been so..."

"Blinded with anger and resentment."

"Blind? No. But there might've been a little glare of resentment," she said. "He asked me to lead a project, to mentor a team developing the Hart specially abled line."

"Wait, what?"

"Yeah, and the kids, more like interns, are pretty amazing, especially this girl, Joya. She's the perfect fit for Keep It Real. So funny. Like me ten years ago, except better employed. You'd adore her."

As Tessa blathered on, Mia stared at her friend until, finally, she noticed Mia's blank look. "What?"

"You're still in love with him, aren't you?"

"In —what? Are you—? No! After what he did to me? How could I? I mean, I couldn't be in...could I? No."

"Tessa, if despair and hurt made women stop loving men, Ben & Jerry's would be out of business. I'm just saying."

"Ridiculous. Besides, he broke things off with me."

"Heartache has zero bearing on how much you love someone. You guys didn't even have a clean break. Along with that Dear Jane card, he left unfinished business."

Tessa shrugged. "I'll admit it. Our parting didn't exactly allow for closure, at least not for me."

"Did you ever think that perhaps he ended your relationship the way he did because he didn't want you to close the door on your future with him?"

"That's ridiculous." She cocked her head to the side. "Isn't it?"

"Your selective memory allowed you to believe it was simple. It wasn't. The man proposed, despite his family's disapproval."

"Now, who's the one selecting memories? I seem to be the only one who recalls that he spent years Jedi mind-tricking me into accepting that we didn't need marriage because our commitment without it meant more. Then he flipped the script."

"People change."

"Not in one night."

"Did you ever think something happened to change his mind? Did you ever ask?"

"No—and why are we having this discussion, again?"

"Because you can't handle the truth," she said, giving her the best Jack Nicholson impression.

"No, what I can't handle is confusion. True love, real love, brings clarity, not confusion. So, I'm going to my office, the only place where life makes sense."

"Quitter," Mia replied.

"Enabler," Tessa added as she folded over with laughter. Then her mind flashed back to the dance with Cody and nothing even mattered. Seeing his face would make all the confusion disappear.

Tessa began texting Cody's office to let him know she wanted to see him again, to dance to K4, and she stopped mid-sentence.

Although she was free-*ish*, he was not. She switched gears and began scrolling through her cellphone mail as she proceeded down the hall before literally bumping a shoulder.

"Oh, excuse me." Tessa lifted her head from the phone screen and saw Chandra—of all people. She felt as if she wore a scarlet letter "G" for guilty.

"I'm so sor—Tessa!" Chandra exclaimed, looking winter chic in her white cashmere coat and some fancy thigh-high boots. "You're just the woman I was looking for."

"You were looking for me? Why?" Tessa swallowed hard and her heartbeat raced.

Did Cody break up with her after lunch? Did Chandra know what happened between them? Maybe she had him followed by a private detective?

Tessa's emotions were knotted in curiosity, anxiety, and confusion. And women were the best performers. Chandra could fake nice and be really angry all at once.

"My visit's unexpected, I know." Chandra kept her voice just above a whisper as if she'd planned to share a secret. "Could we talk in private for a second? In your office, perhaps?"

Tessa replied with a hesitant nod. "Sure. Follow me."

Tessa led her inside, her eyebrows scrunched the entire way. Why in heavens would she want to talk? What could they possibly have to discuss? She'd only been in the presence of a woman for the better part of thirty minutes.

As they passed Mia's desk, Mia's head flinched back, and she blinked rapidly.

All Tessa could do was offer a barely perceptible shrug. Inside her office, Tessa tucked herself behind her desk and offered Chandra a guest chair.

"Now, what can I do to help you?"

"I'm sure you're wondering why I'm here to see you. I mean, we barely know one another."

"The question did cross my mind," Tessa said.

Chandra took her seat, crossed her legs, and pointed her toe as dainty as a prima ballerina.

"About that night at ThaiPhoon, I wanted to apologize. I'd planned to cook a nice dinner for a cozy night at home...mind you I never cook. But I can't help but think if I had made the turkey meatloaf, we'd have been home streaming *The Crown*, not sitting at your table, all up in your face, like we're cousins or something."

"Yeah, well..."

"Helen Keller could see the tension between you two. I don't even consider myself to be that perceptive, and I picked up on it before we sat down."

Tessa chose her words carefully. Yes, she and Cody had indulged in their resurgent emotions, but she had no idea whether that would change anything for them. "We broke up and didn't get much closure. What you witnessed amounted to little more than rigor mortis. In that moment, there was nothing between us except an ambushing and an acquisition."

"He told me as much," she said.

The level of smug in Chandra's voice tweaked Tessa's nerves, but she was determined to remain civil.

"Trust me, he left with a little something extra hanging out of his butt when I got through giving him the devil—and I'm not talking about hemorrhoids"—she snorted— "How did he expect you to react? But, I don't know, after he explained his reasons, I kind of understand."

"Explained?"

"I mean, you're a business owner so you know the purpose of these acquisitions—struggling company, tax write-offs. I'm just a real estate agent so the details are, whoosh"—she waved her hand over her head—"But now he's committed to making the business work, no matter what it takes. I just wanted to make sure you understood that your business isn't in danger or anything. I guess with the board meeting and the vote coming up, he needs to resolve any confusion. Drastic times, drastic measures."

"Hmm. Is that right?" Tessa's heart broke a little. A lot. She questioned everything she'd relished about their afternoon together. Had he taken her to Di'Angelo's as a strategy?

Tessa hadn't sensed Cody's attempt to manipulate her, but she had a long history of being blind to the truth where he was concerned.

"Yes, he explained his plan in almost those terms," Chandra said. "Now that he's acquired your company, he's stuck. Whadaya gonna do?"

"Yeah. He's in a rough position. I don't envy him," Tessa said. "My only hope is to keep the peace. Since we're all in this together for better or worse"—she flashed the Cracker Jack prize on her finger—"I'm hoping we can all peacefully coexist."

"You're right. A peaceful coexistence is best for all—and I will not be the one to rock the boat. Listen, I appreciate you squeezing time out of your busy schedule to stop and chat." Tessa stood behind her desk and glanced at her watch. "Will you look at the time? I've got a meeting with my creative team in two minutes."

Chandra glanced down at her watch. "11:43? Odd time."

"I'm odd...I mean, I have a couple of stops to make before-hand so..."

"Oh, no problem. I'll see myself out. And, again, my apologies."

"It's not necessary...really." She showed Chandra the door and watched her until she hopped her broom.

Before she could process her thoughts, Mia stepped beside her. "So, what was that all about?"

"She came to apologize for Cody's behavior at ThaiPhoon that night...and to happily tell me he acquired Keep It Real for the tax deduction."

"Nuh-uh, hush! Did she really say that?"

Tessa nodded.

"Well, what did you say?"

"What I said is irrelevant. The only thing that matters is what I'm going to do next."

Chapter Nineteen

T essa

AFTER CHANDRA AMBUSHED TESSA, THE COLD WAR RECOMMENCED between her and Cody.

For more than a week, she'd deftly avoided both him and Kyle. Between locking herself in her office under Mabel's guard, teleworking, and cutting herself off from communication with them except pointed emails and text messages, she gave herself some much-needed space to think about the past, present, future —and prepare for the Real Talk launch which she'd planned for the next morning, to her dismay.

Work she estimated would take months had been completed in less than a week. It was too late to stop the project now, especially given all the time her team had invested. But Real Talk was subversive, at least it would appear that way to Hart...and that would explain the text from Kyle.

Kyle: I know you're in your office today.

Tessa: Yes, I am. You're not angry, are you?

Kyle: I'm on my way.

Tessa: Your font looks angry.

Kyle: We need to talk.

Until Kyle's text, no one had confronted her about the rampant rumors or her impending plans. Now the time of reckoning was upon her, and she stood on a path to self-destruction, ready to cross a thin line between misery and regret.

She'd spent the entire morning agonizing over the consequences. Her hasty decisions threatened to change the course of her life—starting with Cody and Kyle.

She blamed K4.

The sweet sound had muddied what used to be clear water.

Unlike Cody, Kyle had never been a source of confusion. His position was clear. They'd shared the sweetest dinner. His words were kind, his heart sincere, and he made her drool more than Ruth Chris's prime rib. He was intelligent, tall, gentlemanly, fine —and tall. Clear water.

Then from the depths of hell (or heights of heaven), Cody swooped in with his extra-large slices of greasy pizza and slow dance to K4 to baffle and confuse her—a state only compounded by Chandra's visit.

After churning over the scene with Chandra in her mind, Tessa concluded it was an enemy attack. However, her intentional malice didn't make the words any less true. Refusing to go to lunch with Cody would've taken the venom out of Chandra's bite, but she couldn't resist the pepperoni. Now Chandra had become an insult to the injury Cody had inflicted on her with his lies about wanting them to become a team. She'd reply to him by releasing Real Talk.

As she awaited Kyle's arrival, she tried her best to calm her nerves. Tessa considered making herself another cup of tea but needed something much stronger— a liquid lunch that included a few whiskey sours.

At once, a series of sharp knocks on her office door startled her out of her thoughts. In a quick motion, she spun around and called for the visitor to enter. She braced herself for Kyle's ire, but when the door opened, she received an unexpected surprise.

"Joya?" Tessa smiled and invited the meek young woman to walk inside. She was dressed in duck boots, a heavy knit sweater, and fashionably tattered and cuffed jeans to fend off the snow's chill.

"I hope I'm not interrupting. You said your door was always open, and I happened to be visiting in the area—thought I'd stop by before heading to Hart this morning. But I totally understand if you're busy."

"This is a very welcome surprise." She had no idea how welcome. "I'm glad you took me up on my offer!" Tessa said with all sincerity. "Please, come in and shut the door. Take a seat. Is there something I can help you with?"

Tessa gestured to her leather guest chair. Joya's long ponytail protruded from under her hat and swung with every step until she sat down.

"Actually, I stopped by to tell you that I'm thinking about quitting the team."

Tessa bent her neck forward and frowned. She couldn't conceal her disappointment. She considered Joya one of, if not the, brightest talent in the group. "Why would you leave? Did I do or say something to discourage you?"

"Oh heavens, no," she replied. "You and everyone at Hart have been absolutely amazing. I could not dream of a better opportunity. The thought that I could get paid to do what I love blows my mind."

"Then I'm confused," Tessa clasped her hands and weaved her fingers together to ease the tension. "Why on Earth would you want to give up your position?"

The sadness behind Joya's eyes was more prevalent than ever. She bit her bottom lip and turned away. Her hands appeared jittery, and she trembled. "May I speak frankly?"

"I wouldn't have it any other way."

"The truth is, during our meeting with you, I left incredibly inspired, but as I looked at the portfolios of the other members—I mean they're all so amazing."

"They really are. I'm in awe," Tessa added.

"I guess...I dunno. I'm afraid my work doesn't measure up. And my deepest fear is that I'll drag the team's progress because I'm so far behind."

"Behind?" Tessa's eyebrows squished together. Then she stood and walked to the front of her desk. "Were you and I in the same meeting? I hate to break it to you, but no one in the room was behind, especially not you."

Joya's head jerked back as if she was shocked by Tessa's reaction. "My boyfriend, Todd and, well, we talked about it, and—"

"And? What did he say?"

"Don't get me wrong, he thinks I'm talented...mostly. He's just not sure if I'm ready...for an assignment of this magnitude. "

Joya's words transported Tessa back five years to the young Cody, who dashed her hopes and dreams. He questioned many things about her commitment to him, to their future, but never her talent. No good man would ever inflict his insecurity on the woman he loved—but a no-good man would. Tessa couldn't point out Todd from a can of paint, but he sounded like an utter and complete jackass.

"Well, I sign the paychecks at Keep It Real, and I've been thriving in this industry for years. I took a close look at your portfolio, did you? Because if you saw what I did, you wouldn't be sitting here; you'd be hovering over your drawing board trying to impress me with new material for the specially abled line."

Tessa struggled to restrain her snarl but revealed a smile despite her best effort.

"Joya, let me tell you a truth to dispel all others. Your portfolio is nothing short of amazing. In the greeting card industry, you're what I consider to be a triple threat—you can write, you can draw, and you're funny. But nothing I tell you will matter if you don't believe in yourself."

"How do you do it?"

"Believe in me?" Tessa replied.

Joya posed a question she'd never been asked before, one she wasn't entirely certain of how to answer. The instinct wasn't automatic for everyone, certainly not for her. "Can I be honest?"

Joya nodded.

"I found that belief wasn't the core of my problem. It was fear," Tessa said.

"What do you mean?"

"Being afraid of colossal failure and ridicule, of not being accepted—or liked."

Her eyes widened, and she slumped back into her chair.

"Scared that people will judge me on my body of work and think it's substandard. On the other hand, there's a fear of success and the attention and expectation inherent in excelling in my field. I understand it. I lived it. Within my comfort zone, I'm in full control over my little piece of the world. Outside, everything is up to fate and chance."

"So, then, you do understand."

"Do I! You've probably got a tornado of thoughts whirling around in your head, and every day you'll allow this storm of self-doubt to build until it destroys every hope and dream in its wake if you don't learn to control it now."

"You've described every moment and emotion I've felt since graduating high school," Joya said. "I was an overachiever, but, there, I had set my course; college is controlled environment, right?"

She fidgeted with her hands.

"I could calculate exactly the amount of effort that would produce the desired result—straight A's. Now, I'm clueless. I could quite literally work myself to insanity and achieve nothing that I truly want or hope for."

"True," Tessa replied. "Or—you could gain experience, lessons learned, and someday, everything. Believing in yourself doesn't mean taking chances in the absence of fear...it means tapping into your courage to try. Getting uncomfortable with being uncomfortable. Putting yourself out there, your work out there, despite the uncertainty."

Tessa checked the time. She feared Kyle would burst through the door any second.

"It means accepting the inevitable—absolutely, you will fail at something, but you won't fail at everything. Understanding that if you don't try, you're assured of having safety but not success."

"I know I won't succeed at everything. But I want to be good. At this."

"And you will. Your job—here, now— is to gain experience and apply your lessons learned so that with each successive try, you inch closer to where you want to be. And if you don't quit, maybe in the next attempt you'll arrive. But, uh, if you don't mind my asking, what does Todd do for a living?"

"Oh, he's a software consultant. Pretty successful, too. Makes the big bucks. He's been trying to convince me to switch careers, move over to the computer industry. He thinks it's more secure, more predictable."

Joya's answer brought all the clarity Tessa needed. She pinched her lips before replying, "I see."

"What? You think that's a bad idea?"

"Not necessarily, not if that's where your heart lies," she said. "But can I offer you a piece of my father's advice?"

She nodded.

"My dad used to tell me that a cat cannot teach a fish how to swim," Tessa said. "You and Todd have different skills, different interests. He can't do what you do or comprehend what you dream. He cannot fathom the vision that the universe has gifted to you and only you. So, how can he judge your capability to succeed in this business—or your art?"

A spark of acceptance glimmered in her, but then it disappeared as quickly. She fixed her eyes on her feet when she should've been looking up.

"If there's one lesson I've learned through all my failures and successes, it's this: Don't ever let anyone talk you out of your passion or your purpose, that thing you're driven to do. The right person will accept you—all of you."

"You're right," she said with a weak nod. "I know you're right. Sometimes my fears and insecurities cripple me. I don't know. Trying feels so much harder than giving up."

"That's the most difficult truth to accept. But giving up guarantees you nothing but regret. Trying offers you the possibility of everything. But I'm not going to lie, it's uncomfortable. Those who succeed get comfortable with being uncomfortable. And I believe, if you work hard enough, if you're willing to learn and persevere, you'll achieve everything you want."

Joya's face brightened, and her brown eyes sparkled with hope. Tessa knew Joya. She'd been Joya and had stood at the crossroads ready to give up everything in the midst of heartache. Somehow, she found the inner strength to save herself.

Joya came back to life.

Tessa glanced at her watch, surprised that Kyle hadn't stormed in. No sooner than the thought crossed her mind did she hear steady strides moving closer.

"Um, I hate to cut this meeting short, but it sounds like Mr. Anderson is approaching." The hard footsteps stopped outside her office.

"Oh, no. I've taken up too much of your time today. I should return to Hart anyway—deadline. First review's tomorrow."

A slow smile stretched Tessa's lips. "The next time you want to give up something—make it the idea of quitting. You belong here, and I'm excited to see what you do with this opportunity."

"Me, too," she said. Then she made confident strides toward the elevator. "Looks like you've got company."

Part of Tessa wanted to ask Joya to stay; she may need a witness statement after Kyle got finished with her.

He greeted Joya as he entered, and she left. Tessa had never seen his expression, so stern or his eyes so narrowed. On closer examination, a pulsing vein in his neck made her afraid. Very afraid.

"How could you do it?" he asked with bark in his voice.

If word of Real Talk had leaked and sparked this reaction from Kyle, what would Cody do?

"How could I? How could you?" she replied.

"This is wrong. Everybody knows it," he said. "Real Talk is a mistake."

"Why is everyone still trying to convince me that I'm crazy? How would you feel if you put your blood, sweat, and tears into a company for five years, and someone bought it to serve as a tax write-off? What would you do?"

"How do you know that, Tessa? Have you even bothered to ask?"

No, she hadn't. Not directly. But who would tell her the truth? She'd been operating in a state of confusion. Kyle met her anger with indignation, and she hardly knew how to strike back. Putting up physical defenses, she folded her arms over her chest.

"The root of the problems between you and Cody stems from a complete lack of effective communication. You two need to talk."

"We're past that point now, but every decision I've made has been in the name of keeping my staff from quitting and saving my company."

"Saving your company from what, success? Keep It Real needed rescuing before Cody acquired it, not after."

"Does he know?"

"Not yet. But he will soon enough. I just hope the damage isn't irreparable—and, unfortunately, there will be damage," he said.

"There's damage on all sides," Tessa said.

"For what it's worth, he handled this situation as poorly as one could handle it. He ambushed you. You have every right to be upset, confused. This is your life's work. But compounding a bad idea with a potentially worse one isn't good for Keep It Real or Hart. You've got to understand that."

She nodded. "I'm sorry if I've put you in a difficult position...and I apologize for ghosting you over the past two weeks. I've had a lot going on."

Part of her hoped he'd ask her to dinner again or even dessert. She found his company soothing, like easing into a warm bath, something she needed, a feeling she craved.

"Well, I just wanted to warn you." He spoke with more frost in his voice than she was comfortable with. "I should be leaving."

"Are you sure you can't stay...maybe for a cup of coffee?"

"No, I can't," he replied. "I guess I'm just not that thirsty."

And with that, he disappeared.

If Kyle's demeanor was any indication of what to expect from Cody, she pitied herself. Typhoon Cody would blow through the door any second. She returned to her chair and, once more, fixed her gaze on the snowfall. There was nothing left to do now except brace herself for the storm.

Chapter Twenty

C ody

CODY POURED A WHISKEY STRAIGHT AT NINE A.M. TO SAVE TESSA'S life. He brooded, still in disbelief. Rumors about her new card line had crept up the grapevine, and now he sat on his hands in his office chair, trying to keep from strangling her with her own hair.

He thought their lunch had changed the dynamic between them. He wanted so much to believe that her accepting the consultant position to oversee the specially abled line meant they had turned a corner.

Apparently, he'd misjudged her in the worst way. Not only had she ghosted him for the past couple of weeks, but she'd allowed her team to create a product that represented the opposite of the Hart brand.

When he visited her office, she had more than enough opportunity to tell him the truth, but she lied straight to his face. Now, as she prepared to launch her latest and biggest mistake, she'd damage the Hart brand while working in direct opposition to his plans to pivot her vision and expand Keep It Real's market share.

To survive the day without losing his mind, he withdrew to his most reliable and safe outlet for his anger. He found a quiet cubbyhole in the old creative suite's darkest corner and allowed his hand to push the pencil across the paper instinctively.

He had no design planned, rather he planned to distract himself until he calmed down. Then he might avoid unleashing the fullness of his fury. An hour later, his abstract mishmash of darkness and anger drawn in zigzags and splotches might constitute art to someone somewhere, but to him, he sketched visual frustration.

As soon as he regained control of his emotions, he abandoned his art. He took several deep breaths, called his car, and made the trip over to Sweet Media.

Cody slipped through the back entrance to escape the notice of her staff. When he arrived at Tessa's office, unlike him, she sat in her seat, appearing unbothered, a picture of calm and ease. He cleared his throat to get her attention, using every bit of his strength to restrain the bite in his bark. Didn't work.

"What's going on? The Real Talk line? What've you done?" The words rolled out of his mouth before he even computed what he'd said.

Surprised at his unannounced presence, her eyes protruded out of her skull. "You're mad," she replied, speaking the understatement of the century.

"Oh, I'm not mad. Dogs get mad. No, I'm ticked. Words have not yet been invented to describe the level of my anger. And the worst part is, if anyone else in Hart had done what you did, I could fire them on the spot. I'm stuck with you."

Hurt washed over her face; his harshness seemed to catch her off guard. "I started the new line as a means to hold on to my staff, to do what's best for Keep It Real. It's not a choice I'd make without careful thought and consideration."

Taking in her expression, the tenseness in her jaw, her

diverted gaze, he knew there was more to her decision than merely doing what she thought best. He knew her.

"That's the problem with you, isn't it? Did you consider, even for a moment, how your choice would impact anyone except you and your little world?"

"I did, but—"

"If this line fails, a loss may mean freedom to you, but it means reduced revenue, smaller bonuses, fewer Christmas presents, less money toward college funds. These are the kinds of things CEOs of major corporations must consider."

"Um, maybe I didn't consider—"

"We don't have the luxury of rash, baseless decisions. You risked hurting your employees, and, for what? Failure and a flurry of I told you so's? The destruction of faith and trust between us? The potential loss of valuable staff not if, but *when* your plan flopped?"

Tessa swallowed hard.

The confrontation was inevitable. Cody figured she probably hadn't expected all of this truth before she downed the full cup of coffee on her coaster.

She seemed to recalculate her response. He could almost see the smoke coming from her ears.

"Quite frankly, I don't understand why you've got a beef with me. Maybe you've played it safe your entire career, but that luxury missed me."

"It didn't miss you. You never wanted it," he reminded her.

"I wasn't favored with the nepotistic silver platter your father handed to you, the big chair, and keys to the executive washroom."

"I proposed to you. You could've taken half."

"Maybe if you'd offered me half instead of a seat in your cheerleading section, I'd have said yes," she said. "I took chances; that's how I made it. I couldn't have come this far without being fearless in the face of risk."

Her voice filled with force and emotion.

"I still run this company," she continued, "and I needed to find a way to increase revenue. I believed Real Talk and a viral social media campaign were the best ways to achieve that goal. I've never been dismissive or condescending about your vision. Why are you so determined to dismiss mine?"

"Because I know you, Tessa. Real Talk is not you. It's not what we—"

He turned his back on her. When he glared at her over his shoulder, he shot a look that could've chilled her to the spine. He'd never looked at her with such shame.

"We agreed, Tessa," Cody said. "At least I thought we did. I saw the words written on your whiteboard. Kinder. Gentler. That was the direction of the new greeting card line."

"First of all, barking orders versus obtaining a consensus are two different things."

"I never barked anything."

"And we never agreed to anything. You attempted to impose your will on me, my staff, and my company. You dictated the request to me—or at least you tried. I never said I'd follow your command."

"Tessa, I have a deep respect for your creativity, and I know, like no one knows, the amount of work and dedication required of you to build Keep It Real. But Real Talk is doomed to fail...miserably. You've lost touch with the market. When is the last time you conducted a focus group? I held one the month before I acquired Keep It Real and the week after," Cody said.

Tessa stood there in shock with her mouth half hanging open. Her face reflected sheer disbelief that he asked.

He could almost hear her launching four-letter expletives in her mind about his audacity to presuppose that he knew her business practices.

"When is the last time you purchased one of your own cards?" he fired off again. "You're not even a consumer of the product you make. My focus groups were barely aware of your brand, yet they were repeat customers of Hart cards. Why? Because people need to connect on an emotional level."

"My brand connects people on emotional levels."

"Yes, but you've got a limited pool of consumers, and your messaging is outright mean at times. We create the cards that people give most often. Don't get me wrong, Keep It Real is a fantastic line, but it's niche."

"There you go with the niche again, like it's a bad thing. I've got news for you. Apple Computers is niche. It's not a curse word."

"The reason I wanted you to enhance your line was to increase your market share. Not encroach on your existing territory; just expand it. And in your unfounded quest to avenge some perceived wrong, you do...what? Destroy the whole company?"

"Arrogant much? Still as self-centered as always," she said. "Our problem is and always was the fact that you think the earth, moon, and stars revolve around you."

"The whole world doesn't revolve around me. Just Hart," he barked.

"My decision to start the Real Talk line had minus zero to do with our history. I did what was best for Keep It Real, in the long-term."

"You need a better strategy."

"And you need better research," she said. "The engine driving the card market looks nothing like you and exactly like me— ninety percent women. And if you don't aggressively integrate social media into your marketing strategy, Hart Enterprises will become the dinosaur of the greeting card industry before you can pour another shot of whiskey."

"All evidence suggests you will release this new line to a resounding thud. Not only is this the wrong way to expand, but it's also not who you are, not anymore."

"This. From a man with no clue as to who I am."

"Fine. This line does not represent the woman I thought you

had grown to be—she's not the woman who I danced with at Di'Angelo's. I thought you were...we were—"

"What? What do you presume to know about me? You never so much as sent me a text after delivering your Dear Jane card via third party delivery service. In no way, shape or form am I the same woman you abandoned back then. She ceased to exist the day you gutted her heart."

"Too bad."

"For whom? Not for me. No, she was young, stupid, and blinded by her love for someone, a man that existed only in her imagination. He's certainly not standing in front of me today. No, you are Chandra's man in every way. You're the one who bought his ex-girlfriend's loser company for a tax break."

"Excuse me?"

"Oh, yeah. Chandra confessed everything under the guise of 'getting along.'"

She used air quotes.

Chandra.

He didn't respond, not right away, only stared at her. He could feel his eyes flood with hurt and contempt. What a performance. She wounded him, brandished her words like a sword, and jammed them like a dagger into his heart.

"Silence. I see your M.O. hasn't changed," she continued.

"Think whatever you want. Nothing I say or do makes any difference." He pressed his hand against his heart. "All I know is I did what I could to—."

"To change me? To turn me into Chandra-lite? Thanks, but no thanks. I'll take a hard pass."

"I didn't try to change you. I tried to change your profit margin. That's my job as the CEO of Keep It Real. But if you're dead set on sabotaging the company and every strategy we devise to spark a turnaround then..."

"Then what?" Tessa barked, hanging on the edge of his words. She seemed eager to hear him say he'd cut his losses and shed the dead weight of Keep It Real.

Perhaps he would've except for the boisterous cheers erupting from the outer offices.

"What's that about?" he asked.

"I dunno," she said with a shrug. "Uh, what were you saying again?"

"I was saying..."

Before the words escaped his lips, Mia flittered inside, beaming like a bright ray of sun. She bumped the door after opening and said, "Knock, knock. May I interrupt?"

"Sure," Cody said.

Tessa gave him a stern side-eye glance. He answered with all of her authority, after all, it was his company.

"Yeah, what's going on?" Tessa followed.

"Real Talk. The sample is going viral. *The Root* and the *Huffington Post* picked it up. In another day or two, our Insta-campaign may hit one million views on social media."

Tessa caught her breath as she nearly stumbled to her seat.

"If today is any indication, the new line will be sold out by the month's end," Mia stammered for a moment. "Before I go back out there and rejoin the group, I'd like to offer an apology to you. I'm so sorry for being a Doris Doubter."

"No, you don't have to—"

"When you introduced the concept, the idea sounded just left of cracked-brained. I thought we'd be unemployed and looking for work next week."

Tessa shifted her gaze to the floor.

"Why I bother questioning your judgment, I have no clue. Everything you touch turns to gold, and early results suggest this idea is platinum."

"I appreciate you. I'll see you guys out there after Cody, and I wrap up here."

Too shocked to display the level of smug he deserved, Tessa pursed her lips after Mia left and gazed at Cody.

"Well," he began. "She's not the only one who owes you an

apology. Look, I didn't think it would take off. Maybe part of me hoped it wouldn't."

"What do you mean?"

"The most critical difference between Hart and Real Talk is how it makes people feel. Your line will hurt people, all under the guise of honesty and authenticity. Words matter. My consumers will cry tears of joy, and yours will cry tears of sadness—a best-case scenario."

"That's not...that was never the intent."

"I offered you the chance to bring happiness to people, to find it within yourself, and you spit in my face, so hell-bent on doing things your own way. You couldn't care less about who you mow over in the process, even if it's your own staff."

"I didn't mean...it wasn't supposed to..."

His eyebrows squished, and he rubbed the scruff on his chin. "Wait a minute. Do you mean to tell me you meant for Real Talk to fail?"

"Not fail. It's taken a life of its own. It moved much faster than I planned. I couldn't stop it."

"Actually, you could've stopped it and, as the head of Keep It Real, it was your responsibility to do so, especially if it morphed into something you didn't want to brand as Keep It Real," he said. "Imagine my shock. All this time, I believed you to be a bitter witch. Color me surprised to learn your situation is worse than I expected— you're a weak one."

His breath got caught in his chest as he realized the brutality of the blow he dealt. He understood the root of the hurtfulness in his tone, but she wouldn't until it was too late—this line was a mistake. He charged toward the door and gripped the doorknob but didn't open it.

"You know what? In the end, that's why we could never work. I was trying to build a life for us, and you weren't strong enough to stay true to yourself in a marriage with me."

"Wrong. Back then, there was only one thing weak about me. You."

"Maybe that thought will keep you warm at night. This line— your actions—they will come with consequences, mark my words. For your sake, whatever they may be, I hope you can live with them."

He turned the knob, marched out to his car, and told his driver to take him home. No way would he return to the Hart offices. He couldn't handle any more drama. He had no desire to speak or think.

If Tessa wanted to come for him again, she'd need to wait until he recovered from this bout. The match was brutal. Yes, he'd won—but he'd thrown a blow that may be too low to recover from this time.

Keep It Real Cards

Congratulations on Your Graduation.
You did it!

Let's Keep It Real— *It only took 7 years and a booty call to Shady McGraderson, but who cares? You finally "earned" that degree.*

Chapter Twenty-One

T essa

THE MORNING'S GRAY SKIES AND WINTERY MIX FIT TESSA'S MOOD, reflected her inner drear, a direct result of her clash with Cody.

She cursed her lottery luck.

An infinitesimal chance existed for Real Talk to succeed, one so small she hadn't even calculated for the possibility. And yet here she sat, sifting through an inbox filled with congratulatory notes while mentally settling on the day's outfit — a casual black suit.

The color would better conceal the blood spatter if she and Cody bumped into one another and descended into an all-out brawl.

Her body ached as if she'd emerged from a double rinse cycle in her washing machine. She turned her eyes to the heavens and thanked them for the coffee brewing in her Keurig. After inhaling the aromatic steam rising from the Colombian Supremo inside her Snoopy mug, she gazed at Kyle's texts with gratitude.

Kyle: Lunch today?

Tessa: You're texting a dead woman.

Kyle: Dead women don't text.

Tessa: We don't lunch either. Meeting at Hart. Specially abled line team.

Kyle: How about dinner?

Tessa: Dead women don't dinner, either. Dessert?

Kyle: Cheesecake.

Tessa: I love you.

She didn't text the last line, but she thought it.

She looked forward to spending downtime with Kyle. Aside from a few stolen whispers and the exchange of starry-eyed glances in her office during integration meetings, their romance had hibernated, like a bear. The Ruth Chris dinner sat in her rearview, but farther than it appeared.

To be honest, she craved intimacy, mental and physical.

The K4 lunch with Cody had worn down her inhibitions so completely that she hungered for affection, a man's arms around her, the heat of his breath on her neck. Why she'd continued to pump the brakes every time Kyle hit the accelerator, she didn't know...or refused to admit to herself.

Cody bit at her during their clash, and, yes, she was wrong about many things. But he'd caught her at the jugular with one salient truth—she'd been a weak leader. In fact, every stride she'd taken to fix her company had been motivated by the exact weakness and cowardice she'd accused him of.

The meeting with the specially abled line team at Hart, which had not been canceled, served as the only evidence that Cody hadn't banished her from the kingdom entirely.

Later that morning, she executed a covert arrival at Hart Enterprises. She'd looked forward to spending time with the team again—her group. The anticipation of it had been a light in her darkness. She'd already begun to take ownership of them, and they, especially Joya, might offer her a renewed sense of purpose after Cody's emotional beat down.

Joya's visit made her recall her own failings and how she overcame them. If Tessa did her job well enough, maybe Joya would give that insecure, shortsighted, unsupportive boyfriend of hers the unceremonious dumping he deserved. As a matter of fact, if Tessa had her way, Joya would end her relationship with a card she designed with her own hands.

Tessa entered the conference room where, to her dismay, the bubbling, happy faces that had greeted her before had disappeared.

Maybe Cody had canceled the specially abled line and announced it to everyone else before her.

"Hey, guys?" she said. "Uh, what's going on? Who died?"

Denesha gasped; horror filled her eyes. Tessa wanted to check her nose; she wondered if a green glob freed itself from her nostril. TiTi's face dripped with tears while the guys' faces drooped, their lips turned down. That's when she noticed the empty seat. Joya's seat was vacant, but her "I can't even" coffee mug was missing from the space she had filled during the previous meeting.

Tessa pointed to the place she expected to see Joya. "Is she in the ladies' room?"

Max shook her head. "She—she's not coming in today. She…" Max struggled to push what should be simple words past her lips.

Why was everyone so down? Sympathy card day was weeks away.

"Joya's mom called. She was depressed, won't leave her room. She quit."

The words "she quit" still hung in the air and rattled through her brain. The subsequent silence compounded her confusion with fear. She didn't bother taking off her coat, but she took a hard tug at her scarf, constricting her already labored breaths.

"Apparently, she and her boyfriend broke up after an intense argument. It caught her off-guard. I think she doesn't know how to handle the pain."

"Oh, no." Tessa understood. She'd been there before. Her jaw dropped in disbelief. "Are you sure she quit? I don't understand?

"They've been beefing for a while now, arguing a lot," Denesha said. "She tried to hide it, but she wore it on her face. Every morning. She always blamed her expression on her lack of coffee. She hid the pain with a smile. Something was always there. Anyone paying attention would notice. So she called me this morning and quit."

Well, she saw something in Joya's eyes, but nothing that would suggest this.

She'd like to believe she could've noticed if she worked with Joya every day, but the sweet girl masked her pain well.

Tessa couldn't fathom the existence in which Joya couldn't withstand the blow from a break up with a guy who, based on Tessa's limited knowledge of him, sounded like a useless excuse for a boyfriend.

What kind of man would make a woman question her own abilities? The answer was in the expression of every member of the team sitting before her.

TiTi opened her mouth to speak, but no words came. Even she understood.

Tessa turned to Max, who reluctantly finished the story in her place. "Their relationship has been on-again, off-again since I met her. Crazy. She couldn't let him go. We all knew she deserved better, but that meant nothing if she didn't know"—she shrugged —"Anyway, yesterday, he called. Might've been around lunchtime. I remember because we were in the breakrooms for one of those brown bag training sessions on brainstorming ideas. Her face cracked after their discussion."

Everyone agreed with the account. They nodded and exchanged uncomfortable glances.

"I asked her what happened, and she said that he told her they need to talk at home. She tried to convince me, or maybe herself, that he would pop the question. Seemed reasonable after all the time they'd been together. But, uh-uh, nope. I knew better."

"Yeah, they talked all right," Denesha added. "I guess she couldn't handle it—or maybe after everything that's happened, she faced the truth. She just checked out of work, checked out of life. Her mom said Todd destroyed her."

Denesha pressed her hand against her chest.

"Her mom called trying to explain that Joya's distraught and to ignore her resignation, poor lady. She doesn't want Joya to lose such a wonderful opportunity."

Tessa couldn't help but wonder if something she'd said had sparked the argument? She immediately replayed their conversation in endless loops in her mind, questioning whether, in trying to offer her hope, she caused Joya to feel hopeless.

Tessa understood the kind of pain that would make Joya want to barricade herself and quit all semblance of normal life. This is the part where Joya needed someone to help her realize how valuable she was and let her know life would go on after Todd. "There's got to be something I can do to help."

More than saying the right words, she wanted to ensure she didn't say the wrong ones and compound an already bad situation.

"I'm going to make sure she's okay."

"I had my appendix removed two summers ago," Max said. "Nobody came to see me...from Hart, anyway. No cards. No flowers. No-thing."

"Well, at Keep It Real, my employees, my team, we're like family. We care for each other, and we take care of business. I'll get her address and visit her."

"I've got it. She and I live in the same development." As fast as Denesha revealed the address, Tessa disappeared.

Joya's resignation took Tessa back to the fateful moment, seconds after she'd read the greeting card, Cody sent that awful day.

She'd experienced the devastation first hand. After absorbing the crushing impact from Cody's square peg and round hole card, something inside her heart wanted to die...at least for an hour or two. Maybe a week.

But time and faith healed all. Although despair turned into hurt and hurt into anger, eventually anger morphed into grit and determination. With a lot of hard work, her determination manifested as the phenomenon known as Keep It Real Cards.

THIRTY MINUTES LATER, SHE ARRIVED AT JOYA'S DEVELOPMENT IN Maryland, a trail of three-story colonials with lush lawns and wrap-around front porches.

A curly-haired brunette wearing UGGs and a bulky green sweater sat on the front porch puffing a cigarette with one hand and wiping her nose with a handkerchief inside the other. Tessa assumed she was Joya's mother because she and Joya practically mirrored one another, except one was at least twenty years older. Tessa's stomach knotted with angst.

The woman's sadness intensified Tessa's own apprehension about being the root of their troubles. The thought paralyzed her to the point that she almost did an about-face and hauled out of there. Instead, she pushed past her angst, and a few tenuous steps later, she stood in front of the woman, who peered up.

She searched Tessa's eyes for something familiar and found nothing. She struggled to smile. As the woman tucked the handkerchief into her front pant pocket, Tessa introduced herself.

"Hi, I'm from Hart Enterprises. Tessa Sweet. You and Joya could be twins. She's on my team." She exhaled when the woman appeared more relieved than irritated.

"Oh, yes. It's nice to meet you. I'm her mom, Rose." She offered a slight wave. "I'd shake your hand, but mine is probably coated in snot." She scanned over her shoulders. "I could use some hand sanitizer."

"I've got some." Tessa dug into her purse, pulled out a small bottle, and chuckled inside. Joya's sense of humor was clearly homegrown. She could see a new wave of sobs building behind the woman's eyes. Her lips quivered as she accepted the bottle.

"Wait a minute. Tessa. Oh, my goodness. Joya mentioned you the other day. She truly admires you."

Tessa smiled, pressed her hand against her heart, and demurred at her kind words. "How is she doing? I just heard the news and rushed over."

"She'll survive this...at least physically. But I haven't seen her so fragile, so vulnerable since I gave birth to her. Doctors can make the blind see. They can make the paralyzed walk. But nobody's figured out a quick-fix to heal a broken heart." The whites of her eyes appeared streaked with red lines as more tears pushed through. The only thing that seemed to keep her from falling apart was the threads of strength and courage she mustered for her daughter.

"I hear Joya's not doing well. She won't leave the house?"

"I told her that Todd boy was no good." She sniffed. "He's got those beady little eyes. You know what I'm talking about? Red flags were flying around like pigeons at a swap meet. He didn't want to meet me. When he finally met me, no eye contact. Zero."

Tessa groaned and nodded.

"Weak, insecure. Todd destroyed Joya from the inside out. She insisted he was 'the one.'"—she used air quotes—"I told her he's not the one; he's a bum. You say that two or three times, you're mildly annoying. By the six-hundredth time, you're ignored. What could I do?" She lifted a single eyebrow and slumped into her chair. "How could he be so heartless? Such a coward?" Rose asked the question more toward the universe than to Tessa.

There were so many things Tessa could've said, but she clamped her lips shut and let Rose release what seemed to be a year's worth of pent up frustration.

"If you don't mind me asking, what happened? I mean, this was all so shocking because we just spoke. I offered her some advice about believing in herself, and I thought—I don't know, something must've triggered this."

Rose replied, "Yes. A card."

"A card?" Inexplicably, Tessa gasped. Rose's words transported her to the minute, the second she received the one from Cody. An eerie feeling crawled through her. The timing seemed too coincidental.

"I'm not old, but I'm just old enough to remember when people bought cards to brighten someone's day, to remind loved ones and friends they had caring, loving witnesses to their lives, you know?" Rose began. "But with all these social media trolls and keyboard cowards, I shouldn't be surprised common decency is extinct. My daughter's condition is proof of that fact."

Rose's spirit seemed to deflate as her purse strap fell from her shoulder.

Tessa sat in an adjacent chair while she retrieved an envelope from her bag.

"Nowadays, they'll make a card for anything, thoughtless jackasses." Rose handed the envelope to Tessa, which she examined for only a second before clenching her eyes shut. "Go ahead. Open it. They call this mess Real Talk," she heard Rose say.

She didn't want to look at it. Her stomach began to quiver. She wanted nothing more than to sprout wings and fly away. Unfortunately, no matter how far she traveled, there'd she'd be, forced to face herself, her truth. At that moment, she heard his voice.

Cody.

Their argument over Real Talk replayed and his words echoed in her mind.

"This line—your actions—they will come with consequences, mark my words," he spat. "For your sake, whatever they may be, I hope you can live with them."

Rose held the card.

Could Tessa live with the consequences?

No, she couldn't.

The thought sparked an epiphany about Keep It Real Cards, about her goal for the company, her vision, and, most importantly—the translation.

Her intent, her heart was in the right place. Through greeting cards, she'd set out to deliver authentic, honest messages that, yes, may hurt at first, but eventually, they would inspire people to become the best versions of themselves. She realized for her vision to materialize, her consumers had to translate her messages the right way.

But what if they didn't?

She envisioned the heart-hurt transforming soul-breaking pain into the kind of grit and creativity that helped her turn her own dreams into reality. However, what if the heartbreak that drives one woman to determination pushes another to the brink?

Pain, hurt, honesty—they did not convert into positive energy for every woman. The wiring in women was as unique as our DNA. The Real Talk line—was mean.

For some, the cards may serve as the cornerstone for rebuilding and growth. But for others, the messages would hit like wrecking-balls, maybe driving them further into the darkness of depression—or something far worse.

Still, she had time to change the line, to be the leader she should've been in the first place. Now that she knew better, she'd do better.

For now, she'd regret the choice.

Chapter Twenty-Two

✦❧❦

C ody

KYLE STRUCK CODY'S OFFICE DOOR WITH TWO QUICK KNOCKS AND poked his head inside.

"Hey! You wanted to see me?"

Cody marched laps around his executive desk, tugging at his already loosened tie.

"Uh-oh, what's going on?" Kyle continued.

Cody waved him inside without missing a step. He could feel the veins in his neck protruding and only imagined the state of his expression. Judging by Kyle's reaction, it accurately reflected his distress.

He snapped his head toward Kyle and replied, "Thundersnow."

In scientific terms, thundersnow, a winter event, occurred when a thunderstorm clashed with a cold front. Emotionally, it was whenever conflict brought him toe to toe with Tessa.

Tessa and Cody lived on opposite ends of the same spectrum, always.

He was illustrations. She was prose.

He was driven and content. She was free and fearless.

He marched to orders. She made her own rules.

He was lightning—he cracked. She was thunder-she boomed. His anger burned hot, while she froze under fire, grew silent, withdrew...and plotted.

The quieter and calmer she became, the more devastating her impact when she let loose.

He'd relearned the lesson many times throughout their relationship. He knew they clashed like thundersnow, and, yet, he'd bought her company from under her nose.

That's when the revelation overcame him.

Before her, he'd never allow emotions of any kind to infiltrate his business decisions. Their breakup was the proof of it. The decision to acquire Keep It Real was not one he would've made. However, under the same circumstances, Tessa would've acquired it in a heartbeat.

In fact, Tessa had not behaved out of character. He had.

And now she dared to conspire against him as if he were the enemy? He couldn't be farther from her adversary. Maybe, after all this time, she needed to know the truth.

The turbulence had overwhelmed him, moved him out of his seat, and pushed his feet to the floor. He'd practically paced a hole in his office rug, trying to diffuse his anger.

"What is she trying to do to me?" he said to the universe in general and Kyle in particular.

"Don't you mean to ask what's she trying to do to Hart?"

"Yeah, Hart." His sheepishness exposed what he really meant. "You know what I'm saying."

He pursed his lips. "I'm sure I know exactly what you meant."

After K4, he thought they had turned a new corner. He let his guard down, believing they'd exchange olive branches. The hope they'd renew a treasured friendship vanished like the wind of a passing storm.

Not only had she failed to heed his advice and shift Keep It Real to a kinder, gentler brand, but she'd also created a cold, heartless line that would fail emotionally, if not financially.

He feared she'd come to regret the line's success. In his estimation, she'd meet a far worse fate. Karma was an undeniable point of convergence. What goes around comes around. Negativity would be met with more of the same.

"Why didn't you tell me about Real Talk when you first heard about it? I'm paying you to keep an eye on what's happening over there."

"Excuse me? I told you weeks ago that Tessa was creating a new line. You told me not only were you aware of the line but also you approved it."

"I wha—" He took slow steps to his chair and sat down. As the scene replayed in his mind, Cody realized Kyle didn't deserve the blame for Real Talk—he did, and for more reasons than he cared to admit, the least of which was failing to consult with Tessa before buying her business.

"I'm sorry, man," he replied after a lengthy pause. "You're right. Absolutely right. This isn't your fault. It's on me."

He expelled a long breath and spun his chair around to take in the wintery view from the window. "You know what? Tessa wins. I give up. One way or the other, I'll rid myself and Hart Enterprises of the headache that is Tessa Sweet for good," he said. "If she thinks she can succeed without Hart, fine. Let her give it a whirl."

"C'mon, man, you know better. You can't dump the company now," Kyle said. His voice went high and then low again. "Talk about vindictive? Now that the going has gotten hard, you want to bail on her?"

Bail on her. Wouldn't be the first time, but the last should've been the last.

"If your conscience doesn't stop you, maybe this will: Cut

Tessa loose, and you may as well hand-deliver to her all the ammunition she'd ever need to mount an expensive legal suit."

"She'd never sue me...I don't think."

"Maybe not, but you're letting your emotions get the best of you. This is not the businessman speaking."

"If not a businessman, then who's speaking?"

"A decent human being. You're respected, not only in this company but in the industry. You want to jeopardize that?"

Cody shook his head and tilted it downward, and Kyle just kept going in.

"The Cody I know wouldn't cause Keep It Real to fail, not intentionally. Tessa will call it a vendetta. She'll call you the *'bitter witch.'*"

Kyle's words caught his attention.

"Even if that's not the whole truth, it's what I would tell my client to say. In fact, I'd go so far as to assert that her success led you to conspire against her all along."

Cody's lips tightened into a flat line, but he listened.

"The Cody I know would say he expected a bumpy integration. Let's give it time," Kyle continued. "The businessman would say neither he nor Hart Enterprises could afford another protracted legal battle after surviving his sisters' war."

"But I nev—"

"Listen, I understand that in the matter of Sweet versus Hart, the truth lies somewhere between fact and perception. I wouldn't be a good COO or friend if I didn't warn you of the consequences."

Consequences. He'd been so busy harping on Tessa's he hadn't taken much time to consider his own.

"You're right," he said. "Let me calm down and figure this out. I expected resistance. But I didn't prepare for outright mutiny."

"Do you want me to talk to her? Maybe I can convince her the line isn't the best strategy for Hart or her own business. If she doesn't listen to me, at least she'll hear me out."

"*Humph.* I realize you two have grown close," Cody grunted. "But, trust me, you don't know Tessa as well as you think you do."

Before Kyle could balk at Cody's assertion, Miss Dee knocked on the door and announced herself before entering.

"Sir?" She locked her eyes on Cody's.

"Yes, Ma'am, can this wait? We're in the middle of...something."

She shook her head. "I wouldn't have interrupted except that I believe this would constitute an emergency."

"Okay, what is it?"

"A Hart Enterprise employee quit today. Apparently, she's not doing well emotionally. Joya Lawson."

"Joya? Wait, that name's familiar." He paused briefly and tapped his chin. "Oh, I remember! She's on Tessa's team. Is she okay? What happened?"

"An unfortunate relationship, depression, and an impulsive resignation. She's a bit distraught. Maybe a first heartbreak. They're pretty rough."

"They are, aren't they. I'm sorry to hear that." Cody winced.

"Her mother called to say she was distraught when she quit. She didn't want Joya to lose her job."

"Of course, we'll hold her seat. That's the last thing she should be worried about."

The news rocked Cody more than he expected. He'd chalk that up to Tessa, too. He'd never suspect Joya was capable of falling into an emotional spiral.

He'd met her briefly only a couple of times, but she reminded him of a young Tessa. He had hopes that she'd become one of the strongest creators on the team, maybe rise to the level of Rice McHugh.

"Did she leave a phone number? Tessa will—"

That's when it struck him—Tessa.

She'd be upset. When she invested her energy in anything or anyone, it became a part of her.

A part of her, he repeated in his mind.

Before his lips could form the question, Ms. Dee chimed in.

"Mia called. Tessa's on the way to visit her; make sure everything's okay."

Instinctively, he wanted to jump out of his seat and run to Tessa's side. Then he took a hard look at Kyle. Maybe Tessa would want him there, in the place that used to be his. "Okay, please keep me apprised of any updates."

"Will do."

When Ms. Dee exited, Kyle peered at Cody. "I'm stunned, but I'm glad Tessa's there."

Kyle didn't budge or ask to leave. There was no urgency in his voice or manner—no effort to check on Tessa's state.

She didn't hire employees. She'd built a family. That's when another realization struck him. Losing control of Keep It Real didn't only threaten her livelihood and her vision but also her ability to protect those who meant the most.

Cody nodded in agreement but realized he was right about Kyle all along—he didn't know Tessa as well as he thought, not at all.

On the heel of his revelation, Cody's cellphone buzzed with a text notification. He glanced at the screen and clenched his eyes shut in disbelief.

What am I going to do now?

His next move—to respond or ignore—would constitute a declaration to himself and his heart.

He studied Kyle, waiting for him to text Tessa, for him to do something, anything. When he did nothing, Cody's next move was clear.

"Uh, I've got some business to take care of. A problem...with a supplier," he lied. "I've, uh, I've also got dinner plans tonight, so I probably won't return to the office until morning."

Kyle's head jerked back. "You sure everything's all right?"

"If you could just keep an eye on things here. Text me if you need anything." He flittered around, grabbing his belongings. "I'll check in with you later. Keep me updated on Joya."

He added the last part to throw Kyle off the scent.

Yes, Kyle was Cody's friend and one of his most important allies, but neither he nor anyone could compete with the desires of his heart.

Only one person, one woman, laid full claim to those.

Chapter Twenty-Three

T essa

WHEN JOYA'S MOTHER, ROSE, HANDED TESSA THE SOURCE OF JOYA'S despair, all sound dissipated except the opening flap on the envelope.

Her soul filled with dread as she read the card and its contents. The backside, the first in her view, contained a familiar marking. Immediately, she recognized Todd's offering as a product in her Real Talk line.

In fact, it was the only one Tessa had designed with her own hands.

Inspired by Cody and conceived the night after the acquisition, she made the card in a place of anger and hate. It wasn't covered with a square peg and a round hole. No, a hand was half-squeezed into an undersized black leather glove. "Since we don't fit, it's time to quit. Let's Keep It Real—We're over."

The card alone was awful, but Todd didn't stop there.

No, on the blank side, the jerk wrote a note with words as

hard and cold as his dead heart. He left no doubt that he'd written each syllable to inflict crippling blows to her hope, self-esteem, and her spirit.

And Tessa, of all people, had unwittingly played the accomplice in his crime. She created the vessel he used to deliver his degrading brand of maliciousness.

"Awful, isn't it?" Rose said. "This day and age has evolved into something I don't recognize anymore. Maybe I'm ancient, but we treated people differently when I was growing up."

"No, you're far from ancient. What you're saying...that's the way it should be."

"I mean, don't get me wrong, life wasn't perfect, not by any stretch of the imagination, but people were kinder. If they had nothing nice to say, they kept it to themselves or talked behind people's backs. Jerks were shunned, not victims."

Tessa nodded. "We blame the people who get hurt instead of those who inflict the pain. Some days, it seems things have changed for the better...and, others, the worst."

"I dunno. I'll never adjust to this. Some days I feel like I'm living in upside-down world." Her voice was laden with despair. "And if the world isn't crappy enough, some genius thought it'd be a good idea to add this card to it."

A wave of guilt overcame Tessa. She felt sick. She wished she could heave and rid herself of the awful feeling, but it was in her blood.

"I suppose it'd be fine if you're heartless, but people like Todd will give them to people like Joya. Sweet souls are aching inside, quietly living on the edge, some hanging on a thin thread between life and death. All they need is a hate card to push them over the edge."—she began to crumble—"What if she doesn't pull out of this?"

Tessa took Rose into her arms and offered a guilty shoulder. Then Rose offered the final dagger to Tessa. "Some people will do anything for cold hard cash. It's blood money and nothing less."

Tessa wanted to explain that she'd never intended to hurt anyone, that she hadn't put enough thought into her plan to be malicious. That she'd created the line out of desperation and the card out of hurt; she never dreamed of breaking a fractured soul.

She wanted to explain to Rose her one true mistake: to judge other people's strength by the depth of her own.

That Cody-card, while devastating, drove her to embrace her passion, to invest a storm of negative energy into a positive cause, building a dream to better the world.

She never once considered her reaction to be exceptional, nor did she expect to find that what sparked her life's light might drive another to darkness.

She was guilty of tunnel vision, not spite.

She gave too little thought to her consumers' vulnerability, to those voiceless people teetering between sanity and hopelessness. With barely a blip, the petty, bitter witch had delivered pain between the covers of a Real Talk card.

At once, she felt powerful and powerless.

Tessa released Rose from her embrace after the poor woman's sobs dissipated. Then she read every word once more. They struck like daggers to even her heart. Joya must've been crushed.

"I can't even express how sorry I am, Rose. May I please go inside, just for a moment? I haven't known her for very long, but I'd like to let her know I came, that I'm here."

"That's very sweet of you. I suppose that would be okay. She's creating. That's what she does when she's upset like this," Rose said. "But, please, not too long."

"I promise I'll keep it brief."

Afraid to disturb Joya's work, Tessa turned the doorknob and softly whispered, "Hello," as she slipped into the foyer. Joya, in the dining room, ignored Tessa's call. Tessa tipped toward Joya's side at the mahogany table and took a seat in one of the wing-back chairs. The brushed nickel geometric light fixture made the whole room glow.

Joya looked okay in her yoga gear, except her ponytail

seemed to sag. She had spread open her Moleskine notebook, and colored pencils were scattered around the table. Her sketch looked like the beginnings of a flower. When she glanced up, she shot Tessa a glare meant to scar her to the soul.

It'd served its purpose well.

"What are you doing here?" Joya barked, a stark change from the appreciative tenor the day before. Tessa knew why; she only hoped she could make Joya understand the truth and ask for forgiveness.

"I-I didn't mean to bother you." She stammered before replying. "I'm sorry about what happened with Todd."

"Sorry? That's pretty rich coming from you, of all people."

Thrown by Joya's damning tone, a frenzy of emotions, mostly guilt, consumed Tessa. The gutting worsened as hurt rained from Joya's eyes. She didn't know how much Joya had learned about Real Talk. Judging from her demeanor— everything.

"I'm not...what do you mean?" Tessa asked.

"I've got to give it to you," Joya applauded Tessa in slow claps. "Your little performance in your office the other day really had me fooled. I thought you cared about people...about me."

"But I—"

"I thought you were real and sincere. I thought your passion was communicating the truth to make lives better. Little did I know, you're just another mean girl, a wolf in sheep's clothing. I hate myself for trusting you, for not realizing you were nothing but a sad, fake, soulless profiteer."

Tessa gulped hard. Joya's condemnation was tough to swallow but probably deserved in some measure, she reminded herself. But one poor decision, in one span of time, didn't reflect the truth of her life.

That didn't stop the souring in her gut.

"Believe it or not, I can relate, Joya. You're angry about what Todd did to you, and you need someone to blame. But I'm not the villain here."

"You're no better than the gun manufacturer or gun store owner that takes no responsibility for the violence."

Joya's face tensed. She turned away from Tessa and grimaced as if she could no longer stomach the sight of her.

"If you hadn't sold the Real Talk line, Todd couldn't have sent it to me. He would've had to buck up the courage to break off our relationship in his own ridiculous way."

Defending herself was futile, so Tessa dropped her head in shame. Her heart ached for the pain she'd caused Joya.

"He told me he wanted to spend the rest of his life with me," she said, pounding her fist on the table.

Tessa thought she'd shifted her ire to the source of her ache. She was wrong.

"Don't you care?" She aimed the question more toward the universe before returning her focus to Tessa. "How can you make a business of words and not understand how powerful they are?"

"Whether you believe me or not, I received a card very similar to yours. The man who sent it, he devastated me at first. But also, without knowing, he saved me. I'd never have tapped into the determination, single-minded focus, or grit it took to start Keep It Real without it."

"Well, for me, it wasn't a Band-Aid. It was a bullet."

Joya spat real talk, truth Tessa couldn't deny.

Tessa had handed Todd the weapon he used to wound Joya. She'd made it possible for Todd to deliver Joya heartbreak, the same way Cody had delivered it to her.

"I'm not as strong as you are," Joya continued. "Maybe if he couldn't select a Real Talk card in the store, things would've been different. After three years of tolerating his secret phone calls, weekend disappearances, late-night texting..."

Tessa sighed. "He's not worthy of you. You're blessed with so many gifts, with so much to offer the right guy. And I think, in your heart, you know your relationship wasn't meant to last, and you knew it long before he sent you that card."

"Well, if you'd designed a card with that message, maybe that's the one he would've given to me."

Tears flash-flooded Joya's cheeks, and she closed her eyes. "Now, get out!"

Tessa froze, paralyzed. She tried to leave but her feet wouldn't move.

"I said—get out!" she barked.

Battered and bruised from the well-deserved tongue lashing, Tessa hung her head and shuffled to the door. She wrapped her hand around the doorknob while Joya lobbed a final shot. "I'm glad I quit. I never want to work with anyone like you."

Without turning, Tessa replied, "I'm so very sorry, Joya."

Two steps out of the door and the tears overwhelmed the fragile dam she'd built to hold them back. She succumbed to grief and dabbed the wetness on her face with the back of her hand.

Rose, distracted by a neighbor, missed Tessa's quick steps past her, down the porch steps, and to her car.

She jumped into the driver seat and drove a few blocks before parking in front of some random house.

Through the blur of her waterworks, she retrieved her cellphone and scanned through unanswered texts and news banners before surrendering to her one heart's desire.

She typed a text, deleted, and retyped it three times before pressing "SEND."

She collected her emotions and returned to Georgetown.

At home, she pushed her key into the lock, and a torrent of tears once again washed over her cheeks and trailed down to her chin and neck. That's when a familiar voice said, "I got your message."

Relieved, Tessa turned, sunk into his warm embrace, and buried her face into his chest.

With him, she didn't need to say thanks or apologize. With him, she didn't need words.

With him, she was at the one place where she could be Tessa, flawed, and accepted. Home.

"It's okay, Tessa," Cody said. "I'm here, baby. I'm here."

Chapter Twenty-Four

T essa

TESSA WAS HEARTBROKEN OVER JOYA, OVER THE IMPACT OF REAL Talk. She thanked the heavens that her dapper knight had come; he arrived straight out of the boardroom and into her home to relieve her misery.

Her fireplace popped with orange, yellow, and blue flames that danced along the red-hot bark. She curled up in her loveseat, awaiting Cody's return. He'd puttered in the kitchen, making her a much-needed cup of Earl Grey. It'd been some time since she'd welcomed the comfort of a man in her sanctuary, but she'd longed for his presence and understanding. He'd gifted her with what she needed. Kyle opened a breach, but Cody burst it wide open. Tonight was different, and maybe, just maybe, Cody was, too.

"Where do you keep the sugar?" he called out above the clink and clank of glasses against the granite countertop. Her teakettle rattled along with the cast-iron stove grates. "Oh, never mind. I found it. You still like a little tea with your sugar, or what?"

"No. My tastes are more refined. Hold the diabetes." She chuckled. "Stevia, please. Two packs are plenty."

"Wow," he said, as the packets ripped and rustled. "Nice coffee bar, by the way. It's comforting to see you're still the same...at least when it comes to your addictions."

"No, my addictions remain unchanged...all of them," she said. "It's my gift to humanity. I still lose all sense of decency if I don't caffeinate first thing in the morning. The coffee bar brings Starbucks a little closer to home."

"The more things change, the more they stay the same." He arrived with her tea seconds later, gently cooling the steam with soft breaths.

Tessa reached up to his towering frame and cupped the mug. She inhaled the aromatic steam and leaned back on her tweed sectional lounge; he pushed aside her mohair throw and filled the empty seat beside her.

One swallow of the warm, soothing fluid released the tension from her shoulders, relaxing her as Cody snuggled in and placed his arm around her. "Feeling any better?"

She nodded. "I'm speaking in coherent sentences. Progress." She shrugged and cast her gaze downward. The more she thought about her confrontation with Joya, the more her shame prevented her from looking Cody in the eye. "It's like I left Joya's house realizing I'm lost. Totally and completely. Somewhere between heartbreak and Keep It Real, part of me disappeared. Now I'm standing in the middle of a mystery of my own making, wondering how I arrived here, at this place, where a plan to motivate people makes them depressed and quit life?"

Between them, suspended in the silence, the question begged an answer Tessa wasn't sure she wanted to hear. Cody thrust his hand up high to offer one.

"I'm not sure I want to call on you," she replied to his gesture.

"Please? I know this one."

She nodded, giving him permission as she set her cup on the coffee table.

"Someone who doesn't know you might say you're stubborn. But I know you're passionate, brilliant, bold, courageous, and hurt."

She rubbed her arms as if she'd caught a chill.

"And your hurt isn't like a surface cut that you can heal with a Band-Aid. When you hurt, you're broken, and the bone's gotta be reset, or it won't heal right...ever. We never broke the bone; I never set things right."

"Wow. Coming from you...of all people." She revealed a sliver of a smile. "Next, you're going to tell me you're eating green vegetables."

"Absolutely," he replied. "Garlic mashed potatoes are the new broccoli."

Somehow in the midst of her sorrow, she'd found a genuine laugh that freed itself from her belly. Cody willed the impossible to be.

She gazed at him and found his light once again, the one that'd been lost for so long she wondered if it still existed. It'd returned at a time and place she'd least expected to find it.

"I hope you never lose that," he said, caressing her with his sweet gaze.

"What?"

"Your ability to laugh through your tears." He reached out with a feather-light touch and traced the line of her lips. Her body felt flush with heat. Her heartbeat quickened. She wanted more than his touch, but she resisted.

"Shh"—she whispered—"You're revealing all of my trade secrets."

He appraised her with a smoldering gaze that made her blush. A palpable heat filled the shrinking space between them. Desire and destiny drew them to each other as much as obligation and history tore them apart.

He leaned in so close she could feel the quickening beats in his chest, smell the spice in his cologne. They sat eye to eye, mouth to mouth, until...he was gone.

Cody bolted out of his seat as if an invisible hand from the heavens snatched him away and broke their trance. His abrupt move reminded her of the last remaining barrier standing between them: Chandra.

Cody lapped the living room to expand the physical distance between them, if not emotional.

"Your place is great...especially compared to the dump we used to live in. You remember?"

"How could I forget? I dunno. There's a thin line between cozy and claustrophobia. I like to think our place was the former. Cozy...lived in."

"You call it lived in. I call it in desperate need of renovation and a little crowded between the mice, crickets, and some mutant insect that flew sideways."

The conversation took a welcome turn toward small talk, her décor, Feng Shei color, and styling—a neutral pallet accentuating earthy tones that falsely promised to bring calm and stability, things that Cody's presence used to bring to her life.

She shuddered and laughed as he turned to the photo display on her side tables. From end to end, he followed her life in stages, beginning after they parted until the present day.

She felt a twinge in her stomach as he did a double-take as if searching for his missing face. She'd abandoned those photos in a pile somewhere in oblivion, and most now contained holes where his face used to be.

He stopped perusing when he reached a single framed item hanging on the wall, replicas of her first Keep It Real card collection.

"Wow, the cards that launched a dream. Do you have any idea how talented you are? How proud I am of you?" His eyes lingered. "If I'm honest, there aren't many moments I wish I could relive. We evolve from our experiences, good and bad.

Regrets are a waste of time. But if I had one do-over, I'd never send you that card. I'd pay to get that moment back."

Tessa examined her feelings as he cut himself off. She questioned whether she was ready for "the talk," wondering if they had anything to gain by confronting the could'ves, should'ves, and would'ves they'd skirted for five years. But he pushed the words out before her heart could decide what it wanted.

"Why did you—I mean, I thought we—in one minute you'd convinced me commitment was bigger than the institution. You said marriage was a staid tradition that would stifle our creativity. I called BS at first, but it didn't matter over time because I loved what we shared. The next thing I know, you ambushed me at dinner with a proposal. You pulled a total one-eighty on me without warning, and I had no idea why."

"You're right. You're absolutely right."

"Something happened to change your mind; I'm certain of it." She rested her mug on the coffee table.

He hesitated to confess it, and then he spoke. "The night before I proposed, my father called me into his office. You remember our fathers were barely speaking? The break was fresh, tempers flared. I had tunnel vision. I was so focused on us that I asked him for the Sweet Hart cards seed money without thinking."

"Wow. Some things never change."

"Exactly. Not only did he refuse me the investment, but he threatened to cut me off, trust fund and all, if I started a business with you."

"Me? He hated me that much?"

"He didn't hate you. He just didn't think you were ambitious enough for me."

"So, you didn't tell him about the business plan."

He nodded. "In his defense, he was afraid I'd leave him, too, and another fracture would leave Hart vulnerable to a takeover or an acquisition."

"It's all coming back to me. Dad loved your father. He just wanted to make a name for himself."

"Oh, I know. After a heated argument, Pops agreed to fund Sweet-Hart, if I dropped the Sweet and built it as part of Hart Enterprises. At dinner that night, he told me to give you up. You were the traitor's daughter. When he couldn't turn me against you, he worked on my sisters. They patronized him for power."

"Wow."

"Turns out, it was all a lie. It wasn't about you. It wasn't about Uncle Brian. It wasn't about Sweet Media. He'd been keeping a secret. I kept my promise not to reveal it...until right now."

Chapter Twenty-Five

T essa

CODY'S FATHER HAD CHANGED THE COURSE OF THEIR ENTIRE relationship with one night, one dinner, one secret. Tessa had always assumed he disapproved of her, of their love. Until now, she didn't know another reason for the break up existed. After all these years, Cody would finally confess the truth.

"Remember the monsoon dinner? While you were in the ladies' room, he whispered in my ear five words that changed my life forever: I'm dying of prostate cancer."

"What?"

"He was dying. Stage four. Inoperable. It turns out the feud was never about leaving. He wanted Uncle Brian to stay and take over Hart Enterprises, but he had too much pride to ask him. Maybe he loved him too much to request that he give up his Sweet Media ambitions."

"I can't believe this."

"Well, I hope you'll believe this," he began. "Before you and I fell in love, the thought of marriage gave me hives. But proposing to you filled me with indescribable...joy."

Joy? She could've fallen over with the breath from a whisper.

"I could envision us exchanging rings and dancing. I could see myself carrying you over the threshold. I wanted to propose, and I wanted you to say yes. But I fumbled my words, I know."

"You? Fumble your words? That's just crazy talk," she said with a snicker.

"It's not intentional," he continued. "I hear the words one way in my mind, and they sound different coming out of my mouth. It's my struggle. If you didn't understand that I wanted a true partnership with you, please, charge it to my head and not my heart. I figured once we got married, Hart would be—"

"Yours."

"Ours, Tessa. Once you took my name, everything I owned would've been half yours. Remember when we were ten, and I wanted to play Big Business?"

"Well, you wanted to be CEO, but you wanted me to be the secretary and didn't want to share the seat."

"Exactly."

"So, I gave you a swift kick in the family jewels to bring you to your senses."

He laughed. "When I asked you to marry me, that was me sharing the seat. I wanted to give you ownership of the company your father helped build. I wanted our families to become one. My father would've been forced to accept us or lose the only heir that wanted the throne, that would run the kingdom the way he did."

"I had no idea, Cody. But I was afraid maybe you were right. Maybe I was weak."

"Stop. You're one of the strongest people the universe ever created. I said that in anger and frustration."

"Since my mother passed away," Tessa began, "my whole world revolved around two people, two men—you and my father." She leaned forward and propped herself on her knees.

"I'd been shrouded in my father's shadow—and then yours. Everything I'd ever done had been a reflection of you and him, even our vision for Sweet-Hart cards to some extent."

"That's not true."

"Yes, it is. Rejecting your proposal was not a refusal to be your wife. I hadn't wanted anything more before you convinced me otherwise. I just didn't know myself; I didn't know my own strength—and I needed to find it. I needed to find out if I could succeed without you...heck, if I could survive without you."

"And you did. You created Keep It Real from nothing."

She glanced at the card he sent her. "Well, not exactly nothing."

"I meant, from your heart."

"Probably more from my pain."

"You were wounded. But you brought much-needed truth to people's lives, and you put food on your employees' tables."

"You can't possibly believe that. Because if you did, then why would you acquire it?"

"You think I acquired your company *despite* my pride in you?" He shook his head. "No, I bought Keep It Real *because of it.* The truth is your father is in deep financial trouble."

"What? But he never—"

"He's struggling to make payroll, and he needed a major cash infusion. That's why he sold Keep It Real to me. He received numerous inquiries, but he entrusted it to Hart because he knew I'd protect it."

She gasped, and the room began to spin. Financial trouble. Cash infusion. All this time.

"Sweet Media was deep in the red and overburdened with debt, at least until I stepped in. I offered a premium to help him. And I wanted to save your valuation by heading off rumors that I picked up a bargain."

That's why he paid the premium? Gratefulness replaced her anger. She glanced up to the heavens to thank the angels that brought him back.

"In another year or two, Sweet Media would've ceased to exist, and Keep It Real would've vanished right along with it. The truth is your revenues were keeping Sweet Media afloat. You're no failure; you never were. I would've told you sooner, but your father knew you'd never consent to leave Sweet Media if you knew he was in trouble."

Shaking her head in disbelief, Tessa pressed for more answers. She wanted to know, needed to know. "So, you bought it to help save my father?"

"No, I bought it because of you. Losing Keep It Real would've broken your spirit, your heart. And standing by and doing nothing to prevent it, that would break mine. I couldn't watch you lose everything you've worked so hard to achieve. And you may have if I didn't step in."

Holding her hand in his, he unearthed her sweetest treasure, one Tessa feared she'd never recover: her faith and trust in Cody Hart. She thought she'd lost them in what felt like an ocean of loneliness, on her own island, surrounded by loss and pain. He'd once been a twinkling star in her darkness, her comfort, her joy, and now, sitting here beside her, he was her savior.

Tears trickled down her cheeks. "Then why break it off and disappear from my life, leaving only a card?"

"My father was dying. Hart needed me. And for us to have any real chance, I had to let you go, to give you the opportunity to pursue your dream, to become the self-made woman you wanted to be. If I didn't, you would've resented me, my name, and everything branded as Hart."

Tessa pressed her hand to her heart; it'd started beating so wildly she thought it might pump out of her chest.

"Losing you was unbearable, but killing your dream—that would've been unforgivable. So, I let you go, always knowing no matter what I did, no matter who I was with at the moment, no matter where in the world I may find myself, I'd be there for you, even if you refused to need me."

For so many years, she wondered why he'd disappeared, this

beautiful man who cherished her, who believed in her. The man who, at one perfect moment in time, was the sun around which she anchored her entire world. Before now, she never quite understood how a star so brilliant could burn away so abruptly, so absolutely.

In hindsight, she understood their parting to be a mercy, an eclipse, a brief darkness to make way for the light. Fate had once more placed him before her, still loving her, still honoring her.

"Believe it or not, sometimes I walk through this world feeling invisible, you know. I mean, physically, people see me every day—but they don't really see into me, nobody does, not the way you do."

He brushed his hands over his face to conceal the tears in his eyes.

"You are the only one who truly sees me, the me inside, the me who always knows what she wants but overlooks the things that she needs. You see me. And, in the way you see me, I see *the me* I want to become."

At a loss for words, Cody smiled as he stroked her cheek with a feather-light touch. She exposed a smile that mirrored his. Then she gripped his hand and pressed his palm against her face.

Tessa whispered, "I've so missed—"

Gently, she dropped his hands and softened her voice to a hush. She hated fighting against the desire in her heart, but she must.

"You missed what?" he asked. Cody now sat on the edge of his seat, anxious for her to speak.

"I wish we could turn back time to the minute, to the second, that you lost yourself in me," he said.

He fixed his eyes on her, willing her to speak.

In the wisp of a flash, she'd embraced the idea of "us" again. The moment was fleeting—reality set in too quickly.

"Nothing," she replied. "You're with Chandra. Married in a

month. I'm not homewrecker material. I'm a front-end tire. I'm not the spare in the trunk."

"What about you and Kyle? You two seemed quite—chummy," he said, trying to deflect.

"I haven't seen dodging that adept since fifth grade. Remember little Jimmy Newman during the Hart Summer Leadership Camp?"

His laugh was hearty and deep, so she continued.

"He got slammed in the back with a dodge ball and peed himself. On the upside, he never got hit again."

They both folded over in laughter. Not that the story was funny. It wasn't. Laughing together just felt so sweet.

"I miss that."

"What?" she asked as her giggles tapered off.

"The sound of your smile. At work, sometimes I stare out the window, and I hear echoes of it in my mind."

Tessa's face warmed into a subtle blush. She shifted her gaze to the ground. "I've made so many mistakes."

He lifted her chin with his index finger. "We've both made mistakes."

"I suppose." She patted his hand one last time. "Thank God for second chances....for friendship."

"Friendship," he said flatly.

Kyle. He came into her life like an autumn breeze, cool, sweet, full of possibility. She needed him in a way. He revived feelings she thought dead. Kyle helped her first prioritize her needs above all others, but Cody made her remember the best of herself.

"Your heart is always in the right place. It's one of those things I've always loved about...you."

The "L" word pushed him upright from his slouch. "But you've got your work cut out for you. I guess that's my signal to leave."

She nodded. "That would probably be for the best, right?"

Her mind went fuzzy, and then, in an instant, it was clear. She agreed with his plan to leave, but she wanted him to stay.

He went through the motions, all of them, stood up, stretched, grabbed his suit jacket, and inched toward the door in stutter steps, seemingly thinking and not thinking, almost saying something and then not saying anything.

He grabbed the doorknob, but he never got the chance to open it. She pressed her hand against his to keep him from leaving. "Please. Don't go. I know I don't have the right to...I mean, you don't owe me...the thing is I—"

"Shhh..." He pressed his finger to her lips to hush her. "You don't even have to ask, Tessa. I don't want to go. I need you, too."

Without a second's hesitation, he pulled her into his arms. His kiss was low and then deep, intensifying with every ebb and flow of their lips, bodies, and minds. Their hands roamed wildly, driven by a tide of emotion too powerful to stem.

Entangled in each other's arms, they drifted in uncoordinated steps to the couch. After allowing the passion to burn for a little longer, they made the only kind of love they needed to make at that moment—they held each other close, fell asleep wrapped up in each other's arms with only their shoes removed.

Tessa spooned against him, knowing they'd come a long way but grateful they'd refrained from going too far. Everything that happened mattered to the future, but nothing happened that they couldn't take back.

The next morning, she awakened cradled in his arms. As her world crumbled around her, he gifted her with the one thing she needed more than the sweetness of his kiss or the comfort of his arms. Without a requirement or request, he gave her his presence, a sense of security. Five years had passed, but their love remained unchanged. All doubt and uncertainty about his heart dissipated. The newfound confidence filled her with the strength to do what she needed to do next.

Tessa slipped out from under him, tipped into the bathroom,

and called Mia. She had a plan to fix the trust she'd broken, and the task started with Keep It Real.

"Sorry to ring you so early, but I need you to set up a team meeting for this morning. Let's make it ten," she whispered.

"With creative?" Mia replied.

"With everyone."

"Mind if I ask what this is about?"

"Not at all," Tessa said, making her bestie cling to the pause. "We've got to get ready. Changes. We're making some changes. Big ones."

Chapter Twenty-Six

C ody

CODY SLOSHED THROUGH THE MELTING MUCK OUTSIDE AND INTO HIS office, cheesing from ear to ear, his pinstriped suit barely containing him. Even in the city's frigidness, the winter sun warmed Cody's face as much as the night spent with Tessa warmed his soul.

"Good morning!" he sang as he floated through the office.

Ms. Dee and everyone with half a clue judged him with suspicious side-eyes as he passed, looks he tried to ignore. He was feeling Tessa's vibe and kill it they would not.

After settling in his executive chair, he spun around to face the window. He leaned back and clasped his hands behind his head, allowed his mind to drift and mentally replay the night in slow-motion—how she pulled him so close, not even air could stand between them, how he'd stood witness to her tears and dried them, how he sensed her pain and relieved it.

He became the man he should be, the man he wanted to be.

Instinctively, he resumed his role as the man who really saw her, who saw the woman she allowed few others to know.

His stomach rippled and flopped as he recalled the feel of her body pressed against his, at the thought of everything about Tessa, the way his hand followed the curve of her hip, to how she twisted her body to hide her subdued snores, to the way she smelled of lavender and jasmine.

In a dream come to life, he awakened next to her and indulged in the softness of her body as it spooned against his in a still-perfect fit.

And she always made him laugh with no effort, like the moment her eyes bulged when she woke up in his arms, apparently shocked he was still by her side.

He couldn't blame her. He should've left, but he couldn't let go.

Chandra forbade him to return home, but Tessa made him remember home is where the heart is, and his heart lie with her. He wouldn't go back, not now, not ever.

After urging Tessa into a hot shower to wash off her sadness, he lost himself in her kitchen, the one place outside of her bedroom where he could display a few new tricks.

"You cooked all of this...for me?" Tessa said, witnessing Cody's culinary genius.

Wrapped in a thick terrycloth robe, Tessa wandered into the kitchen, searching for her morning coffee, and found him wearing her "Kiss the Cook" apron. He'd fried spinach and cheese omelets and homemade hash browns, a long way from the Captain Crunch and toaster pastries he used to serve during their lean days.

"You know how I do," he said in his less than humble brag while thumbing his nose.

"Yes, I know exactly how you do." She waved her hand over her trashcan's motion sensor to pop the lid and peer inside.

"What are you looking for?"

"The delivery bags."

"If you don't sit down and eat! I cooked this beautiful meal, and you're in here talking smack. The only thing you need to worry about is smacking your lips."

She devoured the meal with gusto.

Later, she emerged ready for the office. He couldn't recall what she wore. He only remembered how she looked. Tessa glowed, and her natural-colored lips turned into a wide smile as she shook her head. He was mesmerized by the way her cocoa skin could be so perfect and faultless without a hint of make-up.

If life were kind and perfect, he'd have been free to ask her on a date, and, with each day that passed, he would consume every second, hour, minute of her time. But unfinished business, from both sides, stood between them.

The sound of quick steps toward his office snapped him out of his daze. He paused in the brief silence and then hummed K4. Could it be Tessa? Could she be that anxious to see him again? He was eager for her to enter. But the figure that appeared in his doorway didn't belong to Tessa.

"Chandra?"

Her greeting served as a less than pleasant surprise from a visitor he least expected to see.

She pulled off her all-weather coat to reveal what used to be his favorite mini-dress and knee-high boots. She wanted to get his attention, but someone else had beat her to it.

"Surprised to see me!" she barked. A few surviving flakes of snow sat on her shoulder, so she hadn't been in Hart for long. A quick look around his tidy, pristine office would reveal he hadn't spent the night there. He queued up potential excuses, but only one option sounded right.

"What brings you to my office this morning?"

"I told you not to come home that night, and now you act as if you forgot where you live. Last time I checked, we were still getting married."

He wanted to ask her what time she'd last checked, but he tightened his lips.

"You ordered me out of a home I own, with zero discussion. Last time I checked, that's not what couples do. Now, you want to be Chatty Chandra, and you expect me to talk?"

"Don't," she warned him, cutting the air with her hand for emphasis. "Don't you even try to turn this around on me. You know exactly why I reacted the way I did."

"Tessa and Kyle?" he asked facetiously.

"No." She found a seat on his couch and crossed her legs to reveal the shapely stems he used to find irresistible. Used to. "Just Tessa. I'm not brand new, Cody. You're distant, and I'd be a fool not to connect the dots between you and her."

"I'm not sure what you think happened at that dinner, but what you saw was a bitter clash between business rivals."

"Nice try. I was born *at night*, not *last night*. What I saw was unfinished business between two ex-lovers who still have feelings for one another. Otherwise, neither of you would be so bothered and angry."

"I'm neither bothered nor angry, except by the fact that you visited Tessa and told her I bought her company as a tax write-off. For a realtor who claims to stay in her lane, you certainly veered out of yours."

"You spoke to Tessa?"

"Of course, I did. I'm her CEO."

"Is that all you are to her?" He shifted his gaze and his throat thickened. Instead of saying what he wanted to say, the way he wanted to say it, he pawed at his scalp.

"Mmm-hmm. And I don't believe you, Cody. Not for a second. I'm willing to overlook this, whatever this is, because we love each other," she paused. "You do still love me, right?"

"Of course, I love you...I do." He left a few seconds of silence because there was an exception to his declaration—a major one.

"And I value what we have built together," she continued. "This little thing is nothing but a childhood fantasy of what used to be between you and Tessa. It'll fade away. What's left will be you and me. Then our lives will go back to normal."

She reached out to him, and he came to her, but not for the reason she wanted.

The problem in their equation was not so much in the subtraction than the addition. A new factor had created a complex equation where the simple one between Cody and Chandra no longer existed. He thought his love for Tessa had dissipated, but somehow, even in the face of his neglect, the roots had deepened and grown stronger.

He pulled away and met her gaze with his. As she leaned in to kiss him, he jerked back. The last time they kissed was the last time they kissed.

"Listen, Chandra. Please don't interrupt before I'm finished. I love you; there's no question about that. But I'm no longer in love with you. Honestly, I'm not certain I ever was...not just with you, but with anyone since Tessa."

"Excuse me?"

"The fact is I've been questioning my feelings for you ever since you started moving in. Maybe before then. I'm second-guessing everything I've done, every move I made since the day I broke up with Tessa. I never stopped loving her...and I still haven't."

"You can't mean that. What have we been doing for the past two years? Playing house?"

His heart collapsed in his chest as she frayed at the seams. He had long fantasized his and Chandra's parting would leave them both unscathed. Her tears and trembling relieved him of his illusion almost immediately, bringing to bear the heavy weight of every word he was about to say.

"Our adventure in getting engaged revealed we're not made for one another. I never set out to waste your time. I'm guilty of refusing to admit the truth to myself... at least until now. Please know, I'll reimburse your family for every penny."

"You can't be serious."

"You and Tessa are so different, opposites. She was so out of control, and you were a one-eighty. I truly believe that's what I needed, wanted, at that time. Not now."

"You still need me."

"We're right in so many ways, but not in enough ways to make a marriage. We could pretend every day, but you deserve someone who accepts you as enough, and, despite my failings, so do I."

"It's this easy for you? You can walk away as if I never existed? Because I can't...I won't."

He shook his head. "The old me wouldn't have the courage to confront you with this. The old me would've written a letter or sent a card. I'm trying to stand here and face the pain I've caused. This is one of the most difficult conversations I've ever had, especially with someone I care about. I didn't go looking for this."

"I beg to differ. Not only did you go looking for it, but you also bought it. You bought Keep It Real, and you got Tessa in the bargain. Congratulations."

Chapter Twenty-Seven

T essa

A FROSTY DROP FROM THE WINTERY MIX FALLING OUTSIDE TESSA'S front door plopped on the end of her nose as she headed to work. After her revelatory night with Cody, she lifted her chin into the snow and allowed it to blanket her face.

Everything appeared differently today.

Snowflakes didn't fall; they danced. The chill in the winds lost its bite. She flashed cheesy grins in the faces of every passing stranger, and she found certainty in every doubt. For her, the universe seemed to take an advantageous shift in her favor.

For the first time in a long time, her life's journey no longer felt like an uphill slog. She might be a greyhound on the track, but the rabbit was in reach. Now, she floated on air, on the sweet memories of the night before.

Rather than despise one another, they desired each other. He bought Keep It Real not to sink Tessa but to save her. He put his money, reputation, and sanity on the line to spare her the heart-break of losing her life's work.

Cody predicted she'd face consequences over Real Talk. He could've offered I-told-you-sos, self-righteous finger-pointing; instead, he gave her what she needed most—his ears, his presence, his shoulders, his arms, his compassion. What he offered meant so much more than the feel of a bare body against hers. He helped her to feel safe and protected.

Whatever bliss they'd enjoyed in the comfort of her bed, the reality was never far from her mind. She gobbled down the hot breakfast he served with an extra side of guilt.

One night, however beautiful it may have been, did not change his commitment to Chandra. Tessa reminded herself of the inconvenient fact before they parted.

"I can't find the words to thank you for being here for me when I needed it most. But this is where, whatever this is, has to end. It must."

Tessa waited for him to agree, take a graceful bow for his good deeds, and make a speedy exit.

She never anticipated him grabbing her hands, gazing into her eyes with a wounded expression, and asking her, "Are you saying this because you don't want to be with me? Or because you want to be with Kyle?"

She tilted her head in disbelief. Me and Kyle. "Really? After everything that happened between us? This isn't about me, and it's certainly not about Kyle. It's about you and Chandra."

His eyes pleaded for her understanding before his lips spoke aloud the symphony to her ears. "Maybe nothing sexual happened between us last night, but make no mistake about it—too much has happened. I'm going to make this right—today. I promise."

Tessa couldn't restrain her smile, and her pettiness went into overdrive when she considered ways for him to break it off with the woman who tried to convince her that Cody bought her company as a tax write-off.

A small part of her hoped he'd just send the heifer a card—the small part.

She'd leave the heartbreak to Cody and focus on her own drama—laying to rest the bitter witch in her greeting card business.

Tessa entered her office with a deep breath and prayer. She wore a reddish silk scarf to signal the change she'd prepared to effect.

She dropped her briefcase and coat in her office and wrung her hands while mentally practicing her speech. Her trek through the creative studio ended in the conference room, where her team awaited her arrival.

She entered to anxious faces. She watched their bodies pucker—and it tickled her.

"Good morning, everyone," she announced. "Relax, okay? You're not laid off or fired. Neither am I."

The group released a collective sigh and breathed, making her chuckle. "Today's meeting isn't about you. It's about me."

Eyebrows on half the people in the room scrunched, betraying their confusion; the other half of the room snapped straight in their seats.

"This isn't easy for me to admit, and you may never hear this again...but I'm wrong."

With a less-than-subtle touch of sarcasm, Mia clutched her heart and dropped her jaw, to which Tessa responded with an eye roll and pursed lips. "Really?"

A round of laughter lightened the heaviness that threatened to suffocate the room.

"Anyway, let's get serious for a minute," she said, which ceased the chatter. "I'm guilty of a few sins; disingenuousness and selfishness are the least of them. I've invested so much of my money and myself to build this team that we can call family. But I've failed in the one thing we owe our family—honesty.

"The news about Hart acquiring Keep It Real left me devastated and scared. Not just for myself but because whatever happened to me would flow down to you. Years ago, Cody and I shared a relationship that ended badly. He left me in a dark place, and there I created Keep It Real. I was scared of what he might do to the company. I feared you guys would quit, so I made mistakes, bad decisions. I approved Real Talk out of fear."

A few eyes bulged and murmurs filled the stunned silence.

"The fact is—I never meant to launch the line. I was trying to buy myself some time—to keep you from quitting while conspiring to get my company back. While I expected some blowback, I'd planned to keep it brief, even if I drained my account to guarantee it. I gave zero thought to the messaging we were putting out into the world.

"Last night, I learned that a Real Talk card pushed a recipient off the edge of a breakdown and into a deep depression that made her quit her job...and give up hope for her future."

A collective gasp echoed around the room.

By now, tears streamed down Tessa's face. "I was gutted by the news. Though some may try to convince me I'm not at fault, you'd be wrong."

Everyone shook their heads no, but her heart said yes.

"As the gatekeeper for Real Talk, I am wholly responsible, and for one simple reason: words matter. My words matter. They matter in my texts. They matter in my Facebook posts and tweets. Above all, they matter in the cards we manufacture. I own my part in what happened."

Her audience was captured by the passion in her message.

"Yes, we have the right to say whatever we want, but we must accept the consequences when someone listens. To expect freedom without consequences is not only irresponsible; it's the height of cowardice."

Mia handed her a Kleenex, which she stretched across her fingers and dabbed against her eyes. "I hope someday you can forgive me," she continued. "With that said, my next announcement should come as no surprise. All new production on the

Real Talk line ends today. It's nearly sold out, and we're going in a new direction."

She walked to the whiteboard and first scribbled "kinder and gentler" amid a flurry of murmurs and whispers. When she finished, the board read, "Connect. With Hart!"

"This is our new direction. Maybe for the first time, I'm spearheading an effort that will use your brilliance for the greater good. 'Connect. With Hart' will contain smart, uplifting messages to complement our original Keep It Real cards, which are here to stay."

A sea of smiles greeted her, welcomed her enthusiasm and ideas.

"This new line includes a specially abled collection under production by a junior creative team that I'm mentoring at Hart headquarters. And this brings me to my next announcement— we'll be moving to our new offices inside of a month."

The team exchanged a new round of awkward glances.

"I now realize fighting this acquisition means battling against the best interest of the company. That stops now. Hart has a beautiful facility set up very similarly to what we have here. Not only will this move save operating expenses and overhead for Sweet Media, but it will give us the financial room to strengthen the company as we expand our market share."

That was the message that broke the silence. Now murmurs and muffled grumbles bubbled across the room.

"And, if you can find it in your hearts to forgive me, I promise you I will lead with strength and heart, no pun intended. We're going to the next level...together. On the leading edge, where success lives."

An awkward silence and dead-eye stares swelled to a few slow claps and a standing ovation. In her gratefulness and relief, she pressed her hand against her heart and bowed her head as if offering prayer and thanks.

After the meeting broke and the team dissipated, she met Mia outside the conference room door.

"One terrific speech. I'm proud of you," Mia turned her voice down to a whisper. "So, I want the truth. What got into you last night? Or should I say whom?"

Tessa smirked. "I refuse to dignify your question with an answer...at least, not right this minute. I was so busy letting the words pour out of me that I didn't even tell Cody we were moving. I should probably do that."

"Let's meet for coffee...unless your plans change. One never knows what will happen during a visit to Hart Enterprises," Mia replied with a sideways glance.

"Don't give me that look," Tessa snapped playfully. For the first time since the meeting began, her mouth stretched into a wide smile. She almost bubbled out of her skin.

Not an hour later, Tessa arrived at Cody's suite. With his secretary away from her desk, she walked into the reception area unnoticed. From outside his office door, she heard Chandra and Cody embroiled in a heated discussion.

That's when the heartbreaking words passed Cody's lips.

Keep It Real Cards

Licensed to Drive!
Congratulations on Getting Your Driver's Permit.
Now You're Ready to Explore on Your Own!

Let's Keep It Real—I've seen your driving, and, well...you better call GEICO.

Chapter Twenty-Eight

T essa

SHE STOOD OUTSIDE CODY'S OFFICE DOOR AND CONCEALED HER presence. As he faced Chandra head-on, Tessa could almost feel the chill between them.

"I'm not sure what you think happened at dinner, but what you saw was a bitter clash between business rivals," Cody said.

"I'm neither bothered nor angry, except by the fact that you visited Tessa and told her I bought her company as a tax write-off. For a realtor who claims to stay in her lane, you certainly veered out of yours."

Tessa started to walk away thinking that Cody only said what he needed to speak at the moment to diffuse the volatile situation. But she stopped when she realized that his attempt clearly wasn't working.

"Of course, I love you...I do," she heard Cody say.

She waited in vain for the "but." It never came. All sound dissipated except the crush of her breaking heart. She blamed herself for believing in him again, for trusting in him, and now this.

She should've walked away; she should've run, but her feet mounted to the floor. They'd paralyzed her. She couldn't move. Her mind swirled in deafening confusion until the words that flung the final dagger broke through.

"And I value what we have built together," Chandra continued. "Whatever this thing is between you and Tessa, it'll fade away. What's left will be you and me. Then our lives will go back to normal."

She'd heard enough, but she hadn't seen enough until one last glance revealed Chandra's leaning in to kiss the lips she thought belonged to her once again. Enough was enough.

The speed at which she deflated from her high wilted her. He'd wrecked her, dragged her from beguiled to betrayed in less than a blink.

At first, she took tepid steps out the door, then she took off running to somewhere, anywhere, as far as she could get from Cody.

Her eyes rained and vision blurred as she trucked down the hall, unable to escape the memory of their voices. She ran out of steam deep in the Hart executive suites. As a child, her father warned her that evil lurked there. As an adult, she came to learn that's where the true bitter witches skulked. She turned to retrace her steps, and a familiar shrill sent a chill through her that ached down to her toenails and cut like a razor into her skin.

"Tessa!" the cold, vicious voice called out. "Tessa Sweet!"

One of the Devilment Twins, otherwise known as Cody's sisters Regina and Renee. They emerged from their office doorways. Cody had strategically located their suites on opposite sides of Hart headquarters, a physical reflection of the divide in their relationship. They came from the same family playing for opposing sides.

The twins were cloaked in thousand-dollar suits and bared

their teeth, so they looked more like rabid dogs than smiling women, just as she'd always remembered them.

Five minutes younger, Regina had cut her formerly back-length hair to the shoulder and wore a small diamond in her nose. Renee was slightly less lethal with longer hair.

"Renee and Regina." Tessa made an about-face to give herself a moment of pause. She tried to cool her anger and sadness and then fumbled her words. "I, uh..."

"You okay?" Renee asked Tessa, who was trying to make her escape.

"Oh, I'm fine," Tessa called over her shoulder. "Good seeing you again." It wasn't. "I should—" She gestured toward the elevators.

She found no pleasure in seeing them. Not in any way, shape, or form, and she could feel her mouth twist in disdain. But that didn't stop Renee from calling out to her yet again. "Wait, please."

Tessa stopped cold in her tracks. They'd known one another since they were kids, and the word "please" had never passed their lips in her presence. She assumed the term had been forbidden in the lair.

Forcing a smile into her lips, she turned and said, "Yes? What is it?"

"We'd like to talk to you for a minute. It's important," Regina said.

"And it will be well worth five minutes of your time," Renee added.

Tessa took labored steps in their direction until she reached the interior of Regina's posh office. They joined each other's sides and offered her a choice of executive guest chairs. She took the one closest to the door.

"Make yourself comfortable."

She couldn't find less comfort if snakes were slithering under her chair. It was terrible enough facing two cobras ready to strike head-on.

Renee sat next to her and Regina across from her. In an awkward silence, she waited for them to speak. Just as she opened her mouth to ask why they wanted to meet with her. Regina launched into 'the talk.' "Let us cut to the chase. We want to offer you the opportunity to regain control of your company."

Tessa's eyebrow scrunched.

"We want to make you a deal you can't refuse."

"Why?" Tessa asked.

"To be quite honest, you've got something we need. To us, they're worth the price of Keep It Real," Regina said. She was much more beautiful than her scowl would suggest.

"They're?" Tessa replied.

"We need your votes," Renee followed.

Tessa had understood the power of the proxy from the moment her father gave her control of them. She just never expected the twins to lower themselves to deal with her.

Mr. Hart had intended for her father to use the power in Hart's best interests, whatever they may be. Maybe it was in Hart's best interest for Keep It Real to leave.

"What do you mean, you need my votes? Why?"

"To be frank, we're seizing control of Hart Enterprises, one way or another," Regina said. "Obviously, your votes could make that feat considerably easier. In exchange, we would return Keep It Real Cards to you—and erase your father's debt to Hart Enterprises."

The offer left Tessa flabbergasted. All she could manage to say was, "Wow."

She didn't trust the machine, not the one that tried to put her father out of business. What would they do to her business once they freed her?

"Furthermore, we'll ensure your future success by eliminating the Hart Greeting Card division. We're getting rid of it. Then we'll divert Hart Card resources to our own acquisition —LookBook."

They'd answered the question without her having to ask. But

her next question, "How?" flowed past a knot formed in her throat.

"The formal vote on the acquisition has yet to take place. Cody's been operating as if the purchase is a done deal because your father always voted with him. But the votes are now yours to use as you see fit," Regina said.

"I think it's obvious that we are adamantly opposed to the acquisition. No offense to you," Renee added.

Affronted, she begged to differ. "Yes, an offense to me." Tessa jerked back her head and tilted, stunned by their detachment. She wasn't pleased with their conspiring for obvious reasons, but for them to imply her business was somehow an albatross to Hart was an exaggeration (at least) and insulting (at worst).

"Point taken. The fact is Cody paid a premium for a struggling company. A bad business decision that we need to correct. Cody's judgment is clouded, and, frankly, he's not operating in Hart's best interest."

"Is that right?" Tessa snapped, unable to restrain the bite in her voice. "And you presume that I'm highly motivated to make a trade?"

"Aren't you?" Regina said through tight lips. "Well, I confess, I wouldn't have called you in here today unless I believed so."

Her narrowed eyes suggested she'd prepared to deal the knockout blow. "Besides losing control of your life's work, Chandra's and Cody's marriage must be difficult for you. From what we understand, the wedding's just around the corner. You've been apart for five years, but watching them together can't be easy to stomach, especially because you're still *unmarried and alone*."

Ouch. Her words cut like a machete strike, especially after watching the final betrayal play out in Cody's office.

"This time next year, they'll be man and wife," Renee said, adding a crippling body shot to the deep-cutting wounds. "I suppose that's the bright side, huh? If you get your company back, you can move on, perhaps with Kyle? He's a good man."

Little did Things One and Two know, their messages had plucked all the right strings. Tessa wanted out. If she never saw Cody again, it would be too soon.

Still, she played it cool. "I'll take your offer into consideration. When is the board vote?"

"We've called an emergency meeting. It's tomorrow."

Her mind flashed back to Cody's and Chandra's near-kiss. "Good. Draw up the agreement, and I'll have my attorney look it over before the vote. If you've structured it as you've pitched it here today, then you'll have nothing to worry about."

Their smirks signaled victory as Tessa found her way to the door and fled the lair. She was conflicted.

Hurting Cody had never been her plan, but escaping the pain of watching him marry Chandra was a necessity, especially after the night Tessa and Cody shared.

Once again feeling dizzy from circling the drain, she prayed for one thing and one thing only—to survive the next day without laying eyes on Cody's duplicitous mug.

CODY GAZED OUT OF HIS OFFICE WINDOW AND WATCHED CHANDRA'S Benz break the snow's smoothness with tire tracks. She left heartbroken, but now she could begin the process of separating the lives they had not so long ago joined together.

Plate from Plate. Towel from towel.

Her Nespresso from his Keurig.

What they'd just begun to unite would be parted within a matter of a few short days. The memories with Tessa tempered any pain he might've endured. Holding her in his arms, comforting her as she lay next to him, reminded Cody of the man he wanted to be.

"Deep in thought?" Kyle said, startling Cody out of his solitude. "I noticed Chandra leaving. She didn't look happy."

"Your assessment is accurate." Cody turned and grimaced. "She's gone."

"You say that as if it's forever."

"It is. The engagement is off." Cody hesitated to elaborate more. Rather, he refocused his sights on the object of Kyle's affection, wondering if Tessa would finally break the news to his best friend; her heart was taken.

"I need to run over to Keep It Real," Cody said. "I've got something important to discuss with Tessa." *Last night.*

"If you've got a moment to spare, we need to talk," Kyle said, taking a seat. "I'm here to warn you."

Cody followed his lead.

"I've been so focused on the integration," Kyle said, "that I lost my focus on something more important...the board meeting."

Cody dismissed Kyle's concern with a hand wave. "What are you talking about? We've got the votes. It's in the bag."

"Not necessarily. It seems your sisters have drummed up more support. Unfortunately, neither you nor they hold a controlling interest. Mr. Sweet's votes will be the deciding factor."

"I think we'll be okay." Cody smiled inside but was careful to temper his reaction. Tessa held her father's shares, and she would never give them a proxy, especially after last night.

Kyle scrunched his eyebrows, confused over Cody's lack of concern. "Don't you think you should speak to your sisters? They could oust you as CEO."

"It's not going to happen," he declared. "But thanks for the warning." Kyle's skeptical expression remained steady. "You've got to trust me on this one. I've got this under control."

Kyle exhaled and tightened his lips as if forcing himself to stay silent. "If you say so."

"I do. The best thing you can do for me right now is check up on Joya and please ask Ms. Dee to send flowers. Also, put some fire under Facilities to prepare the Keep It Real space. Something tells me we'll need it to be ready in short order."

"Tessa told you that?" Kyle asked.

"Not specifically. But it's my hope that she's coming around," Cody said to his dumbfounded friend. "You're full of questions today. Just take care of it."

Kyle arched his eyebrows and let out a frustrated breath. "Roger that." He offered a two-finger salute. "Will that be all, Captain?"

Cody laughed. "Man, if you don't scram? See what you can find out about my sisters. I'll concede to one thing: they're always most dangerous when they're quiet. But I really need to pay a visit to the Sweet campus. It's important."

Cody trekked through Sweet's creative studios with the corners of his lips curved upward in a pleasing bend.

He smiled at the hope that this visit would be one of his last times at Sweet Media. Soon, she'd relocate to where she belonged—in Hart's executive offices.

For now, he'd focus on what he'd do the minute he laid eyes on her—close her office door, take her into his arms, and warm her up for the date he'd envisioned for later that night if she was amenable.

He rounded the hall toward her office, spotted Mia, and greeted her with an energetic wave.

She didn't return the favor, not even close.

In fact, Tessa's best friend didn't crack the slightest of smiles. If she had laser vision, she could've burned a hole the size of a moon crater through his torso.

His eyebrows scrunched in confusion as he passed her desk and entered friendlier territory.

The sight of Tessa's face caused his smile to widen to the point at which he had no more teeth to expose. He waited for her expression to reflect his elation, but it never did. Her eyes narrowed, and her mouth squeezed tight, quite the opposite of what he expected.

"Hey, you okay?" he asked.

She nodded and let out an exasperated breath as she palmed her forehead. "Yeah, I've got a headache; I can't seem to shake it."

Pain permeated her expression, but he couldn't discern the source. She appeared tense and uncomfortable. He wished he had the power to make her hurt go away.

He walked behind her, gripped her shoulders, trying to let the magic of his touch release the tension.

At first, her head fell back against his chest, and she leaned on him. Then she abruptly pulled away and took quick steps across the room to escape him. She'd moved as far as possible, as fast as she could without breaking into a full-out sprint. She turned toward him, appearing flustered, but she said nothing.

"Are you ok—what's wrong?" he asked.

"We should probably keep things professional in the office, you know, in case one of our staff walks in."

"You're kidding, right? That's one of the perks of being the boss." He started toward her, but she stopped him with "the hand."

"Tessa, what's going on? Did I do something?"

She opened her mouth to speak but quickly clammed up. Then she closed her eyes and took a deep breath. "Listen, what we shared last night was...*nice*."

"Nice?" he said in disbelief. "Tessa!"

"Yes. Nice is a positive word, and I appreciate you being there for me. Truly. Your presence meant more to me than you'll ever know, but after today—"

"After today, what?" She'd left him completely confused by her reversal. He struggled to keep his footing and took a seat. "Did...did something happen?"

She tightened her lips again. "I think we should...let's just forget last night ever happened."

"What if I don't want to? What if I want to remember it every day—for the rest of my life?"

"I've got a sneaking suspicion you'll have more important things to think about. You'll recover quickly."

"What are you saying?" he asked, now exasperated. He didn't understand what could've happened to cause this stark one-eighty. "Be honest with me, Tessa. Why are you doing this?"

She glanced down at her watch and ignored his question.

"Listen, I've got a meeting in ten minutes. I don't mean to be rude, but..."

"You want me to show myself out? Are you kidding me? Like...you're showing me the exit?"

She held up her wrist and tapped the face of her watch.

After snapping out of his stunned paralysis, he turned to leave and stopped in his tracks. "My sisters invited you to the vote, didn't they?"

She didn't answer.

He turned and glared at her, and she bowed her head in apparent shame. That's when it struck him to ask the question he never thought he'd need to ask. "Can I still count on your support? This change...it's not...you're not going to allow Regina and Renee to take Hart away from me, are you?"

Again, she didn't answer. She replied to him by holding up her watch.

A soulless robot looked back at him. The light in her eyes from the night before had dimmed, dissipated into nothing. Now, a stranger stood in front of him, someone he couldn't depend on to do right by him.

He'd dealt a few blows, but he'd never been on the receiving end of a knockback like this.

Karma traveled on slow paths with winding turns, but Tessa's move was proof positive that her pace was steady and relentless. Karma had caught up to him in her most perfect time. If Tessa's heartache reflected even a fraction of the brokenness he felt, then his regret had deepened in more ways than one. Maybe he'd finally gotten what he deserved.

A wave of regret washed over Cody as he began to mourn the losses of Hart Enterprises and Tessa—the only two loves of his life.

Chapter Twenty-Nine

T essa

TESSA SURVEYED THE KINGDOM OF KEEP IT REAL ONE LAST TIME before heading to her car. Her stomach bound in knots, and her nerves jittered. She planned to make one stop before her later trip to Hart Enterprises for the vote.

She stood a mere three hours from attending the board meeting that would return ownership of Keep It Real to her hands, the hand in which it belonged.

Funny how life changed in an instant. She'd scheduled initial pitches for 'Connect. With Hart' today, a move she'd put on hold. She hoped her surprise announcement later that day would bring relief and cheers: Ownership of Keep It Real would be restored to Sweet Media, which would be debt-free.

Back at Joya's home, Rose allowed Tessa inside, and she left to make a grocery store run. Beyond the front door, she noticed Calvin nodding off on the family room couch as she took tepid steps into the dining room where Joya was still working. She braced herself for more anger.

Tessa had nothing to gain, no hope for relief from her guilt; she just wanted to do the right thing.

Upon laying eyes on Joya, Tessa noticed the return of color in her cheeks, light in her eyes, and the perky in her ponytail. The energetic young woman who visited her office was on the mend, seemingly in more ways than one.

"I come in peace," Tessa said, easing toward Joya's dining room table.

Joya struggled to restrain her smile, but a slight one broke through despite her best efforts. "Thank you."

"Thank me?" Tessa jerked back her head. She was stunned after the brutal dismissal she'd received during her previous visit. "But why?"

"For coming back despite my appalling behavior. For everything. I can't even tell you how sorry I am about the other day."

She waved at Tessa, gesturing for her to come closer. They both clung to the uncomfortable silence; Joya needed to speak, and Tessa wanted to apologize.

"I know it's trite to say, 'it wasn't you, it was me,' but it wasn't you...it was me. In a moment of frustration, you were an easy target, a safe place to direct my frustration and anger. In truth, only one person deserved it."

"Todd?"

She shook her head and pointed her thumb into her own chest. "He and I checked all the right boxes. We had the right look, the right pedigree, but we never laughed or dreamed together. We weren't meant to be. I've known, almost from the beginning, but one thing solidified it for me."

"What?"

"When I sunk to my lowest point, right before I...well...you know. There was one person I wanted beside me, and, to even my surprise, it wasn't Todd. There I was, raw, messy, heartbroken, and the only one I wanted to call was—"

"Let me guess...Calvin?"

Joya smiled love at the sound of his name. She twinkled like holiday lights, in a way Tessa had never thought her capable.

"He came straight to my side, and he's hardly left me since. Funny, isn't it?"

"I've always found true beauty in the midst of ruin," Tessa said. "It's like at the moment your life falls spectacularly apart, you receive the vision and clarity you need to choose the salvageable broken pieces and then use those to build something new, something stronger, something better."

"It is funny, isn't it?" Joya repeated.

Tessa's mind immediately flashed to Cody. In her moment of ruin, she wanted only one person by her side. Regardless of her attraction to...others, he was the only man she wanted to witness her brokenness. She wanted one man to be the ear she needed to listen, to be her shoulder to cry on, to be the arms wrapped around her for safety. What Cody did, the man he became for her at rock bottom, meant something to her. As her mind flashed back to his wounded expression the day before, being there for her meant something to him, too.

"Anyway, I have a reason for showing up here. I wanted to let you know that I'm ending the Real Talk line."

"Because of me?"

"Because it's the right thing to do," Tessa said. "And I refuse to accept any resignation. I want you back to work as soon as you're up to it. How could the team survive without your dry wit and charm?"

"I don't ever want to find out," Joya said.

Tessa smiled and reached out to pat Joya's hand. "Well, I think it's time for me to make my exit. Just let us know when you're ready to come back."

"Thank you...for everything. I mean it."

Tessa's renewed spirit was short-lived. She departed with a smile on her face, but a heavy heart soon found her upon her return to the office.

Even with the Joya visit, she had an hour and a half to kill before the board meeting.

Again and again, her mind churned over what she would say, how she would behave, how she would conjure up the courage to face Cody as she betrayed him.

She wished she'd created a card for such an occasion.

In the past, whenever she needed to tap into negative emotions while creating cards or building emotional walls, she'd rely on flashbacks to the moment she read the card that Cody delivered.

Now, something had changed.

Unbeknownst to Tessa, and without notice, the memory of that pain had been replaced. Hurt and anguish over her uncere-monious dumping had been supplanted by the feeling of his arms around her during her fall to rock bottom; he gifted his presence and security when she needed him most.

He could've been anywhere in the world, including with Chandra, yet, without begging or urging, he chose to fill the cold, empty space beside her.

At once, he'd made her remember...and forget.

She busied herself for a bit, then plopped in her seat and clenched her eyes shut. She tried to push the thought of the vote from her mind as the sound of footsteps drew closer to her office door. Part of her hoped it was Cody.

After a knock, a man spoke. "Meditating? Or clicking your heels three times to get back to Kansas?"

The corners of her lips curved upward at the sound of Kyle's voice. She opened her eyes and allowed herself to see him, perhaps for the first time.

"Hello there, Stranger."

"Can I come in? Or do you need to get back to Toto?"

"Please." She chuckled and waved him inside. "It's good to see you. The past couple of days have been...phew!"

"I'm sure. I tried to call you and even stopped by the other day, but you've been busy. I was concerned."

"The eternal plight of the working executive. As successful as we are, none of us has figured out how to be everywhere at once." She walked to the front of her desk and leaned against the corner. "I've had a lot going on. A member of my team quit after a bit of a breakdown, but she's okay. I just hope I can convince her to come back to work."

"Well, that's a relief, but I thought you were avoiding me...or worse."

Tessa gave him the side-eye. "Worse?"

"To be honest, I feared you might be falling for Cody again."

She returned to her chair to give herself time to come up with a response. "You might've been right for a blink of a second...we have a lot of history. But Cody is firmly in love with Chandra, a fact I confirmed when I overheard them professing their love for one another yesterday. They're still an item and going full steam ahead with the wedding. The time has come to move on."

"You sure about that?"

"My ears don't lie."

He slumped back in his seat, expelled a deep breath, and locked his shining eyes on her. "Does that mean I can take you to dinner again? We can take it slow. Maybe this time we can squeeze in some cheesecake...a walk at the National Harbor? Or we could try your luck at MGM? I just want to help you put yourself first."

"That sounds amazing, Kyle. It's just bad timing. I need to make certain Joya gets back to work and on her feet. And putting myself first all the time, it's not for me. I don't want to lose the best of me. And the best of me is living a life that honors the needs of the many over the few...or the one. Even when that one is me."

"Dr. Spock."

She nodded. "Plus, I've got to"—she glanced down at her watch—"Oh, no. Where'd the time go? The meeting's in forty-five minutes."

"Let me take you."

"Thank you, but no. A quiet drive will help me collect my thoughts, get my head together. But I'd appreciate a text later."

She flittered through the office, grabbing her things. Soon, Keep It Real Cards would be hers, and she'd serve Cody the cold dish of revenge he deserved.

∽

CODY

"Where are you?" Cody half thought about ignoring the intrusive call buzzing his cellphone, especially since he was en route to the most crucial board meeting of his career, but something told him to pick up.

"I'm getting ready to leave Keep It Real," Kyle said. "I came to try and assess your situation. The good news is Tessa's given up the Real Talk line. From all appearances, she'd shifted toward 'Connect. With Hart', but everything came to a screeching halt today."

Cody's stomach turned. "I have no reason to expect her loyalty."

"I thought you'd be more excited that she's back on track," Kyle began, "especially now that you and Chandra have made amends and the wedding's going full steam ahead."

Cody swallowed hard and choked at the same time. "Wait, hold up. Where'd *you* get an idea like that?"

"Tessa told me. Just a few minutes ago before she left for the board meeting."

"Where in the world did *she* get an idea like that?"

"She saw you two together yesterday, at least that's what she told me. Apparently, she heard you reaffirm your love for one another? I don't know...her words, not mine."

Cody stared into oblivion with his mouth hanging open for what felt like a solid minute.

Eventually, Kyle interrupted the silence. "What's going on, man? Everything all right?"

"I've gotta go. If I don't get to the meeting before it starts and explain things to Tessa, we may all be polishing off our resumes tomorrow."

He hung up, and his mind flashed back to the moment in his office just before he broke off his relationship with Chandra.

I'm not sure what you think happened at dinner,
but what you saw was a bitter clash between
business rivals, he heard himself say. Yes, I do
love you, Chandra.

He squeezed his eyes closed and grimaced as he agonized.

He should've been more careful, both about what he said and the way he said it. He easily could understand how Tessa misconstrued their conversation.

She'd only heard part of it.

He cursed himself for trying to break up with Chandra gently.

In hindsight, he should've ripped the Band-Aid, confessed that in the beat of one sweet night, he realized that his love for Tessa remained inextricably woven through every fiber of his being, in every beat of his heart.

Tessa had assessed him correctly. He was a coward. His timidity had cost him five years of building a life with the woman he loved—and now it might cost him Hart Enterprises, the very foundation on which he'd built his life—their lives.

Even worse, Tessa stood to lose more than she realized. Whether she understood it or not, any deal she struck to regain ownership of Keep It Real would eventually lead to its demise. Sweet Media simply lacked the cash flow to bear Keep It Real's debt even with the temporary infusion.

Cody returned to Hart's headquarters and took slow, measured steps toward the board room, trying to appear more relaxed than he was.

He crossed the threshold to take his place in front of the firing squad, and all eyes centered on him.

"Well." Regina had only said one word, but her smugness darn near suffocated him. She had nothing that resembled a poker face, and her wicked smirk spoke every word her mouth didn't. "Looks like the gang's all here. Have a seat, brother dear. We'd like to start. No need to waste everyone's time unnecessarily."

He entered the room and scanned it. He tried to lock eyes with Tessa and give her a little head nod to let her know he needed to speak with her in private, but she looked past him as if he were a piece of furniture, the leg on a side table.

He took a seat opposite her, hoping the chill in her glare would warm. His sisters sat side by side, square in the middle.

"Before we begin," he said, hoping with all faith that Tessa's eyes would meet his. "I need a minute to talk to Tessa alone, just a few seconds."

"Anything you need to say, you should've said before you arrived," said Renee. "We've got the important business of Hart Enterprises to address."

"Yeah, save your inconsequential sentiment for the end of the meeting," Regina added. "Shouldn't take long. This is just a formality now. The deal is done."

"Tessa?" He turned to her, wanting her to look into his eyes to see his sincerity, but she avoided his gaze.

"How long before we take the vote?" Tessa asked. "I'm ready to get this over with."

"I think we all understand why we're here today," Regina said, blustering with her newfound authority. "Cody has run this business well for the past couple of years."

"Officially—five years," he barked. "Including four since our father died and left me in charge, but I've been working for this company for much longer than that."

Regina rolled her eyes and all but ignored every word he said. "Hart is ready for new leadership, a different strategy.

Renee and I are set to assume leadership and undo the damage of some recent, poor business decisions. The shift in direction requires a new CEO—co-CEOs."

He glanced at Tessa, who was now wringing her hands. She must know every venomous word seeping from their lips was based on lies, but she listened, appearing unfazed and impatient.

He'd underestimated the lengths she'd go through to regain control of her company, and everyone at the table had miscalculated him. He would not take the coward's way out. No, if he were destined to lose Hart Enterprises, he'd go down flaming.

"Neither of you spent a day here until Pops passed away, except to collect your shopping checks. I'm the one who's been working alongside him for more than a decade, slaving day and night to learn every aspect of this company's operations. No one in this room is more qualified to serve as CEO than I."

Regina coughed and flashed a coy expression.

"And, yes, I decided to acquire Keep It Real with my heart, but isn't that what this company is all about? Heart. Dad was a strong family man, but what did he ever accomplish or achieve without factoring in his love for us and his legacy, even when he made poor choices that I disagreed with?" Cody pressed his hand against his chest. "But make no mistake about it, I also decided with my head. It was the right thing to do by Hart Enterprises, by Brian Sweet, a man our father very much regarded as the only brother he's ever known, and by Keep It Real,"—he looked straight at Tessa—"which is owned by the only woman I've ever truly loved."

His profession made Tessa do a double-take and took power out of their jabs. "You can eliminate my position, but you can never erase my legacy. You can reverse this acquisition, but you can never change what Tessa's meant to me...what she still means to me." He stared down his sisters like a lion eyeing baby goats. "Now, you may proceed with your little vote." He dismissed his sisters with a sweep of his hand.

"Very well," Regina said, after clearing her throat. She

directed her attention toward Tessa, who now appeared astounded and lifted a weighty folder containing layers of documents between the covers.

"Once we regain control of Hart Enterprises, we will return Keep It Real to Sweet Media per this agreement," Renee said, "and forgive the cash outlay paid to secure the acquisition, as agreed upon by the new co-CEOs of Hart Enterprises, according to the terms set forth herein."

Tessa nodded and at last looked at Cody. He searched her eyes for empathy, for a sign that she'd heard his plea for her heart. He found nothing but confusion.

"Shall we begin?" Regina said. "Tessa, I'd like to offer you the chance to speak, if you'd like."

Tessa nodded as Cody maintained his poker face and tried not to roll his eyes. She locked her eyes on the agreement, as if she needed to maintain eye contact with it to go through with the sham.

Regina was bloated with smugness as she waited for Tessa to finish.

"Keep It Real saved me." Tessa placed both palms on the table and pushed herself to her feet. She began to pace behind her chair. "At the lowest point in my life, when I believed I'd lost everything that matters—my hope for a successful business, a husband, two and a half kids, and a dog—starting Keep It Real gave my life substance, gave me a reason to wake up in the morning and believe in myself. And it was all mine. I never conceived of a time when I'd wake up and Keep It Real would no longer belong to me, not as long as I gave it my all."

"I would like to offer that Cody made an autonomous decision," Renee said.

"Surprise to me!" Tessa continued. "The unthinkable happened, without a second's consultation with me, before I had a chance to think about the ramifications, before I had the opportunity to weigh the opportunities or weaknesses."

"And now I assume you've had the chance to assess the wisdom of this deal?" Regina asked, cutting her eyes at Cody.

Tessa nodded. "Last night, I visited a young girl who nearly gave up on life. I looked around her, and I didn't see things or companies or jewels or money, just the one man who loved her enough to be there for her at her lowest point. She'd taken him for granted but swore she'd never forgotten he came to her when no one else did. At that moment, the teacher became a student."

"I don't understand. What does this—" Regina started before Tessa cut her off.

"Let me make it plain"—she interrupted—"I will not stand against the man who stood beside me at my lowest point. Not for you—or you," she said, pointing to Regina and then Renee. "Keep It Real will stay exactly where it is. And, so will you, Cody Hart"—she allowed her gaze to linger on him—"You are the best CEO of Hart Enterprises—and this is a business decision that is good for the enterprise and the people. I vote to acquire Keep It Real—and if you don't accept my vote, my father will do the same. It's where it belongs...and, Chandra or no Chandra, so am I."

Cody and his sisters sat paralyzed in silence with their bottom jaws dangling low to the floor. Tessa stormed out the door and disappeared with paperwork in her hand.

"What the hell happened here?" Regina's lips puckered in anger.

"I believe this is the part where both of you slither back into your offices while you still have them."—Cody snapped to his feet—"I have some plans to make."

Chapter Thirty

T essa

THE MORNING CAME TOO QUICKLY, RUDELY AWAKENING TESSA WITH
a beam of sun warming her face. After her performance at the
board meeting, she expected Cody to celebrate with Chandra,
but she figured he might at least text a thank you or word of
appreciation—or send a card.

So far—nothing.

While Pepper pawed Tessa's pillow and purred in her ear, she
flipped from her belly to her back and stared at the ceiling. She'd
replayed the day before in her mind. Everything he said, everything she said, trying to figure out what it all meant for the
company, for her future.

She wanted to spring out of bed to greet the new day with a
smile, but heartache anchored her to the mattress.

She reached over and slapped her clock radio into the 'on'
position to drown out the echoes of Cody's speech in her mind.
She failed. Miserably.

Just her luck—K4. *Ugh.*

Even the universe hated her. She wondered if nine a.m. was too early to drown herself in Grey Goose and regret.

Cody had overwhelmed her as he spoke up for her, stood beside her; he did so even as his sisters threatened to take his life's work. She couldn't watch him lose it all. It would've broken his heart, and that would've broken hers.

He saved her and her company—so she rescued him. Suffocated by the overwhelming swell of emotion that followed her speech, she darted out of there like a deer on a country road, ultimately suffering the deer's fate.

Now, she lie in bed alone as she pondered her day. She refused to go into the office and face anyone, especially not Cody. She would see Chandra's lips touching his and hear Cody's voice profess a love that Tessa wished belonged to her.

The workaholic in her hated to make the call, but, for her own sanity, she had to do it.

She picked up the cell and phoned Mia. When her bestie answered, Tessa's performance commenced.

Cough! Cough! She made sure it echoed in the receiver. Then she closed off the airflow to her nose so her voice would sound as nasally as possible.

"Hey, Mia," she said, feigning sickness. "I'm not gonna make it in. I think I have Ebola....or the flu. So, I'll be out today, and maybe tomorrow. Maybe forever. You should probably count on not seeing me for the rest of the week, at least. Call me on my cellphone if you need me."

"Really?"

"What?" She asked plainly, then again with the nasal voice, "What?"

"You had me all the way up to the point at which you stayed home. You must've forgotten I witnessed you drag your pain-ridden stump of a body in here to oversee the release of the first cards."

"I had the sniffles."

"You had the worst case of the flu ever known to man, and we couldn't make you leave. We'd all but planned your burial in the Creative Studios. So, you'll have to come better than that. Up here sounding like Mr. Snuffleupagus."

Tessa held her laugh as long as she could, but it exploded out of her. "Okay, fine." She turned off the act. "So, I'm not sick. The truth of the matter is that I can't face anything today. Not Cody. Not Kyle. I don't even know if I can face myself."

"What Happened?"

"Things One and Two handed it to me on a silver platter, the opportunity to regain sole ownership of Keep It Real. I had one job. All I needed to do was cast one stinking little vote against him in the board meeting yesterday and install the Things as co-CEOs."

"So, what happened?"

"I couldn't pull the trigger. Oh, you should've seen my performance. I mean, it was the stuff of legends. Not only did I vote to retain Cody as CEO, but I also declared my belief that he is the best-qualified person to run Hart Enterprises...this happened, of course, before I darted out of the boardroom like a deer at a coyote convention."

Mia fell out laughing to the point at which Tessa was almost annoyed...then she joined in. She had to admit the entire scene sounded just left of ridiculous.

"You still love him, don't you?" Mia asked as their chuckles tapered off.

"Are you...? Mia, c'mon."

"You not only still love him, but you're so in love with him that you couldn't stop yourself from doing the right thing by him, even when you had everything to lose and nothing to gain."

"How could I, Mia? I mean, he broke my heart."

Mia chuckled. "I've got news for you, Tessa. You slipped up and got over it. After all these years, maybe you realize that the love between you is greater than the hurt."

She pursed her lips. "Right in time for him to declare his love for another woman. They're still getting married. Yeah, I'm not winning," Tessa said. "I wish I could replay his speech. He declared, in front of God and sisters, he made the decision to acquire Keep It Real with his mind and his heart. And that I was the only woman he ever truly loved...but he didn't mean now. He meant from before."

"Whaaaaat?"

"Then he let the sisters have it, told them that they could reverse the acquisition, but they could never change what we meant to one another."

"Wow. *Humph.*"

"Humph? What's *humph* for?"

"Didn't you just tell me that he declared his love for another woman?"

"Yeah. I heard him tell Chandra he loved her with my own ears."

"Well, from what you just told me, *I heard* him declare his love *for you.*"

Tessa opened her mouth to retort, but the words stopped.

Declare his love for me?

She closed her eyes and shook her head. She heard what he said, but she didn't listen, not until this moment.

Maybe Mia was right. But how could she reconcile his so-called profession of love in the face of what she witnessed with her own eyes and ears?

"Pepper got your tongue?" Mia asked.

"Well—" Before Tessa formed her response, the doorbell rang. "I've got a visitor. Probably Dad coming to disown me. I begged him to help me get the company back, and then I caved. Hold on for a sec."

Tessa stopped for a quick check in the mirror. She smoothed her hair, sniffed under her arms, and trotted down the steps. Far from glammed, she declared herself decent enough to answer the door. She peered out the glass panel.

"Mia, let me call you back."

"Who is it? Cody?"

"No. It's...a courier."

She recognized him almost immediately. It was the same guy who'd delivered Cody's break-up card five years ago. He still worked for Hart, she guessed, and he hadn't changed a bit or aged a minute. She'd check on firing him when she returned to the office.

"Can I help you?" She sounded politer than she wanted to be.

His deliveries were like deflated animal balloons, melted ice cream, and broken dreams.

"Delivery for Tessa Sweet."

"I'm she." She waited with anticipation for him to pull a thin envelope from his courier bag.

He passed her a receipt on a clipboard. "Sign here, please."

She signed and watched him drive away and then opened the envelope. It was a card. Tears rushed to her eyes as she read it, walked in the door, and closed it behind her.

On the front of the card: a picture of a round peg and a round hole.

The outside cover read: We belong together.

The inside copy, read, simply: Forever. I Love You. K4.

She knew who'd sent it, and she understood the message.

What she didn't understand is the reason. She was at once elated and confused.

A few moments later, the doorbell rang again. She glanced out of the glass panel, thinking the courier forgot something, perhaps the diamond ring and roses.

But she couldn't be more wrong. The sight stunned her silent.

She reeled back, checked for crust in the corners of her eyes, and smoothed her hair once again before opening it.

There he stood. Cody. Looking like a whole entire snack. He sported a fresh haircut, and his skin glistened with Shea butter. Lord, if he smelled as good as he looked, his mere presence in her home might get her pregnant.

Cody gazed at her as if she were his whole snack, even in her less-than-polished state.

"What are you doing here?" she asked.

"Something I should've done a very long time ago. May I come inside?"

She started to hesitate, to pretend she was going to shut the door in his face, affronted by his relationship with Chandra. But her thought to leave him standing outside looking crazy was as fleeting as her anger. So, she stepped aside and allowed him to enter.

There they stood and faced one another, lingering in a silence that spoke volumes above any words.

"I don't understand. Why did you come here?" she asked again. He still belonged to Chandra.

"Because you're here. Wherever you are, that's where I belong."

She pressed her hand against her heart to prevent it from exploding out of her chest.

As much as she wanted to fall into his arms and declare her undying love and commitment, she held her emotions in check. After all, one major issue remained unresolved.

"What about your fiancée, your wedding? I saw you two together yesterday. I overheard you. You told her you still love her."

Cody grabbed Tessa's hand, sat her down on the sofa, and gently kissed her fingers. Every nerve in her body ignited in a way she scarce believed she could feel again.

"You're right. You did hear me tell her that I love her." He paused long enough to pique her irritation. "But then you left shortly after, am I right?"

"How did you know?"

"Because had you eavesdropped on the entire conversation, you would've also heard me confess to her that I'm not *in love* with her and that I never stopped loving you."

Tessa's eyes widened.

"I don't know what I expected when I acquired your company, but deep down, I know what I hoped. Sitting here with you is more than I ever dreamed."

She stared at his lips. Cody leaned forward until her eyes fell closed, and then he cupped her face in his hands. "I've missed you so much," he whispered.

His eyes welled, and his voice, even in a whisper, trembled with his sincerity. "I'm so sorry, baby. I swear I'll spend the rest of my life loving away any pain I ever caused. Just promise me, you will give me the chance to prove it. Promise me."

She nodded and wiped her tears on the back of her hand. "I just...I can't believe it, after all this time, you're here with me. Loving *me*."

Her hands traced the small of his back and spine as he planted the softest and sweetest kisses on her forehead, then her eyes, her nose, each cheek, and her chin. Then finally, he grazed his lips against hers before devouring them.

Their tongues connected and glided in a perfect, slow, grinding rhythm that intensified with each second of delicious release.

As they slowed to a stop and parted, Cody said, "I love you, baby. I've loved you every day, of every minute since the first day you kicked me in the chicken nuggets."

She snickered through her tears. "Cody?"

"I'm saying that I'm ready to be the man you need me to be." That's when he released her hand, dropped to one knee, and pulled out a Tiffany-blue ring box.

"Wait, are you saying—"

"Will you do me the honor of...sharing the chair with me for the rest of our lives?"

Tessa couldn't stop the tears from flowing. In the wisp of a beautiful moment, her deepest wish, her greatest dream since she was ten years old, had come true. She fell into his arms and landed on top of him on the floor.

He wrapped his arms around her and squeezed her in the sweetest embrace before they looked into each other's eyes.

"Yes," she said through her sniffs and smiles. "*Let's bee* husband and wife. I love you so much, Cody."

"My blue dress with butterflies girl. I love you, Tessa."

"I've got an idea. You know what?" she said to her fiancé. "You should write that on a card."

The end and thank you for reading LOVE IS IN THE CARDS. If you enjoyed this novel, please leave a review at your favorite review site. **To hear "K4," please visit:** http://klbradyauthor.com/romance-novels/seven-minutes-of-christmas-magic/

About the Author

K. L. Brady, a D.C. native, started her writing career in the pages of diaries when she was seven or eight years old. But it wasn't until her fortieth birthday and an Oprah "Live Your Best Life" moment that she finally answered her calling and wrote her first novel–The Bum Magnet. The originally self-published novel was picked up by Simon & Schuster in a two-book deal and K.L. hasn't looked back since, penning the follow-up, Got a Right to Be Wrong and self-publishing the first books in two young adult series and a spy thriller series based on her twenty-year career in the U.S. Intelligence Community.

A certified nerd girl with a love of all things Star Wars, Big Bang Theory and Star Trek, she has a B.A. in Economics and an MBA. She also holds memberships in the Maryland Writer's Association, Romance Writers of America, Sisters In Crime, and International Thriller Writers. She's addicted to writing and chocolate—not necessarily in that order—and currently, lives in the Washington D.C. area with her son.

Website link: http://www.klbradyauthor.com
Facebook link: https://www.facebook.com/KLBRADY/
Pinterest: https://www.pinterest.com/authorklbrady/
Twitter: https://twitter.com/KARLAB27
Instagram: https://www.instagram.com/klbrady_author/

If you enjoyed this novel, please stop by and leave a review at your favorite site. They mean everything to indie authors. And join my newsletter for news on the latest releases, chances to get free books and early review copies, and special contests for newsletter readers only! (Note: We never spam; newsletter issued once every 3 months.)

http://tinyurl.com/klbradynews

facebook.com/KLBRADY

twitter.com/KARLAB27

instagram.com/klbrady_author

bookbub.com/profile/k-l-brady

goodreads.com/karlab27

Other Books by K.L. Brady

Love is in the Cards – A Novel (Clean, Sweet Romantic Comedy)

In this second-chance romance, a greeting card company owner's life is sent into a tailspin when her business is acquired by the ex-boyfriend who dumped her. (Coming October 2020)

Seven Minutes of Christmas Magic (Clean, Sweet Romantic Comedy)

Sparks fly when greeting card company executive ruthlessly steals Mr. Right's parking space before a Christmas party—and then steals his heart. They would be a match made in heaven…if he hadn't been tapped to steal her work and destroy her career. (Coming November 2020)

Trouble's in the Cards (Clean, Sweet Romantic Comedy)

Coming in 2021.

Women's Fiction – Chick Lit

Got a Right to Be Wrong (Some Strong Language)

One week before her wedding day, a woman with a life-long struggle with trust issues finds out a life-altering secret about her fiancée and questions their future.

12 Honeymoons (Clean, Sweet Romantic Comedy)

After a nasty break-up that lands her court, a D.C. socialite, struggling to find her purpose and love, gets arrested (again) and is forced to perform community service.

Christmas and Holiday Romance

Five Golden Rings - A Christmas Novella (Clean, Sweet Romance)

A.J. and Kristie serendipitously "fall" for one another at the National Tree Lighting in Washington D.C. As fast as destiny brings them together, Murphy's Law pulls them apart.

The 12 Daves of Christmas – A Novella (Clean, Sweet Romantic Comedy)

It's a comedy of errors when Dave and Gabby attempt to meet one another face to face after falling for one another due to a misdirected text.

The Bum Magnet (Chick Lit/Women's Fiction - Some Strong Language)

After a lifetime of bad relationships, a woman decides to go on an introspective journey to find out why she attracts to the wrong men—a journey hilariously complicated by a new love interest.

The 007th Day of Christmas (Clean, Sweet Romance)

Coming in 2021.

Sincerely, Santa (Clean, Sweet Romance)

Coming in 2021.

The Playmaker Series – Sweet Romance

Her Perfect Catch (Clean)

A struggling sportswriter finds the story of her lifetime, and love soon follows, during a trip to the Super Bowl.

The Player's Option (Clean)

When sports agent Ty Baker and C.J. meet at a pro-football conference, sparks fly, and they can both see love in the end zone...until disaster strikes. Each learns the other is trying to steal their biggest client and cut-throat competition threatens to tear them apart.

The Eligible Receiver (Clean)

Jet Jamison is hot, successful, wealthy, and can have any woman he wants, the one he truly needs still eludes him, that is, until Veda enters his life. A chance meeting with Jet begins with a sparring match and ends with love at second sight. But she's got a secret that threatens to tear them apart.

The Playmakers – 3-Book Box Set

Her Perfect Catch, The Player's Option & The Eligible Receiver

Are you ready for some love and football? This funny and sweet box set contains heartwarming romances featuring sexy professional football stars who deliver hot, flirty days and cozy nights.

Young Adult - Romance

Worst Impressions (Clean)

In this modern retelling of Pride and Prejudice, shy, basketball loving, tomboy Liz Bennett meets star high school quarterback Darcelle Williams and sparks fly—and she'd like to set him on fire.

Soul of the Band (Clean)

A bullied, inner city teen gets a chance to start a new life when, after her mother's mental breakdown, she is forced to move to a small town in Ohio and joins the high school band.

Spy Thrillers – The J.J. McCall Series (S.D. Skye)

The Bigot List (A J.J. McCall Novel #1)

An FBI Special Agent and her partner are drawn into an unsanctioned hunt for an intelligence community spy when Bureau sources are killed, and an internal investigation threatens to land them atop the suspect list.

Situation Critical (A J.J. McCall Novel #2)

An FBI Special Agent and her partner lead an intelligence community task force ordered to find moles throughout the intelligence community, and its first case targets the White House.

The Shadow Syndicate (A J.J. McCall Novel #3)

The FBI task force heads to New York to shut down a sleeper spy funding network, landing them in the middle of a burgeoning war between a Russian organized crime organization with links to diplomatic spies and the Italian mafia.

SpyCatcher (J.J. McCall 3-Book Box Set)

The Bigot List, Situation Critical & The Shadow Syndicate

Read the first three J.J. McCall Novels in one great set!

www.ingramcontent.com/pod-product-compliance
Lightning Source LLC
Chambersburg PA
CBHW060400260626
47160CB00006B/2376